'You're forththe and have
no desire for a wife either.
Especially one who looks more
like a stablehand than a woman!'

Lothar rubbed his jaw gingerly with his knuckles as Juliana stormed away. In retrospect, he supposed he might have handled the situation better. She was right—their marriage was a greater advancement than any he could have expected—but her accusations had undermined his self-control to the extent that he'd finally lost his temper.

He'd *meant* to say that he'd accepted the offer because he wanted to help her keep her inheritance—not to steal it for himself. He'd *meant* to say that he was a soldier—that when it came to managing a castle she was a far better person for the job. He'd *meant* to reassure her that it would be a marriage in name only, at least insofar as she wanted it to be one. Most of all, he'd *meant* to tell her that nothing about this was a game.

Instead he'd told her she looked like a stablehand. *That* had definitely been a mistake.

Author Note

I first became interested in the Empress Matilda as a child, after reading about her escape from Oxford Castle during the siege of 1142, dressed all in white for camouflage in the snow. Unfortunately that story is often all that gets told about a woman whose incredible biography has been largely—and ironically—whitewashed out of history. The daughter and mother of kings, wife of an emperor and then a count, Matilda was a strong woman for any age, and yet she never managed to regain the birthright that was usurped by her cousin Stephen.

Matilda's problem—as Helen Castor's brilliant book *She-Wolves: The Women Who Ruled England Before Elizabeth* points out—was not that she *was* a woman, but that she was expected to *behave* like one: to be Queen and yet not assert her own individual authority—a contradiction that the Medieval mindset seemed unable to overcome, and that I find fascinating.

This story, whilst not directly about Matilda, is partly about the roles women were and weren't allowed to hold in twelfth-century England—four centuries before Elizabeth I came to the throne. Despite my bias, however, I do have a soft spot for Stephen, who was more merciful than the majority of Medieval kings, and did actually pardon some of those who rebelled against him. At a distance of almost nine hundred years, it's impossible to judge who was the hero and who the villain…but, for the purposes of this story at least, I side with Matilda.

BESIEGED
AND BETROTHED

Jenni Fletcher

Published in Great Britain 2017
by Mills & Boon, an imprint of HarperCollins*Publishers*
1 London Bridge Street, London, SE1 9GF

© 2017 Jenni Fletcher

ISBN: 978-0-263-92621-7

Our policy is to use papers that are natural, renewable and
recyclable products and made from wood grown in sustainable
forests. The logging and manufacturing processes conform to the
legal environmental regulations of the country of origin.

Printed and bound in Spain
by CPI, Barcelona

Jenni Fletcher was born on the north coast of Scotland, and now lives in Yorkshire with her husband and two children. She wanted to be a writer as a child, but got distracted by reading instead, finally writing down her first paragraph thirty years later. She's had more jobs than she can remember, but has finally found one she loves. She can be contacted via Twitter, @jenniauthor.

Books by Jenni Fletcher

Mills & Boon Historical Romance

Married to Her Enemy
The Convenient Felstone Marriage
Besieged and Betrothed

Visit the Author Profile page at millsandboon.co.uk.

To Andy, again,
and my family as always (that includes you, Hilary!)

Also a huge thank-you to Kim, Christine,
Emma and Sharon, without whose help I'd still only
be halfway through.

And to Claudia,
who could give any empress a run for her money.

Historical Note

In 1147 England had been in the grip of Civil War for twelve years.

The tumultuous period now known as The Anarchy was triggered by the death of Henry I in 1135.

After the drowning of his only legitimate son in the White Ship disaster of 1120, the only direct heir to the throne was Henry's daughter, Matilda, although at twenty-eight she'd spent comparatively little of her life in England, having been sent abroad at the age of eight to marry the German Emperor Heinrich V. Widowed at twenty-six, she'd then been married to Geoffrey, the young Count of Anjou, with whom she had three sons— the great-grandsons of William the Conqueror.

Henry's wishes regarding the succession are evidenced by the fact that he made his nobles swear two separate oaths of allegiance to Matilda.

When he died, however, his nephew Stephen travelled immediately to England to have himself crowned King in her place. Unable to leave Anjou due to her third pregnancy, and lacking the support of the nobility, many of whom doubted a woman's ability to rule, Matilda had to wait another four years before pursuing her claim.

By the time she finally arrived in England Stephen's grip on power was already too strong to be broken. As a result, her influence was mainly confined to the south-west of the country, with her base in Devizes in Wiltshire. Despite several victories—most notably the Battle of Lincoln— she was unable to gain a definitive upper hand and the power struggle descended into a lengthy and lawless war of attrition.

By 1147, when this story is set, the majority of the fighting was over. Stephen remained the stronger power in England, but had lost the entirety of Normandy to Matilda's husband. As a result, barons with lands on both sides of the Channel were forced to make peace treaties with both claimants. Most, however, were weary of fighting and simply wanted an end to the war.

In 1153, the ageing Stephen finally agreed to a treaty ceding the throne to Matilda's eldest son— later Henry II—after his death.

Ultimately Matilda lost the battle but won the war, founding the Plantagenet dynasty that was to rule England for the next three hundred years.

Chapter One

❦

Herefordshire—October 1147

One arrow.

Lothar narrowed his eyes, estimating the distance between him and the woman on the castle ramparts. The wind was in his favour and she was facing in the other direction, wouldn't hear the rush of the arrow until it was too late. It was an easy shot, an easy target. One arrow to end a four-month-long siege.

If he gave the order.

'That's her!' His companion's voice was sharp-edged with malice. 'Lady Juliana. She's the one holding the castle.'

'So I assumed.'

'Then what are you waiting for? *Shoot her!*'

Lothar turned slowly, fixing the other man with a cool, charcoal-grey stare. He was known for such looks, had forged a steely reputation based on his inscrutable, hard-boiled exterior. The Angoulême soldiers he commanded called him *guerrier de fer*, 'iron warrior', joking that his skin was so thick that he didn't need armour, that his heart—if he even had one—was buried too deep for any weapon to find it. Most days he didn't care. His reputation was useful. It kept him safe, made other men reluctant to challenge him. It was the reason Empress Matilda trusted him, why she sent him to clear up the messes caused by other men's incompetence. But today...

His gaze drifted inexorably back towards the woman on the ramparts, her long, crimson-red hair streaming in the wind like a rippling banner. Today, his companion's assumption of cold-hearted callousness disturbed him. If he were even half as ruthless as his enemies and most of his friends gave him credit for, he would have given the order already, but he wasn't so cold-blooded, wasn't about to shoot an unarmed woman in the back.

On the other hand, it had been two days since he'd had a decent night's sleep, riding at full pelt from the Empress's base at Devizes, and he was about ready to shoot someone himself. If Sir Guian de Ravenell didn't shut up, it would be him.

'Bring her down!' The Baron's impatience was bordering on hysteria. 'Do it!'

Lothar arched an eyebrow, vaguely surprised that the woman had managed to survive this long with such a voracious wolf at her gates. But then, even a coward like de Ravenell knew that the Empress wouldn't condone such dishonourable behaviour—which doubtless explained why he was trying to make *him* give the order.

He rubbed a hand over his face in disgust, over the livid white scar that ran in a diagonal line from the middle of his forehead, half-hidden by a shock of black hair, through his left eyebrow and down to the corner of his jaw. It always throbbed when the weather turned damp and the autumn mizzle was making the whole side of his face ache.

'You could end the siege right now.' De Ravenell tried a different tack, trying to sound reasonable. 'The garrison inside will surrender without her. Her father was loyal to the Empress, but after he died she surrendered and declared for the usurper.'

He felt a momentary disquiet. After a three-month long siege, William Danville had finally chosen to ride out and confront the usurper King Stephen in battle, but his valiant attempt had ended in disaster. His daughter's subsequent surrender was understandable, though her oath of allegiance to the man whose forces had just killed her father was…surprising.

'She swore an oath to Stephen straight after the battle?'

'Before her father was even cold. The girl's a traitor!'

'Girl?' He didn't bother to hide his scepticism. 'If she's held the castle against you for four months then she's hardly that.'

And as for traitor…

He kept the thought to himself. Between King Stephen and Empress Matilda, two contenders with equally convincing claims to the English throne, it was increasingly difficult to distinguish who was a traitor and who not. Even the Barons seemed to have trouble deciding, given the number whose loyalties seemed to ebb and flow with each passing month. Personally, he had little interest in politics, had his own reasons for serving the Empress, none of which had anything to do with her right to wear the crown. At least Lady Juliana appeared to have a mind of her own. However *surprising* her decision, she'd chosen her side and stuck to it.

Unfortunately for her, it was the wrong one.

'Have you tried bargaining with her?'

'Of course.' The Baron bristled. 'I tried negotiating when we first arrived, but she refused my terms.'

'So you've been inside the castle? What are their defences like? How many men does she have?'

'I'm not certain. That is, not exactly. She came to my tent.'

'Your tent?' Lothar narrowed his eyes interrogatively. 'Whose idea was that?'

'Mine. I offered her a flag of truce and she accepted.'

'And?'

'And nothing.' The Baron's gaze slid to one side evasively. 'She's a shrew. 'Tis no wonder she's still unmarried. She wouldn't listen to reason.'

'Reason.'

Lothar repeated the word flatly, letting the unspoken accusation hover in the air between them. Over the years he'd come to judge other men on their ability to look him and his scar in the face. Sir Guian de Ravenell most definitely could not. The man's reputation as a military commander was bad enough, but with women, it was even worse. If Lady Juliana had gone to his tent alone, expecting to negotiate…

A muscle twitched in his jaw. After more than a decade of soldiering, he'd grown accustomed to all kinds of fighting, but violence against women still made his blood boil, stirring up memories he'd spent most of his lifetime trying to forget. Traitor or not, if de Ravenell had done anything to hurt Lady Juliana, the man would need to find his own castle walls to hide behind.

'She insulted me.'

'Is that so?'

Lothar restrained his temper with an effort. Whatever she'd said couldn't be half as bad as the phrases running through his own mind.

'Have you tried negotiating since?'

'No. I gave her a chance to surrender. Why should I offer again?'

'To end the siege, perhaps?'

'The rules of warfare only oblige me to offer once. She made her choice. Now she can suffer the consequences.'

Lothar ground his teeth, barely resisting the urge to ram a fist in the other man's face. But the Empress couldn't afford to lose allies, even ones as ineffectual as de Ravenell. The way her campaign against Stephen was going, she needed every man she could get—and she needed Castle Haword. Modest though it was, the fortress was strategically vital, holding the only bridge over the Wye for thirty miles. Without a safe route across, the Empress's allies were at potential risk of being encircled, trapped between Stephen's forces and the river. She needed the bridge, however small it might seem to his eyes, and the sooner the better. *That* was why he'd come, to end a siege that had dragged on for too long already. Any quarrel he had with Sir Guian would have to wait.

He forced his attention back to the castle. He hated sieges, preferred open warfare to simply waiting. There was nothing honourable about starving an enemy into submission, still less in fighting men too weak to defend themselves, but he had orders to follow. One way or another he intended to take Haword by nightfall the following day. His duty to the Empress came first, no matter what he might think of her orders.

Methodically, he scrutinised the fortifications for weaknesses. Judging by the design, the original motte was old, dating back to before the Conquest, though the Anglo-Saxon timber had been gradually replaced and strengthened with stone. Even so, the work appeared to have been carried out section by section over a period of years, each wall seeming to represent the era in which it was built. The overall effect was an oddly patchwork, ramshackle appearance, but on the whole, the structure looked solid. An assault wouldn't be easy, but not impossible.

His gaze swept appraisingly back towards the gatehouse and then stilled, arrested by the pair of eyes looking back. He'd been so preoccupied with studying the defences that he hadn't seen her turn around, but now Lady Juliana was staring straight at him, her face ablaze with a look of such searing, hate-filled defiance that he felt the unfamiliar urge to take a step back.

He took a pace forward instead, claiming even more ground as he waited for her to drop her gaze and turn away, but she didn't move, didn't even flinch at the challenge. What had de Ravenell called her—a *girl*? No, she was no girl, in her early twenties he guessed, though from the look of her, if she didn't surrender soon, there'd be naught left but a ghost. The rain was heavier now, casting a murky veil over the space between them, but the effects of the siege were all too evident in her emaciated appearance. Her eyes were too big, the shadowy circles around them too dark against her pale skin, her cheekbones too sharply prominent in her narrow face. Yet he could still feel the heat of her gaze, as if she were channelling all that remained of her energy into that one look of defiance, more eloquent than any words. Something about that look, in the determined set of her jaw and her resolute posture, caught his attention and held it. She looked like a Celtic queen, rebellious and undaunted, the long coils of her red hair tumbling loose over the parapet wall in front of her, the only splash of colour against drab, unrelenting grey. For a fleeting moment, he found himself wishing that they were on the same side of the battlements…

He tensed, surprised by a stirring sensation deep in his chest. He'd seen sieges enough to consider himself hardened to their effects, but this woman's wraithlike appearance disturbed him more than he would have expected. He was accustomed to being the observer, not the observed, used to opponents dropping their eyes in front of him, but she held his gaze like the Empress herself. Standing on the ramparts, windswept and buffeted by the elements, she looked as though she'd rather throw herself into the moat below than concede defeat. He had the distinct impression that she'd stand there as long as it took for him to look away.

Well, he could allow her that victory at least.

'So you have a *girl* holding the castle.' He rounded on de Ravenell. 'Yet you never thought to attack? You have two siege engines. Why haven't you used them?'

'I saw no point risking men in an assault.' The Baron looked taken aback. 'A siege was the safest approach.'

'Under normal circumstances I'd agree, but you were ordered to secure the castle by the fastest means possible.'

'She can't hold out much longer.'

'That's still too long for the Empress. Where are your trenches?'

'My…what?'

'Tunnels. Have you *tried* to dig under their walls?'

'The moat's too wide!'

'You've had four months. You could have dug a tunnel all the way under the river by now.'

'How dare you?' the Baron spluttered angrily. 'I've done everything that could possibly be expected of me. The Empress knows me and my abilities. Who are you? Nothing but an ill-bred, peasant upstart!'

Lothar's expression didn't waver. He knew well enough what Matilda's high-born supporters called him behind his back, though he rarely met one foolish enough to say the same to his face. When the time came, he'd have more than

one score to settle with Sir Guian de Ravenell.
He was starting to look forward to it.

'I'm the peasant upstart sent to finish your job,'
he countered smoothly, 'but you're right, the Empress knows all about your abilities. That's why
I'm here.'

The Baron puffed his cheeks out and then
seemed to deflate suddenly. 'Well, I don't see
what can be done about it now.'

'Then let me tell you.' Lothar gestured towards
a range of oaks on a nearby hillside. 'First, you're
going to order your men to cut down those trees.
Second, you're going to have them build a bridge
and battering ram. Third, you're going to attack.'

'*What?* When?'

'Dawn tomorrow.'

'But we can't! Even if we manage to cross the
moat, the walls are too steep. We can't possibly
scale them.'

'Then you'll need to build ladders as well.' Lothar gave a cynical half-smile. 'Don't worry, Sir
Guian, you'll still get your chance to impress the
Empress. You'll be the one leading the assault.'

He turned on his heel abruptly, calling out orders to his soldiers as de Ravenell gawped after
him. In truth, he had absolutely no intention of
letting the man lead anything, but the look of horror on his face was a small form of revenge, the
very least he could do for Lady Juliana.

Had she noticed? He stole another glance up
at the battlements, but she was staring past him,

out into the distance as if she were searching for something. Help most likely, though if she were waiting for Stephen then she'd be waiting a long time. He narrowed his eyes as he caught a flicker of movement in the shadows behind her. The glint of an arrow, the distinctive curve of a bow... His lips curled upwards appreciatively. It seemed that Lady Juliana wasn't quite the easy target he'd taken her for. Her archer must have been there all along, guarding her back the whole time de Ravenell had been urging him to shoot. Not bad for a *girl*. She might make a worthy opponent after all.

He came to a halt finally, taking up a position opposite the gatehouse. This was the newest part of the castle, twenty feet high, with a heavy oak drawbridge and sloped walls at the base to deter an assault. It would be madness to launch an attack from here, but a battering ram would keep the castle garrison diverted whilst he led an assault from the river, the side that they wouldn't expect.

If it came to it, though he'd try a different approach first, one his own code of honour demanded. Would she listen to him? For her own sake, and for reasons he didn't even understand himself, he hoped so.

'Lady Juliana?' he called up to the battlements, his deep voice reverberating loudly off the thick, stone walls. 'Empress Matilda sends greetings.'

Chapter Two

~~~~~~~~~~~~~~

Lady Juliana Danville leant over the parapet wall and let loose a volley of unladylike sentiments. If she'd learnt anything during her brief tenure as chatelaine, it was a far more colourful vocabulary than that of a typical Earl's daughter, even for one who'd grown up with only a father and soldiers for company. She didn't use the words very often, but looking down at the raven-haired stranger below, she couldn't think of anything more fitting to say.

'My lady?' The archer behind her sounded shocked.

'Oh… Sorry, Edgar. Nothing.'

She bit her tongue, her whole attention absorbed in the scene of activity below. Since the stranger's arrival an hour before, the whole atmosphere of the enemy camp seemed to have changed, become seized with a new sense of energy and purpose, so that the air itself now seemed to crackle and hum with tension.

Why? She narrowed her gaze as if his appearance alone might somehow reveal the answer. Who was he?

He was talking to de Ravenell, apparently about the castle, though his face displayed no more emotion than if they were simply discussing the weather. He looked forbidding and yet, she had to admit, ruggedly handsome, too, with strong, chiselled features marred only by a pale scar running like a streak of white lightning down one side of his face. Dressed entirely in black, with his hair cropped shorter than most noblemen's, he dominated the older man with an air of effortless, imposing authority. Whatever they were talking about, one thing was obvious. The Baron was no longer in charge.

She gave an involuntary shudder. A thin morning mist still hung in the air and it was starting to rain, a lowering drizzle that made her wish she'd stopped to pick up a cloak in her haste to reach the battlements. She'd been asleep in a chair, dozing fitfully after yet another restless night when a guard had brought word of the developments outside. She hadn't even stopped to tie up her hair or put on a headdress, and now her linen tunic offered scant protection against the elements. She'd acted impulsively, as usual, and the last thing she needed was to fall ill. If anything happened to her, what would happen to Castle Haword and all its inhabitants then?

On the other hand, she doubted she'd have time to get sick. Whoever the new arrival was, he didn't look like a man who waited for things to happen. He looked like someone who made them. She'd been confident of holding the castle against a coward like de Ravenell, but this stranger was a whole different prospect. Even with a moat and stone wall between them, there was something unnerving about him, a kind of disconcerting restraint in his manner, as if he were holding some part of himself back, some intangible, inscrutable darkness. Something dangerous.

She clenched her fingers over the parapet wall so tightly that her knuckles turned white, channelling the full force of her fear and defiance into one savage glare. What now, she wanted to scream at the assembled forces below, what did they want this time? Hadn't Haword suffered enough? It was hard to remember a time when they hadn't been beset by one enemy or another. Two sieges in one year was more than enough for one castle to cope with! Never mind everything else! All she, all *anyone* in their right mind, wanted was for the war to be over and for there to be peace again, but the power struggle between Stephen and Matilda seemed no closer to finding a resolution. After twelve long years of fighting, more than half of her lifetime, she hardly cared who wore the crown any more. Bad enough that her home was caught in the middle, but now the Empress sent this fresh foe against them!

The stranger met her gaze suddenly and she saw a fleeting look of surprise sweep over his features and then vanish, like the faintest ripple of air across a still pond. It was so quick that she almost thought she must have imagined it. A split second later and he was completely expressionless again, more like a statue than a man of flesh and blood, hard as stone and just as unyielding. She felt an ice-cold *frisson* of fear, sharp and piercing like the tip of a blade, slide inexorably down the length of her spine. The siege was over. Somehow she'd known that the first moment she'd laid eyes on him. This man wasn't simply going to wait for the castle to fall. He was going to take it. Unless she stopped him.

He dropped his gaze and she felt a brief flicker of triumph, quickly extinguished as he started around the edge of the moat, his long, purposeful strides curving ever closer towards the gatehouse. What was he doing? She held her breath nervously. Was he coming to talk or to threaten her? Either way, she'd only come up to the battlements to see what was happening. She wasn't ready to confront him, not now, not yet! She wasn't properly attired, wasn't even wearing a headdress—and she had the very definite impression that neither excuse was likely to sway him.

Desperately she scoured the horizon for reinforcements she already knew weren't coming, at least not in time. She'd sent word to Stephen months ago at the very start of the siege, but had received no response until just a week before, a brief message smuggled in from the river at night saying that he was heading west, that he intended to reach Haword in another fortnight; reminding her of the debt she owed him, telling her to hold the bridge.

If it were only that easy! She fought against a rising tide of panic. She'd held it so far, had made sure the castle was prepared for a long siege, with food and water enough to last another month if they were careful. But if it came to a fight...

She glanced over her shoulder, into the bailey at the fifty or so men who were depending upon *her* to lead them. She didn't doubt their loyalty, no matter what they might privately think of her change of allegiance from Matilda to Stephen, but they were hungry, exhausted and outnumbered, hardly in any fit state for combat. How could she expect them to fight? How could she expect them to win? Loathe as she was to admit it, if the castle walls were breached then they were doomed. If the stranger's fearsome appearance were anything to go by, he'd forgotten more about warfare than she'd ever known. He had the look of a man who knew little else.

Damn it! She swore under her breath as he came to a halt directly beneath her. Why now? Why had he arrived now? After four long months of waiting for Stephen to rescue them, all she needed was one more week!

'Lady Juliana?' The stranger hailed her in an accent she didn't recognise. 'Empress Matilda sends greetings. Will you discuss terms?'

For a stunned moment she thought she'd misheard him. A besieging army usually offered terms only once, were under no obligation to do so again. After that, if the castle fell, its inhabitants and their possessions became fair game. She'd already been to negotiate terms with de Ravenell at the start of the siege, venturing out under a flag of truce that had failed to provide any protection whatsoever. She'd told him exactly what he could do with his *terms*, though her mind shied away from the memory of that encounter. She certainly wasn't going to trust one of the Empress's men so easily again.

And yet...unbelievable as it seemed, this stranger was actually offering her a second chance, probably a *last* chance to save her men if the castle fell. No matter what her debt to Stephen, how could she refuse such an offer? Besides which, he'd definitely said *terms*, not surrender. The word gave her hope. If the Empress was prepared to open negotiations again then surely it meant she had some new offer, something besides outright surrender, something that might buy them some time?

'Lady Juliana?'

The stranger repeated her name and she gave a start, realising that she still hadn't answered.

'I'm Lady Juliana.'

'Are you willing to discuss terms or not, my lady?'

His voice sounded devoid of emotion and for a moment she was tempted to throw the offer back in his face just to see a response. He even *looked* like a statue, she thought resentfully, as if he hardly cared how she answered. Probably he didn't. Whether she agreed to negotiate or not likely meant nothing to him, but if she refused then she'd be risking more than just the bridge. She'd be risking the lives of everyone inside the castle and she couldn't do that. She was the one who'd got them into this position and she was the one who had to find a way out—had to hear what the Empress was offering at least.

'Stay there!'

She whirled away from the parapet, hauling her tunic up to her knees as she raced down the tower steps, moving quickly so she wouldn't have time to reconsider. If she were going to discuss terms—*if*—she needed to speak with him face-to-face, needed to look into his eyes to see if she could trust him first.

'Prepare to lower the drawbridge!' she called out to the door warden from the stairwell.

'Lady Juliana!' Her Constable, Ulf, seemed to appear out of nowhere, scowling from beneath a thatch of unruly white hair. 'You can't go outside.'

'Only on to the drawbridge.'

'I have to protest.' He followed after her as she dodged around him. 'It's too risky.'

'I won't go far.'

'He looks dangerous.'

She made a non-committal sound. She could hardly disagree with that, but she wasn't about to admit it either. She'd no intention of being intimidated by any man, either the stranger *or* her Constable.

'He won't hurt me while he's wearing the Empress's crest.' She hoped she sounded more confident than she felt. 'You can aim as many weapons at him as you like, just don't shoot unless you have to.'

'I still have to protest…'

'It's not your decision, it's mine! *I'm* the chatelaine, aren't I?'

'Yes, my lady…'

'Then it's *my* choice, isn't it?'

The Constable sighed. 'As you wish, my lady, if you're certain.'

'I am.' She made a swift gesture to the door warden, steeling her nerve as the heavy oak drawbridge creaked reluctantly and then started to descend.

'I'll be watching, my lady.'

'I know you will, Ulf.' She took up a position under the archway and threw a conciliatory look over her shoulder. 'I do appreciate your concern, but this won't take long. I'm only going to find out what he wants, that's all.'

She turned around again, ardently hoping that she was telling the truth.

Chapter Three

Juliana took a second look at the stranger and decided that she'd changed her mind. He was standing exactly where she'd last seen him on the far side of the moat, immense and foreboding, the very intensity of his gaze seeming to bore a hole through the mist between them.

A mistake. She caught her breath unsteadily. This had definitely been a mistake. Outside the protection of the castle walls she felt suddenly exposed and vulnerable, like a roe deer being stalked by a wolf. If this man were truly as dangerous as he looked, then she wouldn't stand a chance. Ulf was right. It was too risky… That thought alone gave her courage. If she turned and fled now, then she might as well admit that she wasn't strong enough to be chatelaine in her own right, without a father or husband or any other man to guide or protect her. And there was no chance in hell that she was going to do that.

She took a tentative step forward and the stranger did the same, mirroring each of her movements until they met, barely an arm's length apart, in the centre.

'Lady Juliana.'

He inclined his head and she dug her heels into the wooden planks beneath her feet, resisting the urge to back down, heart thumping so loudly she was sure his whole army must be able to hear it. She was reasonably tall for a woman, but he towered a full head above her, even bigger and broader than he'd seemed from the battlements, his shoulders so wide they seemed to obscure her view of the enemy camp behind. His stern expression was more forbidding, too, though he was also younger than she'd expected, probably no more than thirty, closer to her own age than de Ravenell's. That fact made her even more nervous. They were as good as alone, out of earshot of her men, so close that she could smell the musky scent of leather and sweat on his skin, could feel the heat radiating from his broad chest, could see it rising and falling just inches from hers…

Her legs trembled unsteadily and she dropped into a token curtsy, glad of the opportunity to lower her gaze, if only for a moment. Everything about him felt overpowering, and the last thing she wanted was for him to guess how strongly he was affecting her.

'You have me at a disadvantage, sir.' She straightened up again, lifting her chin in the air defiantly. 'You know who I am, but who are you?'

'My name is Lothar, my lady.'

'*Just* Lothar?'

'Some call me the Frank.'

'You're from Francia?'

She tilted her head to one side, but the expression on his face didn't encourage further questions. If anything, he looked even more severe. Well, at least that explained his accent… She cleared her throat hastily.

'You said you've brought terms, Sir Lothar?'

'Just Lothar. I'm not a knight.'

'You're not?' She blinked in surprise. From his authoritative manner, she'd assumed that he was a baron at least, but now he mentioned it, she noticed that he wasn't dressed any differently from the rest of his soldiers in a dark leather surcoat, black tunic, black hose and knee-length riding boots. But if he wasn't a knight… She stiffened indignantly.

'Is this a joke?'

'In what way?'

'Is the Empress trying to insult me by sending a soldier to negotiate?'

'A sergeant,' he corrected her, 'and no insult, at least none that I'm aware of. The Empress simply thought that Sir Guian was in need of a rest. Unless you prefer to deal with him?'

'*No!*'

She bit her lip, inwardly rebuking herself for answering too quickly. De Ravenell was the last person in the world she wanted to deal with, but she'd no intention of telling *this* man anything about why.

'My lady?' His grey gaze seemed to flicker briefly.

'I mean, you're here now. We might as well continue.' She tossed her head. 'Do you have the authority to discuss terms?'

'I do.'

'Then tell me, *Sergeant*, what exactly is the Empress offering?'

'A last chance. If you surrender the castle today, you and your men will be spared.'

'Surrender?' Her attempt at composure crumbled at once. 'You said you were here to discuss terms!'

'I am. Those are better than you might expect.'

'They're the same as four months ago!'

'As I said, better than you might expect.'

'But…'

She heard the crack in her own voice. As much as she hated to admit it, he was right. Under the circumstances, they were the best terms she could possibly hope for. The Empress was under no obligation to offer anything at all. If this man wanted, he could simply storm the walls, capture the bridge and ransack the castle. She didn't doubt that he could, but an outright *surrender*? Until that moment, she hadn't let herself even acknowledge the possibility. If she surrendered now then she'd be failing Stephen just when he needed her, after she'd given him her word, her promise, to hold the bridge no matter what. What would he think of her if she gave up now? How else would she ever repay her debt?

'And if I refuse?' She tried to stay calm. 'What then?'

'Then the result will be the same. The castle will fall tomorrow and the normal rules of war will apply.' He paused significantly. 'Do you understand what that means?'

'We can defend ourselves.'

'No. You cannot.'

She caught her breath, fighting the urge to turn tail and run, to flee back inside the castle and hide. She didn't want to believe him, but something told her she couldn't simply hide from this man, couldn't rely on the protection of cold, stone walls. She had a feeling that he'd smash straight through.

'Then I'll destroy the bridge.' She pressed her hands together so that he couldn't see them trembling. 'If you try to take the castle by force, I'll order my men to drop missiles over the walls. We have boulders ready inside. Haword will be worthless to you then.'

'True.'

'Then I mean it! If you attack, then I'll give the order.'

'I believe you, but I wouldn't recommend it.'

His voice was just as cold and expressionless as the rest of him. 'Stephen wants the bridge as much as the Empress does. If you destroy it, I doubt either one of them will be pleased.'

'He'll understand.'

'Perhaps, but what about de Ravenell's soldiers? They've been camped here for months. Do you think they'll simply give up their chance to pillage once you remove the only cause for restraint?'

She stared at him, aghast. 'But why would they still risk attacking us? We've nothing of any value. I'll give them anything they want to go away.'

'Such as yourself?' He leaned forward, lowering his voice as if he were sharing some secret too intimate to be said aloud. 'Men have other motives beside greed and revenge, my lady.'

She gasped before she could stop herself. His breath was warm on her cheek, but his words were chilling. She couldn't deny the truth of them, though she had the distinct impression that he was trying to intimidate her, to frighten her into submission.

'When do you want an answer?'

'You have one hour.'

'One hour?'

'You've had enough time to think, my lady.'

'Not about *this*!'

She staggered backwards, appalled. She needed more than one hour! How could he possibly expect her to make such a momentous decision so quickly? It was no time at all! On the other hand, what choice did she really have? If she wanted to save her men, there was only one thing she *could* do.

He gave a terse nod, as if he knew it, too. 'I'll be back in one hour. No longer.'

She stared at him bleakly. That gave her an hour to make ready, to speak to her men, to tell them to lay down their weapons and hide their valuables as best as they could. If only she could hide the truth about her bargain with Stephen, too, but that was impossible. Once this man took possession of Castle Haword he'd find out exactly what she'd done to keep it. And when he did, he'd likely turn her over to the Empress himself.

Unless... She inhaled sharply, half-alarmed, half-exhilarated by a new idea. Unless she stopped him right now, never gave him the chance to order an assault. Unless she took him prisoner instead!

She bit her lip, struggling to keep her expression calm, gripped by a heady blend of excitement and fear. If she took him prisoner, then in all likelihood de Ravenell would remain in charge and the siege would go on as before. It might not stop an assault in the long run, but it might stall it long enough for Stephen to arrive with reinforcements.

But *how* could she do it? Her mind raced to formulate a plan. She wouldn't be able to overpower him on her own, that was obvious, and if she didn't want to risk any of her men, then she'd have to use another, more insidious means of subduing him. That was *if* she could persuade him to enter the castle in the first place, and how could she do that? There was only one possible method that sprang to mind, though the very idea filled her with horror—a means of entrapping him, too, if she only had nerve enough to try it. If she flirted with him, made him believe that she wanted more than simply to negotiate, that she had a private, ulterior, *personal* motive for inviting him inside the castle walls...would he follow her then?

She felt her cheeks flood with colour and castigated herself inwardly. How could she possibly pretend to seduce him if she couldn't even imagine such a thing without blushing? Beside the fact that she'd never flirted with a man in her life, hardly knew where to begin. Everything she knew she'd learned from overheard snatches of gossip, from watching other people, never participating herself. Her father had made it clear what would happen if any of his men ever dared to so much as glance at her in that way. Not that any ever had. They'd always viewed her in the same way he did—as an honorary man. Certainly never as a woman...

Her heart sank. How could somebody like her possibly hope to tempt someone like this warrior? She had no idea what to say, let alone how to act! What if she did it wrong? Bad enough that she was already damp and bedraggled, and he looked like the kind of man who'd be accustomed to plenty of female attention. If he rejected, or even worse, laughed at her, she'd be mortified. It was a ridiculous idea, too demeaning to contemplate, and yet she had to do *something*, no matter how potentially humiliating. He was already turning away. If she were going to act, it had to be now.

'Lothar!' She called his name out impulsively.

'Lady Juliana?' He looked back over his shoulder, though he didn't turn around.

'I don't need an hour. I'll surrender now.'

'*Now?*'

She nodded, trying to look as innocent as possible as he turned slowly back again, his expression as unreadable as ever. What was he thinking? She ran her tongue along her lips to moisten them, struck by a fresh wave of panic. How could she possibly hope to seduce this man of all men? He seemed to have no emotions at all. Surely a statue would be easier! But it was too late to retreat. If she were going to protect her men *and* keep her promise to Stephen, then this was the only way. At the very least, she had to try. And she *was* a woman after all, no matter what everyone else seemed to think. There had to be something feminine about her, something that might tempt him. Sir Guian had certainly thought so.

She licked her lips again, fluttering her eyelashes in the way she'd seen the castle maids act around her soldiers.

'Why don't you come inside so we can talk?'

'You want me to come *inside*?' Lothar repeated the question to make sure he hadn't misheard.

'Why not?' Lady Juliana tossed her head, sending a cascade of wet ringlets tumbling over one shoulder. 'So we can discuss terms.'

That settled it. That time he definitely hadn't imagined the coy tilt of her head or the glint in those luminous green eyes. For an alarming moment, he thought he'd let his imagination run away with him, distracted by the way her damp dress was clinging to her body in all the right places. But, no, unlikely as it seemed, she was actually batting her eyelashes at him—dark lashes so lush and long they seemed to be catching raindrops on the tips.

'Perhaps you'd care for some refreshment?'

Her voice sounded low and breathy all of a sudden, almost a purr, and he arched an eyebrow before he could stop himself. Normally he prided himself on never being caught off guard by an opponent, but the abrupt change in her demeanour took even him by surprise. He'd known enough women to know when one was flirting with him.

And when one was pretending.

He studied her for a moment, trying to work out what she was doing. He didn't know quite what he'd expected, but she was nothing like the duplicitous shrew Sir Guian had described. Nothing like her father either, except for her eyes. They were the same shade of vivid jade-green, shining with the same spark of intelligence, too. The similarity had disturbed him at first, as if he'd actually been looking into the eyes of his dead friend, though the longer he'd looked at the daughter, the more he'd become aware of the innocence beneath the defiant façade. He'd been deliberately harsh when he'd spoken to her, trying to intimidate her into surrender, though he'd done nothing but tell the blunt truth. It was a tried and tested tactic, one that usually worked, too, even if he'd felt strangely uncomfortable using it on her, as if he'd been doing something wrong. He hadn't *wanted* to intimidate her, even for her own good, though why she was different from any other opponent he had no idea.

He thought he'd been on the verge of success, too, had seen the unmistakable look of defeat in her eyes just a few moments before, quickly followed by something else, a flash of nervous excitement that she was trying too hard to conceal. And now she was playing the part of seductress, though her lack of experience was obvious. Try as she might, she couldn't hide the uncertainty behind her eyes or the heat in her skin—the vivid pink blush spreading all the way up from the throat of her gown to the very roots of her hair. Judging by the way her fingers were toying nervously with the ends of her belt, he suspected it was the first time she'd flirted with anyone. The idea was unexpectedly appealing. If it weren't for the hint of fear behind her forced smile, he might be tempted to find out just how far her blushes spread…

'You should take the time to consider, my lady.'

'You don't want me to surrender?'

She opened her eyes wide and he felt a stirring in his loins, quickly suppressed. For someone so obviously new to the role of temptress, she was surprisingly good at it. She was watching him intently, biting her bottom lip between even, white teeth, though he suspected it was more of a nervous gesture than one designed to entice him. Even so, the effect was surprisingly potent.

'Surrender?' He lowered his voice huskily, responding in kind. Did she even *know* what she was suggesting?

She gave a low murmur, something that sounded like agreement, before spinning on her heel and throwing a beckoning glance over her shoulder.

'Shall we discuss it inside? Out of the rain?'

He watched her go with regret, his gaze lingering on the way her red hair swung loosely against her slender hips and pert behind as she sauntered slowly back along the bridge. It was a shame she was only pretending, otherwise… He fought to bring his mind, not to mention his body, back under control. This was neither the time nor the place for such distractions, but there was something unusually winsome about her. It certainly wasn't the way she was dressed. Her drab brown tunic didn't do her justice at all. A Celtic queen ought to be decked out in jewels— emeralds to match her eyes or rubies to complement her hair. Maybe even gold... He frowned, surprised by the direction of his own thoughts. Since when did he care what women wore? Since when did he notice?

He glanced past her, through the arch of the gatehouse into the bailey beyond. It was a trap. No enemy turned from hate-filled defiance to willing surrender so quickly. She was trying to lure him into the castle, but why? To shoot him? No, if she intended that then she could have given the order from the battlements. More likely she was planning something else, some last-ditch, desperate attempt to take him prisoner—but how would she do it? If the idea had only just occurred to her, as he was almost certain it had, then she was probably making up a plan as she went along. She couldn't order her men to seize him straight away, not whilst he was still armed and with the drawbridge still lowered behind them, providing a possible route of escape. In which case, she'd need to draw him further into the castle, probably into the keep, and if she wanted to avoid bloodshed then she'd need to hold her men off, too... then find some other way to disarm him.

He'd like to see her try. She had nerve, he'd give her that, but how far would nerve take her?

Apart from his sword, he had a dagger in his gambeson and a seax in his boot, not to mention assorted poignards concealed about his person. She'd have to undress him completely to find all of them and he'd definitely like to see that.

On the other hand, what would happen if he *didn't* follow her? If he ignored her invitation and walked away, would she still be willing to surrender the castle in an hour? She didn't strike him as foolhardy, but she'd already proven somewhat unpredictable. If she refused his terms then he'd have no choice but to launch an attack, and then all hell could, and most likely *would*, break loose. Whereas if he went with her, if he pretended to accept her offer, then he'd still stand a chance of convincing her. If she didn't throw him into a dungeon first…

He stole a fresh glance at the fortifications. The castle would make a reasonably effective prison, though not inescapable, and she'd have to catch him first. He hadn't met an opponent who could outwit him yet and he had no intention of starting now. All he had to do was stay one step ahead. In the meantime, the thought of a warm hearth and some female companionship was distinctly appealing. He'd barely had a chance to breathe over the past few months, either fighting or riding between skirmishes on the Empress's behalf. A brief rest, even with a woman who was trying to entrap him, would make an interesting change, and if by some unlikely chance she succeeded…

well, he trusted his men to carry out his orders, no matter what. The attack would go ahead tomorrow as planned, whether he was there to lead it or not. There was no risk to the Empress's plans, only to him—and he was expendable.

'Are you coming?'

He looked down again. Lady Juliana was standing on the very edge of the drawbridge, the sultry timbre of her voice replaced by a nervous quaver that was somehow more powerful than all the fluttering eyelashes in the world put together. He felt a tug in his chest as if she were actually pulling him after her. She looked worried and he felt strangely reluctant to disappoint her. Not that it made any sense. She was a siren trying to lure him into a trap. He ought to stuff up his ears, walk away and leave his ultimatum as it stood—let her surrender in an hour or face an assault at dawn. That was what he ought to do, what his men, not to mention the Empress, would expect him to do. Except that he found it utterly impossible to do so.

He looked down at his feet, vaguely surprised to find them already moving, following behind her like a dog after its mistress. Damn it all, it was a trap, most definitely a trap, but at least he'd go in with his eyes open.

'Welcome to Castle Haword, Lothar.' She gave another coy smile, unable to hide completely her look of relief.

'Lead on, Lady Juliana.'

He rested a hand on his sword hilt, resigning himself to his fate as he followed her under the portcullis and through the great archway. Whatever she intended, it ought to be entertaining at least. Not to mention a far more agreeable way of passing the evening than with de Ravenell. If nothing else, he was interested to see just how far her pretence of seduction would go. He'd no interest in frightening or deflowering maidens, but if she thought she could manipulate him so easily then he'd be sure to give her a lot more than she'd bargained for.

His lips curved in a slow, anticipatory smile. By morning, he fully intended to have both castle and woman exactly where he wanted them.

Chapter Four

~~~~~~~~

Juliana pressed a hand to her stomach, trying to quell the feeling that she was about to be sick.

What was she doing? Her legs were shaking so violently that she didn't know if she felt elated or terrified or both. Had that really been her, flirting so shamelessly with an enemy warrior in full view of the castle walls? She didn't know where the words had come from, but amazingly her siren's performance actually seemed to have worked. Deep down she hadn't really thought that it would, yet there he was at her shoulder, following her into the bailey like just another one of her soldiers. She only hoped that disarming him would be so easy.

She hauled in a few deep breaths, making a conscious effort to swing her hips as she walked. If brazen was what he wanted, then brazen was what he'd get. Up to a point anyway. She'd led him to expect… Her courage baulked at the thought of what she'd led him to expect. She wasn't even completely sure what *it* was, but she was a lady. There was only so far a lady could be expected to go. Wasn't there?

She threw a quick glance over her shoulder and then wished that she hadn't. Of all the soldiers in the Empress's army, she doubted she could have found a more intimidating prospect. With his broad shoulders, Lothar put her in mind of a battering ram, though surely a battering ram would show more emotion. If he was remotely concerned about entering the castle on his own, he didn't show it. On the contrary, his confident stride suggested Haword was already his for the taking. Well, it wasn't, not yet. It was still *hers*, though if her plan failed, she might as well unleash a wild animal in the bailey herself. What would happen if he guessed her deception? How many men would it take to restrain him? More than she was willing to risk.

'My lady?' Ulf stepped out in front of them and her hopes plummeted at once.

'Constable.' She shot him a warning look. 'This is Sergeant Lothar, the Empress's envoy. He and I will be taking refreshments together in the hall.'

'Then I'll accompany you, my lady.'

'That won't be necessary, thank you. We have a great deal to discuss. In private.'

'It isn't seemly…'

'Please see to it that we're not disturbed.' She spoke over him, jutting her chin out as his expression darkened mutinously.

'He ought to surrender his weapons.'

'*Constable*, you insult our guest!'

She whirled around, though to her relief their guest didn't look remotely offended.

'Not at all.' Lothar shrugged, though his stony gaze rested on Ulf a little too keenly for her liking. 'It's a reasonable request. Though there's only one of me and...' he glanced nonchalantly around the bailey '...around fifty of you? Surely you aren't afraid of those odds?'

'Under the terms of a truce, it's customary to leave your weapons outside.'

'If this were a truce I'd agree, but I don't recall anyone uttering the word.' He quirked an eyebrow towards her. 'Did *you*, my lady?'

'I'm mentioning it now.' Ulf's tone was belligerent.

'Did *you*, Lady Juliana?' Lothar ignored him, his voice dropping to an intimate undertone. 'Perhaps when I was distracted?'

She inhaled sharply, taken aback as much by the deep, honeyed tone of his voice as by the fact that he actually seemed to be smiling. The effect was unexpectedly disarming, like the sun bursting out from between storm clouds. For a fleeting moment, his stern features were utterly transformed, still rugged and yet even more strikingly handsome. He looked more like a knight from some chivalric romance than an enemy warrior, a man she might truly be tempted by…

She tore her gaze away, alarmed by the thought. *That* was impossible. She could never be drawn to such a cold-blooded, fearsome-looking warrior. It was only her fear confusing her, not him. *Definitely* not him.

'Our guest may do as he pleases.' She spoke with as much authority as she could muster. She had the distinct impression that Lothar was deliberately trying to provoke her Constable, and her Constable was letting him. If she wasn't careful there'd be bloodshed before they even made it past the gatehouse.

'There's no truce, just…' she groped for a suitable word, 'an understanding.'

'But, my lady…'

'*Stand down*, Ulf!' She held his gaze until he stepped begrudgingly to one side, then gestured towards Lothar. 'Shall we?'

She didn't wait for an answer, marching ahead as quickly as she dared without making him suspicious. It was approaching noon and the castle cooks were busy making the best of their meagre rations, doling out bowls of pottage to a line of soldiers waiting outside the kitchens. She winced as they passed. She hadn't wanted Lothar to see *that*. Bad enough that he could already see the full extent of their defences, but now he could see the condition of her men, too. If he did somehow manage to escape, there'd be no stopping him.

They reached the steps of the keep and she pushed on the door with a sense of relief, glad to be out of sight of her soldiers at last. Judging by their shocked expressions, they were just as scandalised by her behaviour as Ulf. Well, they'd just have to think what they liked. She could explain herself—and accept their apologies—later. *If* her plan worked, that was. Otherwise...

She pushed her misgivings aside, sweeping through the antechamber and on into the hall, her eyes turning at once towards a chest in the far corner. It was where she stored what was left of the wine, as well as other more potent substances in a small wooden box, the key of which she always kept tied to her belt. She wrapped her fingers around it now, gripping the metal tightly as she made her way across the room. Now if she could just open the box, pour the wine and mix one of her remedies into it without him noticing...

She heard a loud scraping sound and spun around, letting out an involuntarily squeak of alarm as she saw her companion draw the last of the iron door bolts.

'So we're not disturbed.' Lothar sauntered towards her. 'Though I'd lay good money on your Constable being right outside.'

Her throat tightened. *Locked in!* Despite what she'd said, it hadn't occurred to her that *he* might do anything to ensure they weren't disturbed. She had no doubt that her soldiers were close by, but if she called for help now, it would take precious

minutes for them to break through. Not that she
needed any help, she reminded herself. She was
the chatelaine and she'd come this far by herself.
She'd work out the rest, too. She had to.

'Of course.' She forced a smile, gesturing casually towards the hearth. 'Won't you make yourself comfortable?'

She turned her back on him again, unlocking
the box and extracting a small leather pouch, taking deep breaths to stay calm. It was only a door
after all, and if—*when*—her plan worked then she
wouldn't even need an escape route. She just had
to concentrate, had to pour two cups of wine and
mix the poppy milk carefully, get the measure-
ments just right and make sure there was no residue left behind. And she had to hurry. She could
already hear the tread of his footsteps crossing
the flagstones, the swoosh of his surcoat as he
cast it aside, the metallic chink of his chainmail...
Chainmail? Her stomach swooped. What was he
doing with his chainmail?

She clasped a cup in each hand and moved
haltingly towards him. To her horror, she saw
that he'd already removed both his surcoat and
chainmail, leaving only his undershirt, hose and
leather boots.

'They were wet.' He jerked his head towards
the discarded pile of clothing.

'Your chainmail was wet?' Her voice seemed
to have become alarmingly high-pitched.

'You'd be surprised at how heavy it gets in

the rain. You should get out of those damp clothes, too.'

She stiffened instinctively before remembering to turn her look of affront into a smile. After all, she was supposed to be flirting with him. This was supposed to be her idea. It was ridiculous to be offended, no matter how insolent he was.

'There's no rush.' She tried her best to sound playful. 'You wouldn't want me to surrender too easily, would you?'

His gaze flickered down to her legs before travelling leisurely up again. 'Forgive me, Lady Juliana, but I was under the impression that you already had.'

She caught her breath, every part of her body tingling where his gaze touched her. He was right about her clothes being wet. She hadn't thought about it before, but they were moulded so closely to her skin that he could surely see every curve of her body. Not that she had many of those, but she might as well have been naked for all the protection her tunic was giving her. Her mouth turned dry at the thought. Now that his warrior's face was finally showing some sign of emotion she wished it wasn't. She wished he *was* a statue again. He was looking at her in a way that suggested he wanted more, far more, than just a drink.

'Some wine?' She held the laced cup out towards him. 'I offered you some refreshment.'

'I don't drink wine.'

His voice hardened abruptly, as if she'd just insulted him instead of having offered a drink, and she froze in panic. Had he seen through her deception already, then? Was that why he'd locked the door? She felt her hands break out in a cold sweat and her scalp tighten with dread. If he didn't drink, then she'd have no chance of overpowering him. What would happen then? What would he do to her?

She licked her lips to loosen them, pretending not to notice the frosty shift in his demeanour. 'It's from one of my father's best casks, for special occasions only. I'm sure you'll enjoy it.'

'Taste has nothing to do with it. I don't drink anything stronger than ale.' Black brows drew together in a fierce line and then suddenly softened again. 'But perhaps just this once. Since we're celebrating.'

He reached for the cup with one hand and caught her fingers in the other, lifting them gently to his lips as her heart seemed to stop and then accelerate again wildly. Alone in a locked room, somehow the gesture felt more intimate than if he'd actually pulled her into his arms. His lips felt surprisingly soft and warm, brushing her knuckles with just the lightest of pressures, and yet somehow making the whole of her insides start to quiver.

It was fear, she reminded herself, fear making her body react in such a new and alarming fashion, as if she were losing control of her senses.

In the flickering firelight, his eyes looked more purple than grey, shimmering amethysts rather than hard granite stones, pinning her to the spot with such compelling intensity that she hardly dared breathe, let alone blink…

On the other hand, the still rational part of her brain argued, at least while he was looking at her he wasn't looking at the wine, wouldn't notice any residue left inside. She was halfway to achieving her aim. He was holding the cup in his hand. Now she just had to make him drink.

She raised her own cup in salute and took a sip, stifling a cry of relief when he did the same. He drained half the liquid in one draught, his other hand tightening over hers as he did so, as if he were daring her to pull away. She didn't move, torn between conflicting emotions of elation and fear. After all, she wasn't out of danger yet. She still had to distract him, had to give the poppy a chance to work whilst she kept his mind off other activities. From the look on his face, it wasn't going to be easy.

'You look worried, my lady.' His voice sounded even deeper than usual, sending a strangely visceral thrill all through her body.

'Do I?'

A black eyebrow quirked upwards and she felt a sudden, faint tingle of suspicion. There was something vaguely mocking about the gesture, something that suggested he knew exactly what effect he was having on her, as if he were toying

with her even. But that didn't make sense. He'd
followed her into the castle because she'd as good
as offered herself to him. He thought she was a
loose woman, a wanton, so why would he make
fun of her? Unless that was what men did, made
fun of their conquests? Though what did it matter as long as he was drinking?

'There's no need to worry.' His thumb brushed
lightly over her knuckles. 'The Empress gave her
word that no one would be harmed if you surrendered. You're perfectly safe, I promise you.'

Safe? She tried not to look too incredulous.
Nothing about him felt *safe*. The way his fingers
were caressing her skin felt distinctly *un*safe!

'Then I thank you...' she grasped quickly at
the idea his words gave her '...though I did wonder *why* the Empress is offering terms again?
Why offer to spare us after what I did?'

'After you swore an oath of allegiance to her
enemy, you mean?'

'Yes.' She gritted her teeth at the accusation.
'I thought that she'd want to punish me. Isn't she
angry?'

'Given your father's loyalty to her cause, she
was mostly surprised. But she has fond memories
of him and would prefer to spare you for his sake.'
His expression shifted slightly. 'As would I.'

'You?' She gaped in surprise. '*You* knew my
father?'

'I met him on a few occasions at the Empress's

court, yes. We even fought side by side at the Battle of Lincoln. He was a good man. Loyal.'

She didn't answer at first, struck with a familiar pang of guilt. If Lothar was trying to rebuke her, to remind her of just how badly she'd betrayed her father's ideals, then he needn't have bothered. She didn't need reminding. She lived with the consequences of her disloyalty every day.

'If he knew what I'd done, he'd be furious.' She answered the accusation before it came.

'Then why did you do it?'

'Why did I swear allegiance to the man who'd just killed my father, you mean?'

The eyebrow quirked even higher. 'Yes.'

She drew a deep, faltering breath. This wasn't what she wanted to talk about, not at all. She didn't want to talk about her father, or politics, or any of the reasons why she'd betrayed the Empress. Her feelings on the subject were still too painful, too raw. She'd made her choice when she'd made her bargain with Stephen, and there was no going back on any of it now. But at least they were talking. Lothar was still holding one of her hands, though he wasn't stroking the knuckles any more. He seemed intent upon what she was saying instead, as if he were genuinely interested in what her motivation had been. Strangely enough she didn't feel frightened any longer. He wasn't a statue or an enemy any more. He was a man who'd fought alongside her father, someone she could talk to about him, even if she probably shouldn't… But perhaps she could tell Lothar *part* of the truth. She wanted to, she realised, wanted to talk about her father to someone who'd known him. If she could make a man like Lothar understand what she'd done, then perhaps it wouldn't seem so bad any more. Perhaps if he understood, then he might even forgive her—and if *he* could, then perhaps she could start to forgive herself, too…

Chapter Five

Juliana straightened her shoulders, trying to look Lothar square in the eye, though with his immense height she had to reach up on her tiptoes.

'You know that King Stephen laid siege to us nine months ago?'

He nodded. 'There were a number of sieges at the time, otherwise the Empress would have sent reinforcements.'

'That's what my father said. He always defended her, no matter how bad the situation became, but the truth was that we weren't prepared for a siege. My father…' she hesitated, searching for a way to explain '…had other things on his mind. We held out for three months, but it was no use. Our only choices were to starve, fight or surrender. Father decided to ride out and meet Stephen in battle.'

'He died like a true soldier.'

'Is that what you heard?'

'Yes.' Dark brows snapped together. 'Isn't that what happened?'

'No.' She shook her head, swallowing the sudden lump in her throat. 'He was injured and taken prisoner, but he never recovered.'

His grip on her hand tightened. 'I'm sorry.'

'I surrendered because I didn't want to lose anyone else. I didn't have a choice.'

'What about your oath of allegiance? Surely you had a choice there?'

She flinched. There was no way to explain *that*, not without telling him the whole truth anyway, and she couldn't do that. But she had to offer some reason, no matter how bad it sounded.

'I'd already lost my father. I didn't want to lose my home and position, too.'

A shadow crossed his face. 'You mean you swore allegiance to Stephen just so you could remain chatelaine?'

'Yes.' She wrenched her hand away, stung by the contempt in his voice. She couldn't blame him for thinking the worst of her, even if, for some reason, she didn't want him to. He actually sounded disappointed—as if he had any right to judge her or whomever she chose to give her allegiance to! She racked her brains, dredging up every argument she'd used to convince *herself* of the validity of Stephen's claim.

'*And* I support him because I want the war to

be over. Stephen's a crowned king. He can bring peace.'

'He's a usurper.' Lothar's tone was implacable. 'King Henry named his daughter Matilda as his heir.'

'Stephen has royal blood, too. They're cousins.'

'He stole the crown.'

'Because Matilda wasn't in the country to claim it! It took her four years even to cross the Channel after King Henry died. England needed a ruler and Stephen was *here*!'

'She had to deal with Normandy first. Not to mention that she was with child when her father died. Absence doesn't lessen her claim.'

'Stephen's an honourable man.'

'Honourable?' Lothar's voice positively dripped with disgust. 'When Henry was alive Stephen swore an oath to accept her as Queen. Twice.'

'Maybe he was coerced.'

'Maybe he's a liar.'

'He can still bring peace! It's Matilda who keeps the war going. If she'd go back to Anjou, then we could have peace again. Isn't that more important than her *claim*?'

'Your father didn't think so.'

'I have a mind of my own!' She flung her cup to the floor in frustration, clenching her fists as the metal clattered loudly across the flagstones. He was infuriating, actually seeming to get calmer the more furious she became. How dare he sound so smug, as if it were all so simple, as if all the choices she'd had to make over the past six months had been easy!

'I can see that.'

She stiffened at once. Her father had always taken pride in having a daughter who could think for herself, but she knew most men were less tolerant. She knew what they called her, too. A virago. A shrew. Unnatural, unladylike, unsuitable for marriage. Was that what Lothar thought, too? Not that it mattered, she reminded herself. She didn't care what he thought of her. If her display of temper had changed his mind about her feminine charms, then so much the better. He'd already drunk the wine. There was no need for him to find her attractive any more. Even if the thought made her feel strangely crestfallen.

'Do you think I should agree with my father just because I'm a woman?' She narrowed her eyes accusingly.

'No.'

'No?'

'On the contrary. I serve the Empress, my lady, I've no problem with women thinking for themselves.' His voice took on a husky undertone as he took a step closer towards her. 'Or with them taking command.'

'Wh-what do you mean?' she stammered, feeling alarmingly out of her depth all of a sudden. She'd been braced for another argument, ready for him to call her an unnatural female, but he was acting as if he *still* wanted her, as if he found the idea of a woman in command appealing. Not that she felt very commanding at that moment.

'I followed you here when you asked me to, didn't I?'

'Yes, but…'

'So, now that I'm here, why don't you tell me what you want from me?'

'What *I* want?'

He stopped a hair's breadth away from her, his voice soft as a caress. 'As I told you, my lady, I'm just a soldier. I'm only here to serve.'

She heard a strangled sound emerge from her own throat, though words themselves seemed beyond her. She had no idea what he meant by *serve* her, though if the tone of his voice were anything to go by, it wasn't something that a lady ought to be doing… Why wasn't the poppy working yet? She'd given him enough to fell an ordinary-sized man twice over! How could he still be standing?

He coiled a strand of damp hair around his fingers, using it to tug her face gently upwards. 'Or you could just show me what you want?'

She dropped her gaze to hide her confusion, though unfortunately that only brought it level with his mouth. Show him *what*? Whatever it was, she'd probably only have to play along for a few minutes at most, but what did he expect her to do? Was she supposed to kiss him? To touch him? She wouldn't know where to start! He was threading his fingers through her hair. Did he expect her to do the same? Not that his shorter style allowed quite the same scope. Perhaps she ought to caress his cheek instead?

She peeked up again, searching for some clue on his face, just in time to see a quickly concealed look of amusement.

Amusement! She felt a jolt, suspicion turning to certainty in an instant. He *was* laughing at her, mocking her pitiful attempt at seduction with a pretence of his own! Suddenly she wished there were a hole she could crawl into. All this time she thought she'd been leading him on, foolishly believing that he was attracted to her, when in fact the very reverse was true. He'd been pretending, too, enjoying her discomfort, letting her make a fool of herself while he simply enjoyed her performance, so arrogantly confident about her surrender that it probably hadn't even occurred to him that she might have an ulterior motive for inviting him inside the castle! Well, she could console herself with *that* at least. In a few moments she'd be the one laughing at *him*!

'My lady?' Grey eyes glinted sardonically. 'Have you changed your mind?'

Somehow she resisted the temptation to slap the smug look off his face. Bad enough that he was toying with her, but now he was mocking her overtly, too, adding insult to injury, as if he thought she wouldn't have the nerve to go through with her seduction. Her temper flared at the thought. How dare he doubt her nerve! She wouldn't back down from a challenge by any man, no matter how intimidating. He could mock her as much as he liked. She'd show him exactly how much nerve she had!

She launched herself forward impulsively, throwing her arms around his neck and her body against his chest with an audible thud as she crushed her mouth against his.

There! She felt a rush of exhilaration as their lips touched and clung. That showed him! It wasn't so hard to kiss a man after all. All she had to do was press her lips against his and hold them there. A few seconds would surely be enough. There was nothing to it, nothing special or terrifying. It was quite ordinary really...

No sooner had the thought entered her head than she forgot it again, startled by the pressure of his lips as they began to respond, gently and unhurriedly at first, then with a deeper, building intensity. For a few moments, time seemed to stop as she simply stood there, stunned, not knowing how to react, unable to draw back even as his tongue slid its way smoothly between her lips, teasing them open before taking full possession of her mouth.

Then instinct took over. She didn't think, didn't give herself a chance to consider as she responded in kind, leaning towards him as he wrapped his arms around her waist, drawing her so close that she could feel every line of his strong, muscular body. He even felt like a battering ram, she thought in amazement, running her hands over the broad expanse of his shoulder blades. If she'd taken a running leap at him from the far side of the room, he probably wouldn't have budged. Not that she wanted him to. She didn't know what she wanted any more. Was she trying to prove something? She couldn't remember. What had started as a gesture of defiance had turned into something else entirely, though as to what it was…

All she knew was that she didn't want it to stop. She'd never even imagined a feeling like it before, this hot, trembling sensation deep in the pit of her stomach, an ache and a need and a longing all at the same time.

He groaned against her mouth and she raked her fingers through his hair, kissing him back just as fiercely—fiercer, even—running her tongue along his bottom lip before twining it back around his. Tasting, exploring…

She froze, suddenly aware that he'd stopped moving. He *wasn't* kissing her back any more. He was barely even holding her, his hands slackening and then falling from her waist as he took an unsteady step backwards. She raised a hand to her mouth, mortified by her own shameless behaviour, afraid that he was about to mock her again before the truth finally dawned.

The poppy was working.

She let out a ragged breath. How could she have forgotten about the poppy? She'd been so wrapped up in the moment, in the heady feeling of his body and lips against hers, that she seemed to have forgotten everything else, including how a chatelaine ought to behave! It was one thing to *pretend* to seduce him—quite another to be seduced right back. Now he was swaying precariously in front of her, staring at his feet with a look of such bleary-eyed confusion that she was almost tempted to grab his arms and steady him. Then he looked up again, fixing her with a stare that had nothing remotely mocking about it, and she tried to jump backwards instead.

Too late. She jerked in mid-air as his hand shot out and grabbed her wrist.

'What have you done?' His tone was menacing.

'Let me go!' She tried to wrest herself free, but his grip was too tight.

'The wine, what was in it?'

'I said, let me go!'

'*What was in it?*' He tugged her roughly back against him, against the same chest she'd flung herself at just a few moments before, though there was nothing welcoming about it now. They seemed to have gone from one extreme of emotion to the other.

'Poppy.'

'*Poison?*'

'A sleeping draught.'

'You *drugged* me?'

'Yes.' She felt an unexpected stab of guilt.

'But don't worry. The effects will wear off by tomorrow.'

He staggered and she caught hold of his arms. No matter what had just happened between them, she didn't want him to fall and hurt himself. Not that she cared, she told herself, but he was no good to her injured. Even if, with the full weight of him in her arms, she didn't know which of them was in more danger.

She stumbled down with him to the floor, inwardly rebuking herself for her own lack of foresight. She ought to have done this next to something soft for him to fall on to. Her plan had worked, and yet ironically she'd managed to trap herself beneath him at the same time. She wriggled furiously, struck by the uncomfortable impression that she was behaving even more shamelessly now than before. His whole body was pressed down on top of hers, leaving little to the imagination. Definitely not a position a lady ought to find herself in.

She gave a push born of desperation and finally managed to half-drag, half-roll herself away. Then she lay on the floor at his side, panting and breathless, studying his face with a confusing mixture of triumph and trepidation. But at least her plan had succeeded. They could discuss *his* surrender tomorrow, though before that happened, she'd better make sure he was tied up tight. After what she'd just done, the last thing she wanted was for him to escape. If he'd thought badly of her before, she dreaded to imagine what he'd think of her when he woke up.

She reached out and trailed a finger along the jagged line of his scar. It made him look dangerous and vulnerable at the same time—as it turned out he was. She'd bested him for the time being, but for how long? She bit her lip, struck again by the sheer hulking size of him, trying to fight off the discomforting feeling that she'd just made an equally huge mistake.

Chapter Six

It was dark when he woke.

Lothar groped his way back to consciousness, opening his eyelids and wincing as a dull pain assailed the back of his eyeballs. Drugged. He'd been drugged. He felt groggy and leaden and stiff all over, the way other men claimed they felt after a night spent drinking. Now he knew what they meant—something else he could blame Lady Juliana for.

Lady Juliana. He swore under his breath. Clearly he'd misjudged the woman. He'd known that she'd been plotting something, that she'd wanted to capture him, but he'd followed her anyway, into the hall where she'd offered him some wine…

What had he been thinking? He must have been mad, following her simply because he'd wanted to help her. Because of her father? Yes and no. Yes, because he'd valued her father's friendship, no, because there was something else about her as well, some other enticement that had lured him over the drawbridge against his own better judgement. It hadn't just been attraction, though that had definitely been a big part of it. If he didn't know better, he would have said he'd felt worried about her...

Felt?

He scowled so ferociously that a stab of pain lanced through his head and down his spine. *Felt?* He'd *felt* worried? Since when did he *feel* things? He'd spent years *not* feeling. He didn't want to feel—not ever! Then again, he hadn't wanted any wine either and look what had happened there. He'd broken one of his own rules by drinking it, letting himself be persuaded by a pair of familiar green eyes in a deceptively innocent face. He had to hand it to her—if he weren't so livid with rage, at himself as well as at her, he might have been impressed. She'd managed to trick *and* to capture him, succeeding where the rest of Stephen's army had failed. He'd barely taken his eyes off her since they'd entered the bailey, but whatever she'd slipped into his drink had certainly been potent. Not to mention long-lasting. Judging by the darkness it was night-time already, the only illumination provided by a few thin slivers of moonlight filtering in through gaps in the window shutters.

Window shutters? He strained his eyes to make

sure he wasn't imagining things. So he wasn't in
a dungeon, then. On the contrary, he was lying on
something that felt suspiciously like a mattress.
Not bad for a prison, though something about his
position felt peculiar. He tried to stretch out, only
to find that he couldn't, and not just because of
the numbness in his limbs either. By the feel of
it, his wrists and ankles were tied together, bound
up tightly with rope.

He paused for a moment, considering what to
do next, then let loose a volley of obscenities, not
bothering to keep his voice down. If Lady Juliana were close by, he hoped she *could* hear him.
They were the very least he intended to say to
her. He supposed he ought to be grateful that she
hadn't gagged him as well, but right now, gratitude was the very last emotion he was feeling.
If—*when*—he got out of this, he'd find a way to
pay her back in kind!

A swell of desire coursed through him, the
more potent for being so unexpected, bringing his
tirade to an abrupt end as the thought of tying her
up brought to mind a very different scenario, not
to mention a far different response to the one he'd
anticipated. He was still furious with her and yet
his mind was beset by a confusing array of im-
pressions—the feeling of velvety soft lips against
his, of a supple body in his embrace, of spiralling
tendrils of hair in his fingertips and the soft pant
of breath on his neck. What the hell?

He heaved at his bindings, venting two very

different types of frustration, but they held tight. Whatever she'd given him must have been even more powerful than he'd thought, making both his thoughts and senses run riot. The image of her in his arms was surprisingly detailed, right down to the silvery sparkle of raindrops in her hair, and so vivid that it seemed less like a dream than a memory, though it couldn't be. In which case, what *had* happened? He dragged himself up to a sitting position, straining his memory for clues. His thoughts were still hazy, but he had a vague recollection of enjoying her company, even of feeling sympathy when she'd talked about her father. She'd argued, too, squaring up to him over the question of Stephen versus Matilda with a spiritedness that had taken him by surprise. Not many people ever dared to argue with him, and the fact that she hadn't been intimidated—not enough to back down anyway—had been oddly appealing. His desire for her had certainly been real, more real than anything he'd experienced in a long time, as if there were more behind it than just a physical response, though as to what he'd done about it…

He shook his head in disbelief. No. Even if he *had* been enjoying her pretence of seduction— a little too much, perhaps—he would never have taken advantage of her in that way. He'd never touched any woman who hadn't wanted him to and he refused to believe that any drug would have affected his behaviour so completely.

The very idea was abhorrent. He wouldn't have touched her, wouldn't have kissed her, not unless... He blinked as another, even more surprising idea popped into his head. Not unless she'd thrown herself at him first...

He gave a hollow laugh, rubbing his wrists together behind his back in an effort to work his fingers loose. Now he was definitely imagining things. The last thing she would have done was throw herself at him, more's the pity. The thought of finding out what those cherry-red lips tasted like was certainly tempting, but she was unlikely ever to offer him the chance. His current situation was proof enough of *that*.

He'd barely reached the conclusion before the door opened and the woman herself appeared, bearing a beeswax candle in one hand and a wooden cup in the other.

'Lady Juliana.' His lip curled at the sight of her. 'Good of you to remember me.'

'It would be hard to forget with all the noise you were making.' She put the candle down on a coffer, though she didn't look at him. 'Your men can probably hear you on the other side of the moat.'

She kept her eyes cast downwards as she approached the bed, walking so slowly that he would have assumed she was doing it on purpose to taunt him if she weren't so obviously exhausted. She looked even more tired than she had before, still dressed in the same nondescript brown tunic she'd been wearing in the rain, though she'd covered her hair with a cream-coloured headdress that only made the rings around her eyes look larger and darker by comparison, almost like bruises. Even so, the subtle sway of her hips was causing a definite physical response in his body. Damn it, what was the matter with him?

He dragged his gaze away from her hips and back towards the window. If he wasn't mistaken, the thin sliver of sky between the shutters appeared to be lighter than before. Hadn't she slept all night, then?

'Your hospitality's somewhat lacking, my lady.' He pushed an unwonted flicker of concern aside, glaring at her instead.

'Then you'll be pleased to hear that I've brought you some ale. Poppy makes you thirsty.'

His scowl deepened ferociously. That was true. His throat felt red raw, though the thought of accepting another drink from her gave him definite pause.

'You'll have to forgive me being suspicious.'

'Why would I drug you again? You're already tied up.'

'Really? I'd forgotten.'

She gave a weary-looking shrug. 'You don't have to drink if you don't want to.'

He shot her a look that would have made grown men quail, though she was too busy stifling a yawn to notice. The sight made him doubly angry. Bad enough that he was her prisoner—she didn't

have to act as if he were an inconvenience as well!
Even if she *had* been pacing the battlements all
night, she could at least have the decency to pay
him a little more attention.

'How do you expect me to drink when I'm tied
up?' he challenged her.

'Here.'

She held the cup to his lips, bending at the
waist and stretching her arms out in an apparent
attempt to keep the rest of her body as far away
from the bed as possible. If it hadn't been for
his own position he might have found such a bizarre posture amusing, though as it was he was
too thirsty to care. After a moment's hesitation
he drank, keeping his eyes on her face the whole
time, though she kept her own studiously averted,
blinking so rapidly it looked as if she were struggling to stay awake.

'Am I keeping you up?' He moved his mouth
away, making his tone as scathing as possible.
'Perhaps you need to go to bed, my lady.'

'I can't.' She put the cup to one side with a look
of relief. 'You're in it.'

'What?'

He was so surprised that for a moment he actually forgot to scowl. Instead he looked around,
reappraising the room in the flickering candlelight, finally noticing the tapestries on the walls
and the small trinket boxes set on a table by the
bed. *Definitely* not a prison, but what on earth
was she doing, putting him in her bedchamber?

He wasn't easily shocked, but he could only imagine two types of woman who would drug a man and then tie him up in their bed—ones who were either extremely innocent or extremely experienced. Under the circumstances, he wasn't sure which alarmed him more.

'This is *your* chamber?'

'Yes. I had my men carry you up. I thought you'd be more comfortable here.'

'Comfortable? Tied up?'

'Apart from that.'

He let out a shout of laughter, anger and shock turning to incredulity. 'Your father always said you were one of a kind. I'm starting to think he was right.'

'What do you mean?' Her eyes shot to his face, meeting his for the first time since she'd entered. 'My father told you about me?'

'He said he had a flame-headed firebrand for a daughter. Foolishly I thought he was exaggerating.'

'Truly? He said that?'

He narrowed his gaze, struck by the flicker of uncertainty in hers. Apparently what her father had said about her really mattered, as if she hadn't known how he'd felt. Strange, but he'd had the impression they were close. Or *had* been anyway...

'Something like that. I forget the exact words.'

'Oh.' Her expression wavered. 'Did he say it like it was a bad thing?'

'A bad thing?' The question took him by surprise. 'No, I wouldn't say that...'

He leaned back against the wall, stalling for time as he wondered what exactly he *would* say. Generally he favoured the truth, no matter how blunt, but this was hardly the time for discussing her father's fears for her future. He certainly wasn't in any position to offer advice. Even if he wasn't tied up, he was the last person in the world to talk to about any kind of paternal relationship.

'He said he'd like to introduce us one day.' That was true, he recalled with a jolt of surprise, though as to *why* William had said it, he couldn't remember.

Her mouth dropped open. 'You mean you were actually *friends* with him?'

'For my part, yes. I told you we fought together at Lincoln, but we spent a lot of time on the march talking, too. He had a way of making people talk. He was one of the cleverest men I ever met.' He paused meaningfully. 'I should have known better than to underestimate his daughter. I won't make the same mistake twice.'

She studied him intently for a moment as if considering whether or not to ask something else, before drawing up a stool.

'Are you hungry? We only have pottage, but I can ask one of the guards to fetch you some if you want?'

He had to stop himself from laughing again. Of all the questions he'd anticipated, *that* hadn't been one of them. She was certainly one of a kind. Now that she'd taken him prisoner, she seemed more concerned with his well-being than in interrogating or making any demands of him. She looked as if she'd rather close her eyes and go to sleep instead, though if the hour were really as late, or as early, as he suspected, then it wasn't long until dawn. Which meant that they were almost out of time. If he were going to convince her to surrender, then he had to hurry.

'You haven't taken many men captive, I presume?'

'Why?' Her expression turned guarded. 'What's wrong?'

'It's not usual to care so much about your prisoner's comfort.'

'Oh… No, I've never taken anyone prisoner before.'

'Then I'm honoured to be your first.' He was gratified to see a faint blush spread across her cheeks. She'd noticed *that* sarcasm at least. 'So what are we doing here, my lady?'

'I'd like to talk.'

'Isn't that what we were doing yesterday?'

'What do you mean?' Her eyes jumped to his again, the look of exhaustion in them replaced by one of sheer, sudden panic.

He arched an eyebrow, surprised by such an extreme reaction. 'You made quite a good defence of Stephen, as I recall.'

'Oh.' The panic receded slightly. 'Yes, of course.'

'Was there something else?'

'No! We talked, that's all.'

'Then what do you want from me, my lady?'

He started, struck by the sudden conviction that he'd said those words before and recently. Judging by the vibrant shade of Lady Juliana's cheeks, she remembered them, too. Her skin was almost the same colour as her hair, as if she were embarrassed about something, but what? Just what exactly *had* happened between them? Surely none of the things he *thought* he remembered…

'I want you to tell your soldiers to go.' Her voice shook slightly.

'Mmm?' He was so busy trying to remember that he barely paid any attention to her words. 'Just like that?'

'Yes. Sir Guian's, too. Tell them they have until noon to pack up and leave.'

'Or?'

'Or there'll be consequences.'

'Such as?'

'Consequences!'

She looked so fierce that his lips twitched involuntarily. 'You'll need to be a bit more specific.'

'It's not funny!'

'No.'

'No, it's not funny?'

'No, it's not and, no, I won't do it. Just no.'

'But you haven't even considered it!'

'I don't need to. No.'

'Stop saying no!'

'Then I decline.'

'You might change your mind when you're hanging by your feet from the battlements!'

'Ah.' He gave a tight smile. There it was at last, the threat he'd been waiting for. He'd been starting to wonder if she'd even thought of one. 'It might, though it wouldn't make any difference. My men have their orders already.'

The colour seeped from her face in an instant. 'What orders?'

'The ones I gave them before we met on the drawbridge. I told you I intended to capture Haword today, though I admit this wasn't quite what I had in mind.'

'You can still countermand the order.'

'I *could*, but it might look a little coerced if I'm hanging from the battlements.'

'You don't think your men will disobey orders to save you?'

'I think they know what will happen to them if they do. I don't tolerate disobedience, my lady. Not for any reason.'

'Not even to save your life?'

'Those are my rules. What kind of commander would I be if I changed them simply to save myself?'

'I'll tell Sir Guian, then.' She sounded desperate this time. 'He'll call off the attack. He never wanted to fight anyway.'

'True, but I think he'd enjoy the spectacle of

me hanging by my feet too much to do anything to stop it. Besides, my men don't take orders from anyone else. With or without Sir Guian's permission, they're coming.'

She shot to her feet so quickly that her stool toppled backwards, landing with a clatter on the floorboards. There were no rushes, he noticed, something else they must have run out of. After four months of siege, it appeared that both castle and chatelaine were reaching the end of their tether. He could see tension in every line of her body, as if she might snap at any moment.

'What difference would it make even if they did retreat?' He kept on pushing, hardening his heart against the bizarre urge to offer comfort instead. 'You'd only buy yourself a few days, a week at the most, before the Empress sends them back again.'

'Maybe that's all I need.'

It was only a murmur, but enough to make his brows snap together at once. Was that why she was so determined to hold out then, because she was waiting for reinforcements? The last he'd heard, Stephen's forces had been busy fortifying coastal defences against the threat of Angevin landings, but perhaps she knew something he didn't. If Stephen were heading back into Herefordshire, then it made capturing Haword even more vital. In which case, he had to persuade her to surrender *now*...

'What's that?' She twisted her head at a clamour-

ing sound from outside, the clanking of metal over
the dull hum of voices.

'Take a look.'

He nodded towards the window and she ran
towards it, unlatching the shutters and flinging
them wide. Even from across the room he could
hear her sharp intake of breath.

'What are they doing?'

'Hard to say from here, but at a guess I'd say
they're preparing for battle. I'd suggest that your
men do the same.'

'But I don't want to fight!'

'Then surrender. My offer still stands.'

She spun around, eyes widening with amazement. 'You'd forgive me after I drugged you?'

'Apparently so.' He surprised himself with the
answer. He *could* forgive her, though mercy alone
knew why. 'Although I think we can keep that
part between ourselves.'

She stared at him mutely for a few seconds,
her expression veering between defiance and uncertainty, before she reached into the folds of her
gown and drew out a slim, though still lethal-
looking dagger.

'No.' Her face took on a look of resolve. 'I'm
the chatelaine and this is still my castle. We're
going to the battlements.'

Chapter Seven

Lothar watched her approach in silence, wondering just how badly he'd misjudged her, before she reached down to his ankles and sliced through the rope bindings.

'Time for my swing over the battlements?' He lifted an eyebrow sardonically. 'Am I allowed to wear my boots at least?'

She hesitated briefly and then walked to the end of the bed, picking up his leather boots and sliding them warily over his feet, as if she expected him to kick out at any moment.

'Your hospitality's improving, my lady.'

She didn't answer, her face set with a look of grim determination as she made for the door and murmured something to the guards outside. She gestured back into the room as if she were telling them to fetch him, but he stilled their approach with a scowl, heaving himself unsteadily to his feet and making his own way across the floor. After a night spent lying in one position, his legs felt numb, but he'd be damned if he was going to be dragged around like a prisoner. Even if he *was* about to be hanged from the battlements, he'd bloody well get there himself.

He reached the doorway at last and leant his shoulder against the jamb for support, surprised to hear a faint sound like moaning coming from elsewhere in the tower. From the way Lady Juliana's head snapped around, he could tell that she'd heard it, too, though it stopped almost at once.

'I thought I was your only prisoner?' He looked up and down the gallery suspiciously. As far as he could see there was only one other door. 'Or do you keep a few of us for your entertainment?'

'It must be one of the guards having a nightmare.'

She tossed her head and moved on again, leading him part of the way down the stairwell and through a side door out on to the ramparts. He limped stiffly behind her, peering over the walls to survey the battle preparations going on below. The sky was still a gauzy purple, but the army camp was clearly illuminated by the combined light of dozens of campfires, revealing the dark silhouettes of men carrying planks of wood towards the moat, ready to erect makeshift bridges and ladders. Most of them were already armed and armoured for battle. Not long until morning then.

They climbed up a few steps on to the gatehouse roof and Lady Juliana waved a hand, dismissing her archers.

'You, too.' She gestured at the guards behind him next.

Lothar watched them go with surprise. What did she intend to do, haul him over the side of the battlements by herself? Not that any of the men argued with her, he noticed. They obeyed her commands as if she were a seasoned battle commander and not an exhausted-looking slip of a woman clutching a dagger, though he had to admit there was an aspect of inner strength about her, that of the Celtic queen she'd first put him in mind of, the lone woman facing an army below. Under other circumstances, he might have admired her. As it was, all he could think about was getting her to surrender as quickly as possible—preferably before the first volley of arrows hailed down on them. Not that she seemed in any hurry to talk. Just like before, now that she had him where she wanted him, she seemed to have nothing to say.

'You know, if you're going to hang me over the edge then you might need some help.' He broke the silence at last.

'I'm not.'

She said the words in a flat, defeated-sounding voice, standing in the exact same spot where he'd first seen her the day before, though this time she looked desolate, her shoulders slumped so low that he was half-tempted to countermand his orders after all. Glancing down at his feet, he realised he was standing in the same space where her archer had been, as if he were the one protecting her now.

He shook his head, trying to rid himself of such an unsettling idea. Clearly the poppy was still affecting him, reawakening that strange worried *feeling* that had made him follow her into the castle in the first place, and he had no time for feelings. She was close to surrender, he could sense it. A few brutal truths ought to do it. If he could bring himself to say them...

He took a cautious step closer, poised for any sudden movements, half-afraid that she was about to jump over the edge. He wouldn't be able to catch her with his hands tied behind his back, but he could knock her sideways and pinion her beneath him if he had to. He'd tumble over the ramparts with her rather than let her surrender *that* way.

'You're outnumbered, my lady, and your defences won't hold for more than twelve hours.'

'I know.' She turned her head, looking vaguely surprised to find him standing so close. 'But I made a promise.'

'To Stephen?'

'Yes.'

'The man who killed your father?'

She pursed her lips. 'You don't understand.'

'No, but I do understand war. Once a battle starts, it's hard to stop. I can't vouch for Sir Guian's men and I can't change the rules of combat either. If you surrender after the assault begins, they'll have the right to do whatever they want with your home and your belongings. Your women, too.'

'There aren't any women.'

'None?' He frowned. 'What about your maids?'

'I sent them away for their own safety.' She gestured vaguely towards the river. 'There's a village on the other side. The water protects them better than our walls can.'

'You're telling me that you're the *only* woman here?' He closed his eyes briefly. 'Sweet mercy! Surrender. Now.'

'A commander shouldn't surrender just to save themselves, isn't that what you said?' She jutted her chin out, though the flash of fear in her eyes gave her away. 'Tell me something about my father.'

'What?' He blinked at the abrupt change of subject.

'I need to know if I can trust you. You said that you were friends. Tell me something that proves it.'

'You want *me* to prove that I'm trustworthy? I'm not the one who drugged your wine, my lady. Trust works both ways.'

'I know, but…*please.*'

She gave him a pleading look and he rolled his eyes in frustration. What next? First she tricked him, then she took him prisoner and now she wanted *him* to prove himself? Never mind the fact that they were running out of time! Next she'd be asking him to console her…

'He was supposed to marry your aunt.' He dredged the memory up from somewhere. 'Your mother was a younger sister, but he said that once he saw her, he couldn't marry anyone else. He said she had hair like a sunset.'

'Red.' She lifted a hand to her head self-consciously. 'But my father liked it.'

'Then we've something else in common.'

He stiffened, taken aback by his own words. Why had he said that? He *never* said things like that! It had to be her proximity affecting him, recalling his dreams from the previous night. He was so close that he could smell the delicate honeysuckle scent of her hair, or was it her skin? He was tempted to bend closer to find out…

'Surrender.' He cleared his throat huskily. 'Now, while you still can. No matter whose side you're on, Matilda's or Stephen's, your father would have wanted you to be safe.'

'That's all I wanted for him, too.' Tears welled in her eyes suddenly, bright and glistening like diamond drops. 'But I failed him. I should never have let him go.'

'Go where?'

'Into battle!'

'How could you have stopped him?'

'I don't know. I just should have.'

'He was an experienced soldier, Lady Juliana, a good one, too. He must have thought there was a chance of victory for him to engage Stephen in the first place.'

'There was, but not the way that it happened. I should have realised…' She bit her lip abruptly. 'If I surrender, do you *promise* that my men won't be harmed?'

'They won't even be prisoners. They can join Sir Guian's men or they can leave. Whichever they choose.'

'All right. As long as you understand that every decision I've made since the battle has been mine and mine alone. I take full responsibility for everything. Any punishment should come to me.'

He felt vaguely unsettled again. What did *that* mean? The solemn way that she said it suggested there *was* something else, something he didn't know about, that she took responsibility for.

'I'm not here to punish anybody, Lady Juliana. I told you, the Empress only wants the bridge.'

Her expression wavered in a way that he couldn't interpret, before she reached around him, cutting the bindings on his wrists before holding the dagger out in both hands.

'In that case, I surrender.'

He bent his head in acknowledgement, trying to dampen the hot swell of desire that seemed to have been unleashed in his body as she reached past him. For a fleeting moment, the soft curve of her breast had pressed against his arm and it had been all he could do not to push her up against the battlements right there and then. Now that his hands were free, he could do it, too...

'Does it have personal value?' He reached for the blade instead, weighing it in one hand as he waited for his blood to cool again.

'The dagger? No, it's just a—' She stopped mid-sentence, gaping in shock as he tossed it over the ramparts.

'Now take off your headdress.' He curled his fingers to stop himself from doing it. The urge to touch her seemed to be getting stronger every moment. 'You need to signal your surrender.'

She nodded and took it off at once, waving the material like a flag at the soldiers below.

'Better.' His gaze drifted admiringly over the loose tresses before he realised what he'd just said. He'd meant to say good, not *better*—even if the other word seemed far more appropriate. What in hell's name was wrong with him? He couldn't remember any woman ever affecting him so strongly. 'Make sure your men see you waving it, too.'

She gave a murmur of assent, moving from one side of the roof to the other as he watched one of his soldiers run off towards Sir Guian's tent. There. That ought to be enough to call off the attack. He felt more relieved than when she'd cut his bindings.

Felt?

'What next?' She came back to stand in front
of him, covering her hair up again as she did so,
tucking away the brightly coloured strands with
deft fingers.

He grimaced. He knew exactly what he wanted
to do next. He wanted to haul her into his arms
and pull that headdress back off again. He wanted
to find out if her hair and lips felt as soft as he
imagined them. More than that, he wanted to find
out where that honeysuckle scent was coming
from…

But he had orders to follow—and he had a
strong suspicion that she was going to like them
even less than he did.

'Next you need to lower the drawbridge and
surrender to Sir Guian.'

Chapter Eight

'*Sir Guian?*' Juliana felt as though he'd just pressed the dagger to her throat, not hurled it into the moat.

Lothar nodded stiffly. 'He was the one sent to capture Haword. The Empress wants him to hold it.'

'But he was never going to attack!'

'None the less, those are the Empress's orders.'

'But... *Sir Guian?*'

She spat the name in disgust. Of all the men in the world, how could Lothar expect her to surrender to *him*? The very thought of his smug, gloating face was repellent. The same face that she'd slapped and scratched at in her haste to escape from his tent four months before. If she surrendered to him now, then he'd think that he'd won, that she was yielding more than just a castle, that she was surrendering *herself*, too. She felt as if her blood were turning to ice.

'You tricked me!'

His features hardened at the accusation, as if he were turning back into a statue before her very eyes. 'I've told you nothing but the truth, my lady.'

'Not all of it! I agreed to surrender to you, not him! You knew that.'

'And you knew that I'm not a nobleman. As you pointed out yesterday, I'm only a soldier. I can't hold a castle with any authority.'

'So you're going to let *him* get all the acclaim?'

'There's little enough of it to be had in war. He's welcome to any he can get.'

Welcome? She mouthed the word back at him, though he didn't respond, didn't flex so much as a muscle. If he'd truly been made of stone, then he couldn't have looked any more rigid.

She whirled away from him, biting back a cry of frustration as she peered down into the bailey below. Her men were already gathering together by the front gate, a pale and emaciated group compared to the soldiers outside, piling their weapons in a heap as they prepared to surrender. She ought to go down to them, ought to say something, not that she knew what. Her thoughts were in turmoil, dominated by the one overwhelming idea that Lothar had tricked her just when she'd decided to trust him. And she'd let him, exposing herself as the gullible, inexperienced *woman* she clearly was! Maybe she wasn't fit to be chatelaine after all. Behind that stony façade, he was probably laughing at her. Just like he'd laughed at her before...

She felt tears well in her eyes again and blinked them away furiously. She wasn't going to lose control in front of any man, even if all she wanted to do was throw her hands up and scream. He must have known how it would be all along. The whole time he'd been trying to convince her to surrender, he'd known that it would mean to Sir Guian, but he'd kept silent about that, waiting for her to agree before revealing the horrible truth. Friend of her father or not, if she hadn't already given him the dagger then she would have shown him exactly how she felt about *that* deception!

At least he didn't remember what had happened between them the previous evening. Memory loss was a common side effect of poppy, though she'd never been so glad of it before. She'd hardly dared look at him that morning in case it somehow triggered a memory and the last thing she wanted was for him to remember just how wantonly she'd behaved. She didn't want to remember herself, even if standing so close to him now made it impossible not to. The most shameful part of all was that *she'd* started it. *She'd* thrown herself at him, flinging her arms around his neck like the most flagrant, unashamed strumpet! She hadn't even been the one to stop it. Only the poppy had done that.

So much for maidenly modesty, never mind her reputation. Her men seemed to have forgiven her behaviour once she'd explained herself, though a few had still seemed unable to look her in the eye. All in all, she'd done an excellent job of shocking them and compromising her honour at the same time, gambling everything on a plan that had apparently been doomed from the start. Lothar had given the order to attack before he'd even met her on the drawbridge. If she'd tried, she couldn't have failed any more spectacularly. Now Stephen would find out that she'd broken her promise and the Empress… Well, there was no telling what the Empress would do once she found out the full extent of her betrayal. Her change of allegiance might be forgiven, but as for the rest of it…

'You should be wearing a cloak.'

'What?' She spun around, trying to reconcile Lothar's concerned tone with his inscrutable expression.

'It's cold. You weren't wearing one yesterday either.' His forehead creased slightly. 'You should take better care of your health.'

She glanced up at the sky. *Was* it cold? She hadn't thought to notice the weather. What on earth did it matter when she'd just surrendered her home?

'I doubt if the Empress will care if I catch a chill.'

'On the contrary, she specifically asked me to report on your health when I return to Devizes.'

A shiver that had nothing to do with the temperature raced down her spine. 'You mean you're *leaving*?'

He inclined his head. 'Now that you've surrendered, my work here is done. The Empress will have another commission for me.'

'So you're just going to abandon me—*us*—to Sir Guian?'

He paused briefly before answering. 'Those are my orders.'

'When?' Her lips felt so dry that she could hardly utter the question.

'As soon as you lower the drawbridge.'

This time she felt as if he'd actually taken the dagger and stabbed her in the heart with it. No matter how angry she was with him, the thought of being abandoned to Sir Guian was ten times worse! How could he? Didn't he know what kind of lecherous snake the Baron was?

Her heart sank. Of course he knew. That was probably the reason he hadn't told her the whole truth in the first place. He knew and he didn't care. Why would he? He hadn't even known what she looked like twenty-four hours ago. He'd probably forget her in less time—as soon as he rode back over the drawbridge most likely. Why *would* he care who he left her with? She was the one reading too much into one kiss—a kiss that he didn't even remember! No wonder he had no compunction about leaving her. It would be strange if he did. She was the one behaving as if their encounter had meant something, which it most definitely hadn't!

Briefly, she considered pushing past him, rushing down the steps and calling her men back to arms. But it was hopeless. Even if she did somehow manage to get past him, the possibility of which she seriously doubted, everything else he'd told her was true. He hadn't lied about their being outnumbered, nor about the strength of the castle's defences. If she reneged on her surrender, it would scarcely delay the inevitable and put her men in even more jeopardy.

'Lady Juliana?' Lothar's expression seemed to shift slightly, betraying the faintest hint of some emotion. 'Do you have any cause to object to Sir Guian?'

She held back a snort of derision. Aye, she had plenty of cause, not that she was going to admit it to *him*. She hadn't told anyone what had happened that day in the Baron's tent when he'd tried first to seduce and then to force himself on her, hoping that silence might make the feelings of humiliation and rage go away. They hadn't, but she wasn't going to tell anything to a man who'd just proven he couldn't be trusted! He'd already tricked her into cutting his bonds and surrendering. She wasn't going to show him any more weakness.

'Would it make any difference?'

'It might.'

A muscle jumped in his cheek as he answered.

He looked different suddenly, less rigidly controlled, as if she'd inadvertently found a crack in his stone-clad exterior. His grey eyes were narrowed to slits and yet somehow they seemed to be smouldering, too, like coals newly stoked into life.

'What do you care?' She felt a strange tingling sensation start to build in her toes and move up through her body, something between fear and excitement.

'If you have cause...' the muscle in his cheek twitched again '...then I could speak to him before I go. Make him understand the kind of behaviour the Empress expects.'

Her cheeks flared. That proved it. He *definitely* knew what kind of a man the Baron was, as if he already knew what had happened between them. But he couldn't, no one did. In which case, he must only suspect. And yet he seemed to be offering to help her, too, to talk to Sir Guian, for all the good it would do. The man was too arrogant to pay heed to anyone else. Though if anyone *could* persuade him...

She folded her arms, refusing to consider it. There was no point anyway. Even if she could bring herself to admit the shameful truth—that she'd been naive enough to agree to a private negotiation, what could a soldier, a sergeant, do against a Baron? No, she'd taken care of herself then and she'd keep on doing it. She didn't need any man to protect her. Now that she knew what to expect from Sir Guian she wouldn't be caught off guard again, could fight him off a second time if she had to. And at least she knew the kind of man he was...unlike Lothar. She had only the vaguest idea of who *he* was. For all she knew, he might be even worse!

No, she conceded, that wasn't fair. He wouldn't be worse. Even when she'd been pretending to seduce him, he'd barely touched her, up until the point when she'd kissed him anyway. She'd given him more opportunity and far more encouragement than she had the Baron, yet Lothar was the one who'd behaved like a true knight. If he were the one holding the castle, then she'd have no cause to fear him, not in that regard anyway, though that was probably just because he *wasn't* attracted to her. He'd made that clear enough when he'd laughed at her pathetic attempt at seduction. He'd probably only kissed her back because he'd been drugged and she'd thrown herself at him, responding by instinct rather than inclination. A wave of mortification washed over her. Of course a man like him wouldn't be attracted to a woman like her. She'd been a fool to think otherwise and if he intended to leave then the sooner he was gone, the better! Her secret would be safer with him gone anyway...

'It's none of your concern.' She turned her back on him, heading for the stairwell. 'You're leaving and I have a castle to surrender. We ought to get on with it.'

'Did he touch you?'

She froze mid-step, arrested by the tone of his voice. It sounded deep and threatening, like the rumble of thunder before a storm. Nervously, she peered back over her shoulder, struck by the same impression of danger she'd felt when she'd first glimpsed him over the battlements, of darkness held in check. Except that now, the darkness was there on the surface, barely restrained any more. His question seemed to offer her the power to unleash it, but why? Why would he care what the Baron had done, or tried to do, to her? Why would he want to avenge her? And yet he looked about ready to maim someone. The skin over his jaw looked so tight she was half-afraid it might tear—as if *he* might snap. If she wanted revenge on Sir Guian, then she wouldn't get a better opportunity. It would be one way of making sure he didn't touch her again and she'd only be telling the truth.

She caught her breath, appalled by the temptation. They might be at war, but there'd been enough violence already and she had the sudden, powerful conviction that she didn't want to know how dangerous this man could be. The look of raw, unrestrained fury on his face made her wish that his impenetrable mask were back on again. Clearly that was all it *had* been—a mask. The force of emotion beneath was truly terrifying.

'Lady Juliana?' His whole body seemed to bristle when she didn't answer. *'Did he hurt you?'*

'No. He didn't touch me.' She said the words quickly but firmly, starting down the stairwell at once so that he couldn't read the lie on her face, acutely aware of his footsteps following close behind.

'Where are my weapons?'

'Why?' She felt her heartbeat accelerate with panic. 'I thought this was going to be a peaceful surrender?'

'Where are they?'

'In the keep.' She turned to face him as they reached the bottom of the stairwell. 'Just where you left them, but...'

Her protest faded away as he stormed off, marching towards the keep as if she hadn't bothered speaking at all. From the murderous look on his face, she had the distinct feeling that he couldn't hear anybody. Despite all her efforts, it seemed that she'd unleashed a wild animal in the bailey after all.

She glanced towards the drawbridge and then back at the keep again. What had she just done?

Chapter Nine

'*Is* it true, my lady? Are we really surrendering?'

Juliana met Ulf's dour gaze and nodded regretfully, raising her voice so that the rest of her men could hear her, too.

'We're surrendering, but Sergeant Lothar has given his word that no one will be harmed.'

'We can still fight.' Ulf glared in the direction of the keep. 'You know we'll follow your commands to the end, my lady.'

'I know.' She put a hand on his arm. 'And I'm grateful, but if we can surrender peaceably then we ought to do it. I only hope that Stephen understands.'

'You did your best, my lady. No man could have done better.'

She smiled weakly. 'You're a loyal friend, Ulf. Did the guards do as I asked?'

'Yes, my lady, but I don't know if it will work. If they do a thorough search…'

'Then hopefully they'll see an empty store-room and move on,' she forestalled him. 'I know it's not the best plan, but it's all we can do. It's the safest place for now. Maybe later…'

She faltered. Maybe later *what*? She didn't have an answer to that. All she could do now was take things one step at a time and try to keep Haword's secret for as long as she could.

Ulf grunted, lowering his head like a bull. 'This is all *his* fault.'

She looked around to find Lothar already striding back towards them, his stormy temper showing no sign of abating as he fastened his sword belt with a vicious-sounding snap.

'Lady Juliana.' His gaze narrowed perceptibly at the sight of her hand on Ulf's arm. 'Are you ready?'

'Yes.' She pulled her fingers away, reluctant to inflame his temper any further, though it seemed already too late for that.

'*Sergeant.*' Ulf took his sword from its scabbard and tossed it into the dirt. 'It seems you're the one disarming me after all.'

'So it seems.' Lothar's pale gaze fastened on the Constable interrogatively. 'Ulf, wasn't it?'

'Aye.'

'Do you have any skill with that?' He nudged the blade with his foot.

'As much as you, I'll wager.'

'Then you must be truly exceptional.'

Juliana held her breath, wondering how best to intervene. The two men were eyeballing each other in a way that made her skin crawl.

'In that case, you'd better keep it.' Lothar flicked the blade up with his foot suddenly, catching it in mid-air and tossing the hilt back towards Ulf. 'Stay with your lady. Do you understand?'

'Understand what?' A jolt of surprise turned into a fresh stab of panic. Why would Ulf need to stay with her?

'Tell them to lower the bridge.'

She dug her heels into the dirt, resenting the order. 'Not until you tell me why Ulf needs to be armed.'

'He doesn't. It's a precaution.'

'Against your own men?'

'Not *mine*.'

'Sir Guian's, then?'

He didn't answer and she put her hands on her hips angrily. 'This is *my* castle, I have a right to know!'

'It *was* your castle. Now lower the bridge.'

'It's *my* castle until I surrender it to Sir Guian and I don't want there to be any fighting, not for any reason. Do *you* understand?'

She held his gaze as a tense silence stretched out between them. Out of the corner of her eye she could see her men watching, waiting to see what would happen. She wasn't sure what the outcome was going to be herself, but she refused to back down.

'No fighting,' she repeated the order, more firmly this time.

'As you wish.' He spoke tersely, as if he were forcing the words past clenched teeth. 'Now lower the bridge.'

She sucked in a breath. *Did* he understand? She hoped so, though whatever was about to happen was already beyond her control. She might as well lower the bridge and find out what it was. She was tired of sieges and arguments, tired of everything… A wave of exhaustion rolled over her, making her legs teeter unsteadily.

'Lady Juliana?'

Lothar's voice prompted her and she blinked a few times, trying to wake herself back up again. She was supposed to say something, wasn't she? Something about lowering the bridge? The words were there in her head, but the idea of putting them together seemed like too much effort all of a sudden. When was the last time that she'd slept? Not at all the previous night and only a light doze the one before that. No wonder words weren't making sense any more. What was she supposed to say again?

'Oh… Lower the bridge!'

'Are you feeling unwell?' Lothar's face swam into view, managing to look angry, exasperated and concerned all at the same time.

She shook her head, fighting an ill-timed

and incongruous desire to laugh. She *definitely* couldn't remember the last time she'd done that. But at least he wasn't looking quite so ferocious any more. If she wasn't mistaken, he and Ulf had just shared a look of mutual confusion. That was a definite improvement in their relationship. Perhaps he thought she'd been drinking her own poppy milk medicine, she thought with amusement. The idea had certainly tempted her often enough. If she drank just a little then she could sleep through a whole night for once. Sleep and let somebody else take charge, just for a while...

'Juliana!'

His hand gripped her arm suddenly, pulling her backwards and out of her daze as a bay-coloured destrier thundered to a halt in front of her, followed by a troop of armoured soldiers. She gave a small yelp, shocked less by the spectacle than by the intimate use of her name, not to mention the feeling of Lothar's hand wrapped around her upper arm, close to her breast. They'd barely touched since their kiss the previous evening, all except for one unintentional moment when she'd reached past to cut his bindings, and the spontaneous thrill that raced through her body made her heart start to pound as heavily as the destrier's hooves.

'Lady Juliana.' Sir Guian dismounted in front of her, his expression even more smug than she'd anticipated. 'I see you've come to your senses at last.'

She stiffened, trying to maintain some sense of equilibrium as the quivering sensation in her stomach was replaced by a violent churning. She squeezed her hands into fists, digging the fingernails into her skin as she fought the urge to lash out. For a moment, she thought she felt Lothar's grip tighten as well, as if he were experiencing the same impulse.

'I've agreed to surrender on condition that no one is harmed, if that's what you mean, Sir Guian.'

'Very well. I'm prepared to be lenient as long as no one interferes with my business.' The Baron threw a contemptuous look around the bailey before beckoning his soldiers forward. 'Not that there's much here to take.'

'Hold!' Lothar's voice arrested them. 'There won't be any looting.'

'What?' Sir Guian looked as if he'd just been told to take a running leap into the moat.

'I said there won't be any looting. Lady Juliana and I have come to a different arrangement.'

'What *kind* of arrangement?' The Baron's gaze flickered from her head to her feet in a way that made her feel nauseated. 'I should have been party to any discussion.'

'You had that opportunity four months ago.'

'You had no right to agree anything without me!'

'I think you'll find that I do.' Lother's voice

took on a dangerous edge, though the Earl seemed not to notice.

'We've been waiting here for months! My men deserve a reward.'

'For doing what exactly?'

'For the siege!'

'You want a reward just for waiting?'

'It's more than that and you know it! I've spent my own time and money…'

'And the castle is won. Surely that honour is reward enough.'

'The Empress will hear of this.'

'Then go back to Devizes and tell her.'

Juliana followed the exchange with a growing sense of amazement. This was—or had been— her castle and yet Lothar seemed to be the one fighting for it. No matter what he'd promised, she hadn't expected him to actually take sides *against* Sir Guian, though now she was afraid that his aggressive manner was only making a bad situation worse. His grip on her arm was becoming tighter the longer he spoke, as if he were barely controlling his temper. Even more alarming was the fact that his soldiers appeared to be thinking the same thing. Easily distinguishable in black, they were gradually detaching themselves from the Earl's men and positioning themselves defensively in front of hers.

'As you wish.' Sir Guian suddenly seemed to notice the threat, too, his lips twisting in a smile as frigid as the atmosphere between them.

'Then I accept your terms, Lady Juliana, whatever they are.'

'Thank you, Sir Guian.' She did her best to sound conciliatory. 'Then Haword is yours.'

'I'm honoured.' A triumphant gleam appeared in his eye. 'In that case, Lothar, *you* may give *my* greetings to the Empress. I believe I can take over from here. It's time Lady Juliana and I became better acquainted.'

She felt bile rise in her throat. The way he was looking at her made it abundantly clear what kind of acquaintance he had in mind. Apparently the way she'd fought him off last time hadn't deterred him at all.

Then she noticed the silence, so heavy it seemed to shroud the entire bailey. No one was moving either, as if all of the soldiers had frozen where they stood, all of them looking in one direction—towards Lothar and the expression of utter, unmitigated rage on his face.

'No!' She reacted instinctively, spinning around and placing herself in front of him as the Baron seemed belatedly to realise the danger he was in, backing away with a look of horror. Lothar's grip on her arm was painfully tight now, but she forced herself to smile, grasping at the first words she could think of.

'You can't go until we've said farewell. I bid you a good journey, Lothar... *Lothar?*'

She stretched up on her toes, trying not to quail before the full force of his tight-lipped fury, forcing his gaze to meet hers. Merely smouldering before, his eyes were positively blazing now, as if there were actual fires behind them. She didn't understand his reaction, but if it was something to do with her then she had to be the one to appease him. Tentatively she reached up and put her hands on his shoulders, felt the muscles strain beneath her fingertips. Every part of him seemed coiled and ready to do battle.

'Lothar?' She repeated his name softly. 'No fighting, remember?'

For a moment, she thought he hadn't heard her. Then his gaze shifted, his pupils honing in on her face before gradually focusing, the swirling, Stygian depths fading from stormy black to pale grey.

'Juliana?' His voice sounded strained.

'Yes.' She practically sagged with relief. 'Goodbye, Lothar. Please send my greetings to the Empress.'

'I will.' He seemed to bring himself back under control finally, clenching his jaw as he looked past her shoulder. 'But not yet. Perhaps I didn't make myself clear, Sir Guian, but I won't be leaving immediately.'

'What do you mean?' The Baron's voice held a distinct trace of fear.

'I mean that my men need a rest. We'll stay another night, if that's acceptable to you, my lady?'

He looked down at her, his breathing still ragged, and her heart seemed to skip a beat. *Was* that acceptable to her? She'd only just come to terms with the idea of him leaving. Now she had no idea how to feel about him staying.

'Yes.' She hardly recognised her own voice.

He nodded, his expression softening briefly and then turning inscrutable again. 'In that case, it's time you got some sleep, my lady.'

'What?' She pulled her hands away from his shoulders, shocked to realise that they were still there. Somehow she'd forgotten that she was standing with her arms around him in full view of *all* their soldiers! Even Sir Guian was looking at her strangely.

'You need some rest. Ulf and I will take it from here.'

'Ulf?'

She turned to her Constable, but he only shuffled his feet. So much for following her orders to the end!

'No.' She folded her arms, glaring at both of them. 'I'm not a child to be sent to bed.'

'It would be best if you did.' Lothar's tone was implacable again.

'No!'

'Would you prefer to be carried?'

'You wouldn't dare!'

'Wouldn't I?'

He arched an eyebrow and her cheeks flamed with indignation. He didn't look like a man who made idle threats, but how dare he threaten to humiliate her in such a way! After *she'd* calmed him down! After *she'd* prevented a fight! After *she'd* been prepared to deal with Sir Guian in her own way! She felt as if she'd just been stabbed in the back. He would never dream of doing such a thing to a man. If he was trying to demonstrate that she wasn't chatelaine any longer, he was certainly making his point.

'Last warning, my lady.'

She summoned as much contempt into her gaze as she could muster and then spun on her heel, muttering a string of invectives as she stormed furiously back towards the keep. She'd retreat for now, but if Lothar thought that she was simply going to follow his orders then he could think again. She had far more important tasks to occupy herself with than sleep and she was determined that he wasn't going to find out about any of them!

Chapter Ten

Lothar took one look at the crowded hall and fought the urge to start shouting at the top of his lungs.

Sir Guian's men were lounging on and around the trestle tables in varying degrees of inebriation, the worst disciplined group of soldiers he'd ever laid eyes on. They'd been no help in securing the castle, though his own men had surpassed themselves, carrying in fresh provisions, scrubbing floors, laying fresh rushes and replenishing the wood stores. It was a marked improvement, as if a gust of wind had blown through the bailey, blowing away all trace of the siege and making it fit for purpose again. In a better temper, he might have felt satisfied. As it was, he wanted to pick up the nearest table and hurl it against the wall, Sir Guian's soldiers along with it.

He shouldn't be there. That one thought had

dominated his thoughts all day. He ought to be halfway back to Devizes by now, back by the Empress's side where he belonged. If what Lady Juliana had murmured that morning was true and Stephen's forces were really heading back into Herefordshire, then he ought to report it himself, not simply send a messenger. Instead he was wasting his time in a ramshackle castle in the middle of nowhere, guarding a woman who'd deceived, drugged and imprisoned him, all because, for some inexplicable reason, he couldn't bring himself to leave!

He glanced towards the stairwell that led to the private chambers above, nodding discreetly to the two soldiers he'd stationed there as guards—one to detain anyone who attempted to get past, the other to fetch him. Judging by the fact that neither had moved, he could only assume that Lady Juliana was still sleeping upstairs. His body stirred at the thought, though the memory of what he'd almost done in the bailey that morning was enough to banish the feeling completely. The leering expression on Sir Guian's face had turned his suspicions into crystal-clear certainties. The fact that Lady Juliana obviously hadn't wanted to talk about what had happened between her and the Baron had only made matters worse. Lothar's imagination had run riot, making the red mist descend even faster and more forcefully than usual. He hadn't lost control of himself to such an extent for years, but he'd been about to do something

definitely *not* in the Empress's best interests, until
Lady Juliana herself had stepped between them.
She'd urged him to calm down, her green eyes
boring deep into his until he did. *How* had she
done it? Usually when he lost his temper, someone was bound to get hurt, yet she'd managed to
bring him back to himself.

Not that he'd thanked her for it. He'd ordered
her to bed instead, ignoring her look of outrage
as she'd stomped away, muttering a string of surprisingly imaginative insults. He didn't think he'd
ever seen any woman, the Empress included, ever
look or sound more furious, but he'd needed to put
some distance between them. *She'd* needed some
sleep, that had been obvious, and *he'd* needed to
calm down and work out what the hell had just
happened.

After taking the whole day to clear his head,
he was no closer to finding the answer. Whatever power she had over him, whether to lure
him inside a castle and hold him there, or to calm
his temper, it wasn't something he'd ever come
across before. He didn't know how to feel about
that either.

He climbed the dais to the high table and
muttered an oath. Now that he finally felt calm
enough to confront Sir Guian it seemed that he'd
waited too long. The Baron was already slouched
in one of the large wooden chairs, an empty cup
dangling from one hand as he looked around the
room with bleary, red-rimmed eyes.

Damn it. He took a seat at the opposite end of the table, scowling fiercely until one of his men appeared with a trencher and some ale.

'Have the castle garrison been fed?' He practically barked out the question.

'Yes, sir, just a small amount as you ordered.'

'Good. They can have bigger portions tomorrow.'

'What about Lady Juliana, sir? Shall I bring her a trencher?'

'Mmm?' The very mention of her name set his nerves on edge. 'Yes, when she wakes up.'

'She's here now, sir.'

'What?' He jerked his head up, surprised to find her already mounting the steps to the high table beside him, *still* dressed in the same brown tunic she'd been wearing when they'd met. He was starting to wonder if she had any other clothes.

'Lady Juliana.' He pulled out a neighbouring chair, surprised by a feeling of eagerness. 'Are you feeling well rested?'

'Rested enough.'

She sat down without looking at him and he sighed.

'I see you haven't forgiven me yet then.'

'Why would I?' She shot him a venomous look. 'If I were a man, you would never have humiliated me like that.'

'If you were a man, you would have been

clapped in chains and held for ransom. Would you have preferred that?'

'More than being insulted, yes!'

'Then I apologise. If I'd known you would have preferred a dungeon, then I could have obliged, but I did what was necessary at the time.'

'It was *necessary* to send me to bed?'

'Yes. You'd just surrendered the castle and your men needed to know Sir Guian was in command. Remaining downstairs would only have confused matters.'

She looked slightly mollified. 'You could have explained that at the time.'

'I could have, but I thought anger might keep you awake long enough to reach your chamber. You looked like you were about to collapse.' His gaze narrowed suspiciously. 'You still do.'

'I look no such thing and you're the last person who ought to criticise anyone else's temper!'

He made a wry face. It was a fair enough comment, he supposed, though he wasn't used to such forthright honesty. Not many people dared to criticise *his* behaviour, especially his somewhat unstable temper regarding certain subjects. He wasn't accustomed to criticism, or to explaining himself either. He never had to, except to the Empress, but Lady Juliana seemed to have no fear of him. Paradoxically her defiance only added to her appeal. He wouldn't have thought he would like it, but judging by the way that his body was responding again, he most definitely did.

'You're right.' He inclined his head. 'I lost control earlier. It won't happen again.'

'Good.' She gave him an arch look, then gestured disdainfully towards a particularly rowdy group of soldiers. 'I see you're making yourselves at home.'

'Some of us are.'

'If you don't approve of their behaviour, then why don't you stop them?'

'They're not my men. I'm not in command.'

She peered down the length of the table. 'Sir Guian doesn't seem in a fit state to do anything.'

'Then I'd call that an improvement, wouldn't you?' He watched her face as one of his soldiers placed a fresh trencher in front of her. 'Hungry?'

'Ravenous.' She leaned forward eagerly, breathing in the aroma before favouring the man with a wide smile. 'It smells delicious. Thank you.'

'You're welcome, my lady.'

Lothar watched his soldier depart, seized with an irrational surge of jealousy. She'd never smiled at *him* like that, as if she truly meant it, not even when she'd been pretending to seduce him—and she'd spent most of the time since glaring at him.

'Better than siege rations?'

'I never want to eat stockfish again in my life.' She picked up a piece of cheese and then paused with it halfway to her mouth. 'Have my men eaten?'

'Of course.'

'Where are they?'

'We've set up tents for them in the bailey.'

'Tents?'

'The keep and stables are full and the store-rooms are full of Sir Guian's supplies.'

'What about your men? Are they going to billet here with Sir Guian's?'

'No, they're in tents, too. Now eat.' He nudged the trencher closer towards her. 'Questions later.'

She looked faintly rebellious for a moment, then seemed to change her mind, tucking into the food with relish.

'Slow down,' he reprimanded her. 'You shouldn't eat too quickly after a diet of stockfish.'

'I know.'

'You'll make yourself sick.'

'Probably.'

'Lady Juliana…'

She put down the piece of chicken she was holding with a sigh, licking the juice off her fingers with such enthusiasm that he had to look away quickly.

'You know, you give a lot of orders for a man who says he's not in command.'

'That was advice.'

'Good. Then I can ignore it.'

She gave an exaggerated smile and then continued eating with gusto, leaning back in her seat and giving a satisfied sigh as she popped the last sweetmeat into her mouth.

'Is there any more?'

'Not for you. You shouldn't eat too much either.'

'*More* advice?'

'As you wish.' He sighed and gestured to one of his soldiers. 'Just don't say I didn't warn you.'

'I won't.' She pursed her lips with the air of a person who'd just won an argument. 'So why are your men sleeping outside?'

'Because they prefer to.' He threw a pointed look around the hall. 'I can't say that I blame them. In any case, this is Sir Guian's command. It makes sense for his men to billet here.'

'Sir Guian's command?' She repeated the words mockingly. 'Whenever I looked, you were the one giving orders.'

'Whenever you looked?' He put down his ale with a thud. 'You were supposed to be sleeping.'

'I was some of the time, but I had to make sure my men were being looked after. Surely you didn't expect me just to forget about them?'

He cocked an eyebrow. He knew a lot of barons who would have done just that.

'And are you satisfied with their treatment?'

She waited until a fresh trencher was set in front of her before answering.

'You sent them to bathe in the river.'

'Yes.' He wondered what she was getting at. 'They needed a wash. Their clothes, too.'

'I know. It was thoughtful of you. I just…'

'Didn't expect me to think of it?' He finished the thought for her. 'They're not prisoners, my lady. I told you that.'

'I know. Thank you.'

'Thank you?' He couldn't keep the surprise out of his voice.

'Yes! I can say thank you!'

'So it seems.'

He saw her grit her teeth as if she were trying to control her temper.

'Thank you for keeping your word, too. About the terms of surrender, I mean.'

'Did you think that I wouldn't? I always do what I say, my lady.'

'So do I—or I try to anyway. That's why I didn't want to surrender. I made a promise to the King. It wasn't easy to break.'

He nodded solemnly. He could understand that. He'd made his own promise a long time ago, to a woman who'd taken him under her wing when he'd had nowhere else to go. A promise that had taken him away from his homeland and into a foreign war that seemed to have little hope of ever reaching a conclusion, though even then he'd never once thought of reneging. He could hardly blame Lady Juliana for feeling the same way. If anything, it made him feel closer to her... He clenched his jaw. *That* was the last thing he needed.

'There's no shame in surrender, my lady. Half the castles in England have surrendered and been recaptured at some point during the last ten years. Stephen himself surrendered at Lincoln. He'll understand why you did, too.'

'I hope so.'

She twisted her head suddenly, distracted by a commotion in the direction of the stairwell. He followed her gaze, annoyed to see a group of Sir Guian's soldiers arguing with his guards.

'Don't you think they've had enough to drink?' Her voice sounded tense. 'There's nothing left in the cellars.'

'My men have orders not to let anyone through. They won't get past.'

The taut line of her jaw relaxed slightly, though her face still looked anxious.

'Speaking of surrender...' she seemed to notice him watching her suddenly '...has the Empress ever done so?'

'Has *Matilda* ever surrendered?' He gave a shout of laughter. 'No. She doesn't believe in the word.'

'So there's no shame in it for me, but there is for her?'

'It's different.'

'Why? She's fighting for her home just like I am.'

'She's fighting to reclaim her country and fulfil her father's wishes.'

She winced as he said the word father and he berated himself for his own tactlessness. 'I didn't mean—'

'Perhaps if her father had known what would happen, he wouldn't have wished it,' she interrupted before he could apologise. 'Perhaps if he'd known how much suffering it would cause, he would have given the crown to Stephen.'

'Perhaps, though from what I've heard, Henry wasn't a man who tolerated his wishes being thwarted.'

'No.' Her expression of defiance faltered. 'Perhaps not. My father said he was a strong ruler and Matilda takes after him.'

'She does.'

She gave him a sharp, sideways look. 'I heard a rumour that she was almost captured at Oxford.'

'That's true.'

'It *is*? What happened?'

'The King's forces caught us by surprise and surrounded the town. The siege lasted three months, but eventually there was no choice. The garrison had to surrender. Matilda escaped over the walls the night before.'

'Wasn't there a moat?'

'It was frozen. She crossed the ice, then walked six miles through the snow to reach safety.'

'What about her guards? How could so many men escape without being noticed?'

'There were only three of us, few enough to pass unseen, and we wore white cloaks so we wouldn't be noticed.'

'*We?*'

He shrugged, wondering why he was telling her any of this. He rarely told anyone anything. Taciturn was an understatement for him—even Matilda said so. He'd spoken more in the past twenty-four hours than he had for weeks, though that was probably only because she reminded him so much of her father, with the same intent manner of listening, as if she were absorbing every word. He'd only met William Danville on a handful of occasions, but he'd still counted him as a friend. Fighting side by side had a way of speeding up friendships. The older man's keen intelligence and perceptiveness had led him to reveal more about his past than he had to anyone besides the Empress. Apparently the daughter had the same gift for drawing information out of him. On the other hand, he'd never found William quite so intriguing, nor felt such a compelling desire to move any closer towards him. He'd certainly never wanted to touch him, to reach under the table and stroke his leg…

'The Empress must value you very highly.' She tipped her head to one side like a curious bird, mercifully oblivious to the direction of his thoughts.

'She trusts me. I've served her for most of my life, since I was seven years old.'

'What about your family?'

'I don't have one. I was living on the streets of Bamberg, a city in Francia, scavenging to survive when the Empress found me.'

'What happened?'

'She was visiting Bamberg with her husband, Emperor Heinrich. I was sitting on the roadside when her carriage went by, but she saw and sent a soldier over to fetch me. She was still young herself, but I thought she was the most beautiful woman I'd ever seen.'

'My father said that, too.' Her voice sounded wistful. 'Then what happened?'

'She asked me a few questions. I told her the truth and she asked if I'd like to come and serve her. I've been at her side almost every day since. She saved me. She knows I'd give my life to protect her if necessary.'

'So you've been a soldier since you were *seven*?'

'At first I was more of an errand boy. My talents in that direction became obvious later on.'

He grinned, but she didn't react, studying him intently as if she were trying to make sense of something.

'So you serve her because she saved you, not because she was Empress of Austria?'

'I suppose so.'

'And now she wants to be Queen of England?'

'Yes.' He drew his brows together. What was she implying?

'So your being here has nothing to do with England itself. What about *your* home? Did you want to leave? Don't you *care* about England at all?'

He stared back at her in surprise. What kind of questions were those? What did *caring* have to do with anything?

'I swore an oath to the Empress. My home is with her, just as my duty is to her.'

'So not to England.'

'When she becomes Queen of England, they'll be the same thing.'

'*If* she becomes Queen.' Lady Juliana leaned back in her chair, popping another sweetmeat into her mouth with a cynical expression. 'My father said she never would be.'

Chapter Eleven

Lothar quirked an eyebrow in surprise. William had been one of the Empress's most dedicated supporters. That he would ever have said anything quite so disloyal was hard to believe.

'You think I'm lying, don't you?' Lady Juliana's lips curved tauntingly.

'Yes. Your father was loyal to the Empress. He chose to meet Stephen on the battlefield rather than surrender. Why would he have done so if he'd thought her cause was hopeless?'

'Because he believed in her claim. He would have been loyal to the end, just like you.' A hint of bitterness crept into her voice. 'But he still thought she'd never be Queen.'

'Because?'

'Because she tried it and failed. When Stephen was captured at Lincoln everyone thought she'd won, that the war was over, but the Barons never accepted her.'

'There were plenty who supported her cause.'

'Her *cause*, yes, just as long as she didn't tell them what to do. When she behaved like a man—a *king*—they rebelled. The city of London rose against her. Then when the Earl of Gloucester was captured and she had to exchange Stephen for his release, we were right back to where we started.'

Lothar set his jaw uncomfortably. There was enough truth in what she'd said to make him wonder if the words really *had* come from William.

'What about you then, my lady?' He turned the challenge around. 'Do *you* think a woman can't rule?'

'No!' She sounded shocked. 'I'd never say such a thing! Of course a woman can rule.'

'Then doesn't that put us on the same side?'

She pursed her lips as if she were choosing her words with care. 'In principle, yes, I believe in Matilda's claim, but in practice I have to support Stephen. I want peace more than I want to prove a point.'

'The Empress can bring peace, too.'

'Can she? My father didn't say that she *couldn't* rule, just that she wouldn't be allowed to. Most men aren't ready to accept a woman giving orders.'

'There are a few exceptions among us.' He paused meaningfully. 'Your soldiers, for example.'

She made a dismissive gesture. 'They're just used to me. No one here thinks of me as a woman.'

'Then they must be blind. Perhaps you under-estimate your charms, my lady.'

Her lips parted slightly, a pink blush spreading over her cheeks as if she were genuinely shocked by his words. A memory stirred at the back of his consciousness. She'd blushed like that when she'd first invited him inside the castle, yet the image in his mind now was different, as if it had taken place in darker surroundings, somewhere like this very hall...

He shifted in his chair as his groin tightened uncomfortably. Hell's teeth, but the dreams had been vivid. He could almost taste her lips again.

'Forgive me...' he fought to regain focus '...but if your father really believed that a woman wouldn't be permitted to rule, why did he raise his daughter to follow him as chatelaine? He clearly trusted *you* to command.'

Her gaze flickered. 'Maybe because he didn't have any sons.'

'He could have found a suitable son-in-law.'

'He would never have done that!' She tossed her head as if the very suggestion offended her. 'He trained me for the same reason that he kept on supporting the Empress, because he knew things would never change if no one stood up for what was right. He had a higher opinion of women than most men do, though people said he was foolish.

First in marrying for love, then raising his daughter to act like a boy, but he wanted me to be free to choose my own path.' She pulled her shoulders back. 'In any case, I doubt he would have been able to find a husband for someone like me.'

Lothar looked her up and down speculatively. It hadn't occurred to him to think of her as boyish before, though he supposed most men wouldn't want a bride who was quite so independent. Not to mention one who seemed oblivious to the idea that she could actually enhance her appearance by changing her gown occasionally. Not that she needed to enhance anything. Those flashing jade eyes were enticing enough on their own. On second thoughts, perhaps it was better that she didn't change her gown after all... His breeches were straining enough as it was.

'What do *you* think?' She rounded on him.

'What do I think?' *That he'd like to see her without any gown at all!* 'I think he was a cleverer man than I am.'

She gave a bitter-sounding laugh. 'I think that maybe everyone else was right. I *did* let him down in the end. I surrendered the castle to his enemy, Stephen. Maybe he shouldn't have left me in charge.' Her face crumpled suddenly. 'And now I'm not fit for anything else.'

He felt a tightening sensation in his chest, struck by the uncharacteristic urge to say or do something comforting, to wrap his arms around her and whisper words of reassurance. For all her defiance, it seemed that deep down she was more vulnerable than he'd realised, doubting her own ability to be chatelaine after all. He even half-raised a hand before he stopped himself.

'I told you, my lady, there's no shame in surrender. You had no choice at the time, but considering your oath of allegiance...' He forced the words out reluctantly. 'Perhaps you ought to go to Stephen.'

'What?' She looked as horrified as if he'd just struck her.

'You gave him your allegiance and lost your castle because of it. He'll take care of you.'

'You mean *leave* Haword?'

'Of course.' Surely she knew that? 'The Empress will want to appoint a new lord.'

'But this is my home!'

'It *was* your home,' he said the words as gently as he could, 'but you can't remain here indefinitely. You ought to leave as soon as you're ready. Your men, too, unless they're willing to serve Sir Guian.'

'What am I supposed to do at Stephen's Court?'

'Doubtless he'll arrange a marriage for you.'

Green eyes flashed like emerald studs. 'I've just told you I'm not the kind of woman men want to marry.'

'Stephen should still reward you for your loyalty.'

'And that's what you call a reward—marriage?

Obeying a man for the rest of my life? A prison would be more honest.'

'I believe that many women find happiness in marriage.'

'Like the *Empress*?'

He frowned at the sarcasm. Clearly rumours about Matilda's tempestuous relationship with Geoffrey of Anjou were more widespread than he'd realised.

'She did with Emperor Heinrich, her first husband.'

'What about you?' She looked at him askance. 'Are *you* married?'

'No.'

'Have you ever been?'

'No.'

'Then what do you know about it? You say that you serve a woman, but would you allow your wife to have a mind of her own?'

'I've no intention of finding out. I've no desire to get married.'

'But you think it's a good idea for me?'

He took a swig of ale in frustration. Damn it all, it wasn't as if he *wanted* her to get married! The very idea evoked all kinds of images he didn't want to dwell on, but he was trying to help! She was only too stubborn to see it.

'It would be a means of protection.'

'I don't need protecting!' She raised her voice, almost shouting at him. 'You're just like every

other man. You think it's all right for *you* to be free, but not for a woman!'

'I didn't say it was right. It's just the way of the world.'

'A *man's* world!'

'A woman can still have power in marriage.'

'Says the man who doesn't want to be shackled!'

He swallowed the last of his ale before answering. 'I have my own reasons for not wanting to marry.'

'Such as?'

'They're private.'

'They're excuses!'

'Perhaps it's because I don't want to spend my evenings arguing with a harpy!'

She shot out of her chair at once. 'Then allow me to relieve you of my company. As for the rest, there's no need to concern yourself about *my* future. I'll leave when I'm ready.'

He fixed her with a hard stare. 'I thought that my remaining an extra night would give you time to prepare your departure. I can't delay any longer.'

'So that was why you…?' A look of surprise flitted across her features before she cut herself off mid-sentence. 'None the less, I intend to stay a while longer.'

'With Sir Guian?'

'Yes.'

'And his soldiers?'

'I can take care of myself.'

He clenched his jaw, trying to restrain his temper. 'Very well. I'll speak with him before I leave.'

'There's no need.'

He sighed. Was there anything she wasn't going to argue with him about this evening?

'Would you prefer that I didn't?'

'I'd prefer that no one gets hurt.'

'Then I promise only to talk.'

She regarded him dubiously for a moment before the arrival of two new soldiers at the stairwell seemed to distract her again.

'There's nothing to worry about.' Lothar frowned, perplexed by the sudden look of anxiety on her face. What was it about the stairwell that bothered her so much? She seemed to get jumpy every time anyone went near it. 'They're just relieving the guards. No one will disturb you upstairs, you have my word.'

'Thank you.' She avoided his gaze as she picked up the remains of her second trencher. Despite her earlier protestations, she'd hardly touched any of it.

'Still hungry?' He lifted an eyebrow.

'I might be later. Will I see you again before you leave in the morning?'

He threw a quick glance in the direction of Sir Guian. It seemed highly unlikely that the Baron would be in a fit state to talk about anything before noon. Beating some sense into him would be far easier, but now that he'd promised…

'Yes. We'll break our fast here.'

'Then I'll see you in the morning. Goodnight, Sergeant.'

'Goodnight, my lady.'

He tapped his fingers on the table-top as she hastened away, unable to shake the feeling that he was missing something. Despite their conversation, she seemed more of a mystery than ever. Why hadn't she slept? She'd said that it was because she'd been keeping watch on her men, but that didn't make any sense. She must have realised they weren't in any danger quickly enough, so why hadn't she taken the opportunity to rest? Something was definitely worrying her, too, even more than the threat of Sir Guian. She seemed more anxious about the stairwell than she did about him, as if she were afraid of anyone else going upstairs. As if she were hiding something…

He remembered the sound of moaning he'd heard earlier, the one that she'd dismissed as one of her guards having a bad dream. In all the commotion he'd forgotten about it, but now he felt a tendril of suspicion. Not what, but *whom* was she hiding?

He waited another minute and then pushed his chair back, lighting a candle in one of the braziers before making his way towards the far corner of the hall, nodding at his guards as he followed her up the curve of the stairwell.

· The tower seemed deserted as he made his way silently past her chamber door and turned the handle of the one opposite. He'd half-expected it to be locked, but it opened without any resistance, swinging wide to reveal a large made-up bed, two sturdy-looking coffers, and a small desk in one corner. Other than that, the room was completely empty.

He stood stock-still in the doorway, feeling as though he'd just invaded something private. This was clearly her father's old chamber, kept the way it had been when he'd last ridden out to battle, though it retained a strangely lived-in feeling. Even so, it seemed highly unlikely that Lady Juliana would let one of her guards sleep there. He must have been mistaken in what he'd heard earlier. Either that or the sound had come from elsewhere...

'Do you want to sleep here?'

Her voice at his shoulder almost made him drop his candle in surprise.

'No, my lady.'

He turned around slowly. How had she known he was there? He hadn't creaked so much as a floorboard—though neither had she, for that matter—and yet there she was watching him, *still* fully dressed, though she'd removed her headdress at least, revealing two loosely tied braids falling over each breast.

'This was your father's chamber?' He grimaced as she nodded. 'Then I'm sorry for disturbing it.'

'Were you looking for something?'

She sounded wary and he paused, trying to gauge her reaction. She looked as suspicious as he felt, her green eyes glowing like a cat's in the candlelight, fixed on him with an intent feline gleam. What would she do if he confronted her with his suspicions directly? Would she bolt or unsheathe her claws? Either way, he doubted that she'd tell him anything.

'I was looking for clues.' He settled on a different excuse. 'Something to remind me about what happened last night. I don't like mysteries.'

'Last night?' Her voice jumped up a few octaves. 'I told you, we talked. There's nothing else to remember.'

He raised both eyebrows, struck by the sudden, powerful conviction that she was lying. The look of panic in her eyes was as good an admission of guilt as if she'd said it aloud. Which meant… He was struck dumb for a moment, struggling to adapt to the unlikely realisation that his dreams hadn't been dreams after all.

'It's late.' She brought her voice back under control, though her expression remained guarded, as if she were afraid of what he might be thinking.

He didn't answer, his memory flooding with remembered sensations. The smooth plumpness of her lips, the exhilarating feeling of her body moulded against his, everything he'd thought he'd imagined made real. He could hardly believe it. He'd known that she'd lured him into the castle under false pretences, but he'd never expected her to go so far as to actually kiss him, let alone to throw herself into his arms with such wild abandon. Had it *all* been a pretence? Her first kisses perhaps, though the way her body had responded when he'd pulled her against him had certainly *felt* real. Either that or she was the best actress he'd ever seen. Judging by the heat burning her cheeks now, she definitely wasn't that.

'Lothar?'

He looked past her before he could stop himself, into her chamber and the bed he'd slept in the previous night—heard her breathing hitch in response. His own breathing sounded uneven, too, as if the air between them had suddenly become thicker and heavier, picking up every stray sound and movement. He felt as if all his senses were on the alert, as if he were aware of every hair on her head, every small tremor in her hands as she clutched them together in front of her. Most of all, he was aware of the fact that she wasn't moving away. He didn't think he'd ever been so aroused in his life, fighting the urge to pull her into his arms and see how she'd respond to his kisses a second time. They were alone in a tower with no one to disturb them, no one to even know they were alone together. The only people sober enough to have noticed him enter the stairwell were his guards and they knew better than to say anything. If he drew her into his arms again now, who was there to object?

He forced the temptation away. No matter how

powerful the attraction he felt for her, she was an innocent. He definitely hadn't been mistaken about that. A woman on her own without a father or guardian to protect her. If he kissed her, then he'd be taking advantage of that vulnerability. Never mind the fact that he was leaving in the morning. If he kissed her now, it would only make his departure more difficult and it was becoming hard enough already. Whatever strange power she seemed to hold over him, he had a feeling that touching her would only strengthen, not break, it.

Besides, even if she wasn't moving away, the look on her face spoke volumes. No matter what had happened between them, she clearly didn't want *him* to remember any of it. Was she ashamed? Embarrassed? Whatever the reason, if she didn't want him to remember then she obviously didn't want it to happen again.

He closed the door to her father's chamber and made a formal courtier's bow, heading for the stairwell before he could do anything he might regret.

'Goodnight, Lady Juliana.' Somehow he forced his feet to keep moving. 'Sleep well.'

Chapter Twelve

⁂

'It's a fine day, my lady.'

Juliana stood on top of the keep steps and stared down at Ulf in surprise. Was he ill? He didn't look ill. On the contrary, he looked better than he had for months, his wrinkled face and white hair illuminated by the reddish-gold autumn sunshine. If she wasn't mistaken, he was actually smiling. She blinked, trying to remember the last time she'd seen her Constable look anything other than dour. The sun might be shining for once, but what was there in their present situation that he could possibly find to smile about?

'Ulf?' She descended the steps cautiously. 'Are you all right?'

'Better than that. See for yourself.'

She looked up, though it took her a few moments to fully appreciate the sight of Sir Guian's men lugging sacks and barrels from one end of the bailey to the other. If the sound of groaning, not to mention the greenish tinge on most of their faces, was anything to go by, they weren't accustomed to such hard work.

'What are they doing?'

'Sergeant Lothar ordered them to move the supplies to a different storeroom. He made them muck out the stables first.'

'Did the supplies need moving?'

Ulf's smile spread into a grin. 'No one dared ask.'

'Oh.'

She bit her lip, not quite knowing how to react. On the one hand, the sight of the men who'd sat around taunting them for months being forced to do manual labour was more than a little amusing. On the other, since they were the same men who'd be staying once Lothar and his soldiers left, humiliating them probably wasn't the best idea. Bad enough that she was going to be stuck with Sir Guian. She didn't want him feeling vengeful as well…

'Where are *our* men?'

'Behind the smithy. Sergeant Lothar sent them to do weapons' training with his soldiers. He said they needed to get back into shape.'

'Did he?'

She glowered at the insult. Not that it *was* an insult really. He was right. After months of being trapped inside the bailey, her men *did* need to get back into shape, however much it rankled that someone else was giving them orders now.

'What about you?' She glanced towards Ulf resentfully. Judging by his newly cheerful disposition, he appeared to have no problem with the change in command.

'He told me to stay and look after you.'

'I'm not a child!'

'He said you might say that, my lady, and that I should send you back to bed if you argued.' Ulf held his hands up quickly. 'Not that I would.'

'And where is *he*?'

'He went out for a ride an hour ago.'

'Where to?'

'I don't know. He's not the kind of man who shares all his thoughts.' Ulf glanced at Sir Guian's soldiers again and chortled. 'Not that he doesn't make them obvious sometimes.'

Juliana made a harrumphing sound. She only wished that Lothar had been clearer about what he'd been thinking last night. What had he been doing upstairs? After he'd said that the best thing for her was to run off to Stephen and get *married*, she'd thought there was nothing left for them to say to each other. He couldn't have made it any clearer that he'd no personal interest in her—not that she wanted him to—so what had he been doing in her father's chamber afterwards? Had he been looking for her or something else? If it was her, then why? And if it was something, or *some-*

one else, then what had made him suspicious? She didn't know which idea worried her more.

The feeling of panic had increased tenfold the moment he'd mentioned wanting to jolt his memory. The idea that he might remember their kiss had been alarming enough. The way his gaze had altered, as if he just *had* been remembering it, had been even worse. Not that he'd said or done anything, and if he'd remembered then surely he would have...wouldn't he?

Even so, she'd been aware of something, some undercurrent of tension between them. For a heart-stopping moment, she'd even thought he'd been going to kiss her again. His eyes had lingered on her lips as if he'd wanted to. Standing face-to-face in the near-darkness, she'd felt her own treacherous body start to betray her again, too, as if the air of danger that had frightened her so much about him at first had actually started drawing her towards him now. If he hadn't left when he had, she might have made an even bigger fool of herself than she had before—and this time, there wouldn't have been any poppy-laced drink to make him forget.

'Did you get any rest, my lady?'

'Mmm?' Ulf's question brought her back to the present with a jolt. 'Oh, yes, I dozed a little.'

'In the taproom?'

She glanced around surreptitiously, checking to make sure no one else was in earshot before answering.

'I stayed there most of the night, but I was afraid of being summoned this morning so I went back upstairs as soon as I heard noises in the hall. Just in time, too.'

She could still hardly believe the narrowness of *that* escape. She'd got back to her chamber only minutes before two of Lothar's soldiers had arrived carrying a large bath tub, then proceeded to fill it to the brim with steaming water. Once she'd got over her relief at such a close call, it had felt wonderful. She'd stepped out of her clothes and into the tub with a feeling of intense, heartfelt relief. She'd been wearing her old brown tunic for two days straight and it hadn't been particularly flattering before that. Practical was probably the best word to describe it, not that there had been any point dressing up for a siege. No wonder Lothar had treated her more like a girl than a chatelaine. She hadn't exactly looked the part. Whereas now... She'd soaked herself for as long as she'd dared, then pulled on one of her best gowns, a respectable velvet bliaut in the same shade of muted green as most of her clothes, determined to prove that she could at least *look* like a chatelaine, as well as a lady, even if the once snug material now swamped her gaunt frame like a sack. She'd had to bunch the material over the top of her girdle just to stop it from trailing on the floor, though overall she'd been reasonably pleased with her appearance.

One glance at her reflection in the polished

metal bowl she used as a mirror had put paid to
that. Her only hope was that the change of gown
would distract from the huge black rings around
her eyes. They looked bad enough in her dimly
lit room. In broad daylight, they'd only provoke
more suspicion than ever.

'We can't use the taproom for long.' She
pushed her apprehensions aside. 'It's too cold.'

'You don't think we could tell Sergeant Lothar the truth?'

'What?' She gawked at Ulf in surprise. 'I
thought you didn't like him?'

'It's not a question of liking, but he seems fair-
minded.'

'When he doesn't look like he wants to wring
someone's neck, you mean?'

Ulf gave her a strange look. 'That was for you,
my lady. If *he* hadn't, then I would have.'

She looked away quickly, refusing to acknowledge that particular debt amongst all the others.
But Ulf was right in one way. Ironically, Lothar's honourable behaviour in preventing any
looting had kept her secret safer than she could
ever have hoped. No one beside him had ventured
any further than the hall of the keep. Still, even
if he *was* as fair-minded as Ulf seemed to think,
she couldn't risk telling him anything. He was
still one of the Empress's men, practically her
right-hand man if everything he'd said last night
was true. If she told him her secret, then he'd tell
Matilda and they'd all have to suffer the conse-

quences. He was clearly in love with Matilda after all. What had he said, that his only home was with *her*? The words shouldn't have affected her, but they had, causing an unwonted stab of jealousy. *The most beautiful woman he'd ever seen.* Somehow it hadn't bothered her quite so much when her father had said it...

'There's no need to tell him anything.' She lifted her chin stubbornly. 'He's leaving today so we won't have to use the taproom much longer. We'll use Father's chamber again. Sir Guian won't notice what's under his nose if I make up an excuse.'

'As you wish, my lady.'

Her chin dropped slightly. 'You don't approve?'

'It's not my place to say so, my lady.'

She bit her lip anxiously. She wasn't afraid of Ulf betraying her, but she would have appreciated his—or *anyone's*—support. Not that she needed it, she reminded herself. *She* was the chatelaine, or at least she had been. She could make her own decisions without any man's advice or support—and she could start by confronting the Baron herself.

'Where's Sir Guian?' Her gaze searched the bailey. 'Has he gone for a ride, too?'

Ulf didn't answer and she looked up in surprise. If she hadn't known better, she would have said he looked secretive, though he'd never kept secrets from her before.

'Constable?'

'I believe he's feeling unwell, my lady.'

'I didn't see him in the hall.'

'That's because he's in the gatehouse. Sergeant Lothar summoned him there just after dawn.'

'And?'

'I don't know, my lady. He still hasn't come out.'

Her mouth fell open. 'Is he hurt?'

Ulf shrugged as if the answer didn't particularly bother him. 'I didn't hear any sounds of violence.'

'Has anyone gone in to him since?'

'Not as far as I know. I'm not sure the Sergeant would approve.'

Approve? She picked up her skirts and strode determinedly across the bailey. Approval be damned, what had Lothar done? Even if he was trying to protect her, he had absolutely no right to take matters into his own hands! Hadn't she told him she could take care of herself? Hadn't she demanded that he didn't use violence? And if Ulf said the word *Sergeant* one more time she would scream!

She was within arm's reach of the gatehouse door when a grey stallion burst through the archway suddenly, rearing up on its hind legs as the rider drew rein in front of her.

'Lady Juliana.' Lothar's eyes flickered briefly over her loose-fitting gown before settling on her face with a faintly baffled expression. 'You seem to look more exhausted every time I see you.'

'Sergeant.' She folded her arms belligerently. There was no explanation she could give him for that—besides the fact that her appearance was none of his business, *especially* when she'd put on her best gown and all he could do was find fault!

'Where have you been?'

'Out.' He swung down from his saddle, landing at her feet with a thud. 'Have you eaten?'

'My habits are none of your concern.'

'But you want me to tell you where I've been?'

She glared at him. 'What have you done to Sir Guian?'

'Nothing permanent.'

'Have you hurt him?'

'Do you care?'

'Yes! Especially if you make him angry and then leave us to bear the brunt! I told you I can take care of myself.'

'So you did, but in this case there'll be no brunt. I didn't lay as much as a finger on him. We talked, just like I promised. He even gave me a present for you.'

'What is it?' She narrowed her eyes as he reached into his gambeson and pulled out a rolled-up piece of parchment.

'A letter of safe conduct for when you finally decide to leave.'

'Oh.' She reached up slowly, wrapping her fingers around one end of the parchment while he still held on to the other, so that for a moment it seemed as if they were holding hands. The very idea was enough to make the breath catch in her throat. 'That was thoughtful.'

'He also intends to give you and your men enough supplies for the journey.'

'He *does*?'

'He was feeling generous.'

'But...' her gaze drifted towards the gatehouse door '...does he need any help?'

'Why would he?'

'Ulf thought that he might be feeling *unwell*.'

He dropped his hand from the parchment abruptly. 'Still so mistrustful? I just told you that I didn't touch him.'

'Then why hasn't he come out?'

'Perhaps he's still recovering from last night. He wasn't best pleased at being woken up at dawn. Or perhaps he's just taking some time to consider what we talked about.'

She gasped as the truth dawned on her. 'You threatened him?'

He shrugged. 'I made him aware of the re-percussions of *not* listening to me, if that's what you mean. I wouldn't call it a threat as much as a warning. He knows I'm a man of my word.'

She felt a quivering sensation in her stomach, something between fear and excitement. She didn't approve of his methods, but she had no doubt that they would be effective. And if he was telling the truth then there was no need for her to go inside and deal with Sir Guian. That was a relief, even if it did leave her alone with Lothar again. She could feel him watching her, waiting to see what she would decide, as if her decision might actually matter to him, though it was difficult to concentrate under the force of that piercing grey stare.

'All right.' She took a step back into the bailey.

'I appreciate your trust, my lady.'

She narrowed her eyes at the sarcasm. 'I thought you were leaving.'

'So eager to be rid of me?'

'I want things to be settled, that's all. It's got nothing to do with *you*.'

She walked ahead of him, biting her lip on the lie. That wasn't true at all. He had everything to do with the way she was feeling, as if her head and heart were in conflict. The sooner he was gone, the safer her secret would be, yet the thought of him leaving caused a pang in her chest that she'd never experienced before. Perhaps Ulf was right and she ought to tell him her secret. He *did* seem fair-minded. Procuring a letter of safe passage for her had been thoughtful, too, and he'd already proven that he had no problem with serving a woman, in which case he ought to treat *her* as an independent woman as well. Could she tell him her secret and trust him to hold only her accountable and not her men? Could she trust him to persuade Matilda of that, too? If he was leaving, then this might be her last chance...

'You have a fine estate.'

She blinked, startled out of her train of thought.

'Yes, though it's not what it was. The crops on this side of the river are ruined. We had to plant them late after Stephen left, then we couldn't bring in the harvest once Sir Guian's men arrived. We're just lucky to have the other side of the river as well.'

'I'm glad of it.'

'So am I, though I know others haven't been so fortunate.' She threw him a sideways look. 'I don't suppose either Stephen or Matilda are starving, no matter how much everyone else suffers.'

'The Empress would relieve the suffering if she could.'

'She could surrender.'

'So could Stephen.'

She pursed her lips with a vague sense of disappointment. If she'd hoped that he might say something disloyal about Matilda, then clearly she was wasting her time.

'I hope your horse isn't too tired.' She changed the subject instead as one of his soldiers took charge of the reins. 'I would have thought you had a long enough journey ahead without a morning ride, too.'

'It wasn't far. I just wanted a look around.'

'For anything in particular?'

'Just Stephen and his army.' He said the words so nonchalantly that it took a moment for them to sink in.

'What?' She almost skidded to a halt.

'I heard a rumour that Stephen was coming into Herefordshire again. I wanted to take a look.'

'What rumour?' Her mouth felt dry all of a sudden. 'What made you think that?'

He gave her an eloquent look. 'You did, my lady. Yesterday when I asked what difference a week would make to the siege and you said that it was all you needed. I assumed you were expecting reinforcements.'

She cringed, inwardly berating herself for her own stupidity. She'd muttered something to that effect under her breath, but she'd never imagined he might have noticed. How could she have been so thoughtless? He'd remembered what she'd forgotten herself. In all the upheaval of the past day she hadn't even thought about Stephen!

'I don't know what you're talking about.' She tried to feign innocence.

'In that case I admire your loyalty, but the castle still needs to be ready just in case.' He jerked his head in the direction of the smithy. 'I thought your men might need some weapons' practice. You never know when they might be called on to fight.'

'For Sir Guian?'

'I'm afraid so. I told you last night, if they want to stay here then it's their only choice. Perhaps you'll allow me to show you whilst my horse is resting?'

His gaze locked on to hers, his eyes seeming a whole different shade suddenly, their granite depths shimmering like crystalline violet in the sunlight. No, she warned herself, she ought to say no. It wasn't just a bad idea, it was a dangerous one. Reckless. Imprudent. Completely irresponsible. No matter how thoughtful he'd been, they were still on different sides in a war. He was her enemy, sort of. Then he extended an arm and, for a moment, she forgot to breathe.

Chapter Thirteen

Juliana stared at Lothar's elbow, taken aback by such an incongruous gesture. He seemed too big, too austere, too much the soldier to behave in such a courtly fashion. Especially considering the first time they'd met. There hadn't been *anything* gallant about that! She wasn't accustomed to acting the lady either—couldn't even remember the last time a man had offered her his arm—and yet somehow she couldn't resist the temptation.

'Very well.'

She placed a hand on his bicep, twisting her face away as a thrill of excitement raced through her body, building in strength as it went. She had to place her spare hand on her stomach to try to calm it.

'This way, Lady Juliana.'

They crossed the bailey in silence, following the same path they'd walked the day before, though she could hardly believe it had only been that long. She felt as if she'd known him for longer. So much between them had changed. When they'd first entered the castle she'd been afraid of what he might do to her, but all of her fears had turned out to be completely unfounded. Now she was scared in a whole different way, of herself as much as of him. She didn't understand why she responded to him so acutely, but she couldn't seem to help it either. Not that it meant anything on *his* part, she was certain. She was deluding herself to think that a man like him would ever look twice at a woman like her. Even if it *seemed* as though he already had.

'There they are.'

She jumped as they rounded the corner of the smithy, so deep in thought that the sound of his voice, not to mention its close proximity to her ear, actually startled her. She turned to find his face leaning in towards hers, so close that she could feel the heat of his breath against her cheek.

He gestured ahead and she looked, excitement turning to horror as she saw a group of his black-clad soldiers bearing down on her thin, emaciated-looking ones. No! She took half a step forward, seized with a rush of panic. Her men were weak and tired, no match for his warriors. They weren't evenly matched!

She opened her mouth to protest and then closed it again, her panic gradually ebbing away as she started to make sense of the scene before her. There was no antagonism or aggression about it. On the contrary, there was an air of camaraderie, as if the soldiers were sharing advice rather than blows. A stranger would never have guessed that they'd been facing each other as enemies just two days before.

'Sparring, not fighting.' Lothar's tone was reassuring.

'Yes.' She let out a sigh. 'That's a relief. It would hardly have been fair.'

'No, but your men are well trained. I'm sure they'd make worthy adversaries.'

'I wasn't talking about them. Though yours aren't bad either.'

'Not *bad*? They're some of the finest soldiers in the Empress's army.'

'As I said, not bad.' She bit her lip, struggling to keep a straight face. 'But you know my father raised me to have high standards.'

'So it seems.' The coals behind his eyes seemed to spark with amusement briefly. 'He was a fine soldier. One of the best tacticians I ever met.'

'A good teacher, too. He was always patient with me.'

The muscles in his arm seemed to flex slightly beneath her fingertips. 'He taught you to fight?'

'Of course. He believed that a woman ought to be able to defend herself.'

'Did he think that you'd need to?'

'I don't know, but I suppose he thought that I

should be prepared just in case. He taught me to use a sword and a bow like the rest of his men.'

'I thought ladies were taught poetry and sewing.'

'Most are, but there was no one here to teach me. My mother died from the sweating fever when I was three.'

'I'm sorry.' The muscles in his arm twitched again. 'I lost my own mother when I was a child. I know how painful the loss is.'

'To be honest, I don't remember much about her. I wish I did, but at least I had my father.'

He made a strange sound, something between a grunt and a protest, the muscles in his arm flexing so violently this time that she thought he was about to pull away.

'Do you remember your mother?' She asked the question warily.

'I remember everything about her.' His voice sounded different suddenly, rougher and more guttural, as if he were struggling to speak at all. 'She was the whole world to me.'

'Oh.' She squeezed his arm, touched by the note of anguish in his voice. His face looked less like something carved out of granite now, more like flesh and blood. Like that of a man in pain. 'Was it a sickness as well?'

'No.'

'An accident?'

'No!'

She leapt backwards instinctively, recoiling from the anger in his voice.

'Forgive me.' He rubbed a hand over his face, as if he were forcing the emotion back down again. 'I don't like to think of it. What happened to my mother… They called it an accident, but it wasn't.'

'Oh.' She bit her tongue, fighting the urge to ask what *it* was.

'But I know what it's like to grow up without one.' He lowered his hand and his face was like granite again. 'Weren't there any other ladies in your father's household?'

'No.' She shook her head, relieved that the moment of crisis seemed to have passed. 'One of my aunts came to live with us for a while, the one my father had originally been supposed to marry, but she hated it here. She said that we were in the middle of nowhere and I was too unruly.'

'*You?*'

She couldn't repress a smile. 'Actually, I think he might have asked her to leave. After that it was just father and me so I learned what he taught me. Do you want to see?'

His expression clouded over again. 'I don't think that's a good idea.'

'Why not? Haven't you ever seen a woman wield a sword before?' She pulled her arm away from his, scooping a leather gambeson off the floor. 'Or are you afraid that I'm better than you?'

'Lady Juliana…' He cleared his throat. 'I'd prefer if you didn't.'

There was a note of warning in his voice, but she felt too exhilarated to pay any heed. At least this was one way to prove that she was an independent woman—fit to be chatelaine, even if she wasn't any more. For some reason, his opinion on that score seemed to matter to her.

She borrowed a weapon from one of her soldiers and issued a challenge to one of his, tapping her foot impatiently until, after a moment's hesitation, the man lifted his own sword in response. Then she didn't hesitate, springing forward at once, catching the man by surprise as she thrust her sword up towards his shoulder. He dodged backwards, veering to one side, but she was faster, anticipating the move and swinging her blade around in an arc to catch him on the other arm before flicking it up towards his face, stopping barely an inch from his cheek.

'I yield.'

The soldier looked impressed and she grinned triumphantly, twirling around on the spot to face Lothar.

'You next?' She pointed her sword at his heart.

'Put. It. Down.'

She tensed, her hand wavering in mid-air, though she refused to lower anything. Lothar's expression was almost as animated as it had been when he'd confronted Sir Guian, though this time he didn't look so much angry as pained. Why? Surely he wasn't upset with her just for fighting when he'd asked her not to? Why couldn't she fight if she wanted to? How dare he give her an order!

'Afraid I might beat you?' She tightened her grip on the sword hilt.

'No.'

'Then why won't you fight me? Because I'm a woman? Aren't I worthy?'

'Worth has nothing to do with it. I don't fight women.'

'But you'll fight *for* one?'

'There's a difference.'

She took a step closer, pushing the tip of her sword against his chest, though he didn't so much as blink. She felt a wave of resentment, building to fury. If she were a man, he might have accepted her as an equal and acknowledged the challenge. As a woman, he deemed her of so little importance that he could simply refuse to fight her without any dent to his honour. Was he *determined* to humiliate her in front of her men, to show them how little authority she now had? Or was he just trying to make her feel as powerless as possible? Worst of all was the fact that, short of impaling him on her sword, there wasn't a thing she could do about it.

She dropped her weapon at last, passing it back to its owner with as much dignity as she could muster. The intractable expression on Lothar's face was the final straw. She'd hoped that he might be impressed by her sword skills, but he was just as disapproving as every other man she'd ever met outside Haword. Somehow, she'd thought that he might be different—she'd *wanted* him to be different—but clearly he thought her father had been wrong in the way he'd raised her, too. *That* was why he'd mentioned sewing and poetry. Those were the skills he thought she ought to be practising, the ones Matilda had probably mastered! *That* was the kind of woman he'd be attracted to, the kind he was prepared to serve, not an unnatural woman like *her*.

'Go back to your Empress, then.' She jutted her chin out, refusing to show how much the realisation hurt. 'Go back and serve a real lady. You've *wasted* enough time here.'

'Lady Juliana…'

'Goodbye!'

She didn't wait to hear what he was going to say, swallowing her tears as she fled across the bailey. This was the second time he'd humiliated her in front of her men, but she wasn't going to cry, no matter how great the indignity. She wouldn't give any man that satisfaction. Bad enough that he'd taken her castle and her position, but now he was trying to take away the only skill she had any pride in! If he didn't leave soon, she'd have nothing left, nothing except her secret— and she'd be damned if she was going to give him that, too! After what had just happened she'd rather take her chances with Sir Guian. With any luck, she'd never see Lothar the Frank ever again!

Chapter Fourteen

Lothar watched her go with a pang of regret. He wasn't accustomed to the feeling. Most of the time he didn't care what people thought of him. He was answerable to the Empress. No one else's opinion mattered. Yet the fact that Lady Juliana had misunderstood him, that she'd interpreted his refusal to fight as an insult, bothered him in a way that made him want to run after her. *Almost.* He set his mouth in a stern line. But what would he say if he did? If he explained his reaction, then it would only lead to further questions and he had no desire to answer any of those. No, it was better to leave it this way. He'd done what he'd come to do—ended the stalemate, restocked the castle, made sure the fortifications were in good enough condition to withstand another siege, and advised Lady Juliana to go to Stephen. He'd even dealt with Sir Guian, terrifying him even more thoroughly than if he'd used actual violence, using his *peasant* upbringing as a blacksmith's son to describe what could be done with a few tools and a branding iron. That was all he could do, all he could be expected to do, and the sooner he put some distance between himself and Lady Juliana, the better. In all likelihood, he'd never see her again, so what did it matter how he left things between them? He had neither the time nor the ability to soothe hurt feelings. Far better to stop thinking about it and go before he could change his mind.

'We're leaving.'

He summoned his men, surprised to see disapproval on the faces of both sets of soldiers. Apparently they thought he'd been overly harsh, too.

'Now!'

He stood to one side whilst they packed up their weapons, trying and failing *not* to think about her. He oughtn't to think about her and definitely not in the way that he wanted to. Even if he *did* like her, she wasn't the kind of woman he could ever aspire to. Unladylike as she was, she was still a lady, part of the nobility, whilst he was a peasant by birth. He'd no right to think of her other than as someone to serve. Not that she'd think of him in any other way either. The more he thought about their kiss, the more he decided it *must* have been a pretence. In all likelihood, he'd simply mistaken his own ardour for hers. It wasn't as if she'd ever looked pleased to see him since, and now…well, judging by the look on her face as she'd stormed away, she never wanted to see him again.

He felt a constricting sensation in his chest. It didn't matter how much he was attracted to her. Nor that her sword skills were equal to most of his men. Her eagerness to show them off had been strangely endearing, though the very idea of it, coming so close to what he'd told her about his mother, had made him sick to his stomach. Her sparring with his soldier had been bad enough, but when she'd challenged *him* to fight, a grey pallor had seemed to descend over the scene, as if winter clouds had suddenly obscured the autumn sunshine. It was the same icy feeling of horror that always accompanied any thoughts of violence against women. Fighting her was the one thing he would never do—never raise a finger, let alone a sword, to any woman, never behave in the way that his father had done.

He pushed the memory aside as he led the way to the stables, surprised to find Ulf already waiting with his stallion.

'Lady Juliana said you were leaving, sir.'

'Did she?' He scowled. Apparently she really *was* keen to be rid of him. 'Where is she?'

'Back in the keep.'

He took hold of the animal's reins, trying to ignore the feeling of mounting pressure in his chest, as if there were actually a band tightening around it. Perhaps he'd ridden too much that morning after all...

'In that case, tell her I said goodbye.'

'I will, sir.'

He put a foot in the stirrup and then paused, arrested by a gleam of something in the other man's eye. 'What is it?'

'Nothing, sir.' The gleam vanished at once.

He looked around. His men were busy fastening packs to their saddles. Some were already mounted. He ought to mount, too, ought to get on his horse and ride away. He rarely deviated from his purpose, but this time he felt as if his body were actually holding him back. Every time he tried to climb up on to the stallion the pressure in his chest only seemed to get worse. This was ridiculous. Why was he finding it so hard to leave?

'Damn it.' He rested his forehead against the saddle for a moment before dropping the reins with an oath. 'Wait here, all of you.'

'Sir?'

He heard Ulf call after him, but he kept going, taking the keep steps three at a time. He didn't want it to end like this. At the very least, he wanted her to know that he hadn't meant to insult her. More than that—*worse* than that—he couldn't leave without seeing her one last time.

He stalked back through the hall and across to the stairwell, already mounting the steps to her chamber when he heard a noise coming from the opposite direction, from the stairs leading down to the cellars. It sounded like moaning again, the same as he'd heard the day before. He turned around instantly, going back to the hall for a candle, before heading down into the darkness. The stairs looped around twice before he found himself in the cellars, but the space was barren and empty, the castle provisions long since exhausted. Slowly he made his way around the cavernous chamber, but there was nothing suspicious—though nothing that might explain the noise either.

Perplexed, he started back up the stairs, one hand trailing along the wall, so that when it fell away suddenly, he almost tripped in surprise. Looking closer, he found a small archway hidden in one of the embrasures. He must have missed it on the way down, taking it for just another wall sconce, but peering through the darkness he could see that it was actually the entrance into another empty storeroom, nothing of any interest... He was just turning away when he heard the moaning sound again, accompanied by the faint murmur of a woman's voice—Juliana's voice, in a soft tone he'd never heard before, as if she were soothing someone...

He took a step inside and looked around, belatedly noticing another small door in the side wall. Cautiously, he moved towards it, ducking his head under the archway before stopping abruptly, rooted to the spot by the sight before him.

There, lying on a straw mattress on the floor,

illuminated by the light of a single candle, was the unmistakable figure of William Danville, ashen-faced but still very much alive. And bending over him, holding a cup to his lips and murmuring softly, was his daughter.

He must have made a sound, though he wasn't aware of doing so, because she looked up suddenly, letting out a small shriek at the sight of him.

'What are you doing here?'

What was he doing there? If it hadn't been for his friend's wasted, almost skeletal appearance he might have laughed at her indignant tone—as if he had no right to be there, as if she had every right to keep her father hidden away like a prisoner, as if she had any right to be indignant at all! He didn't know if he felt more stunned, outraged or horrified. All three emotions were clamouring so loudly in his head that he could hardly think straight. He'd suspected her of hiding something, but never in his wildest imaginings had he conceived of anything like *this*!

'It's not what you think!' Her voice held a distinct quaver of panic.

'Really?' He took a step towards her, the red mist descending like a veil over his eyes. 'Then tell me what I *should* think, my lady, and then tell me what the hell is going on!'

Juliana leapt to her feet with a mounting sense of alarm. What was Lothar doing there? How had he found her? Hadn't she told him to leave? He *had* been leaving! She'd heard the trample of hooves in the bailey just a few moments before. So what was he doing there now, looking at her as if she were some kind of monster? She'd just finished giving her father a sleeping draught, much as she hated to do it, but from the look on Lothar's face it might as well have been poison.

'It's not what you think.' She repeated the words helplessly.

'I *think* it's your father. Or are you going to tell me it's one of your men having nightmares again?'

She flinched, desperately trying to come up with a way to explain. How could she say that it was *and* wasn't her father? He'd think she was mad.

'So *this* is the bargain you made with Stephen?' He looked her up and down furiously. 'It's one thing to want to be chatelaine, my lady, quite another to hold your own father prisoner!'

'He's not a prisoner!' She felt appalled by the accusation.

'No? According to you, an hour ago he wasn't even alive!'

'I never said that! It was Stephen's men who spread the rumour.'

'You never corrected it.'

'I couldn't. I made a promise.'

'To let everyone believe your father was dead?'

'*Yes!*'

She took a deep breath to calm herself down. Losing her temper wasn't going to get her anywhere. She couldn't exactly blame him for thinking the worst, but she had to find a way to make him understand, to make him see that the situation wasn't as bad as it appeared, even if he seemed too angry to listen.

'I can explain.'

'Can you? Or will you just lie to me again?' His eyes contracted to slits. 'What were you giving him just now?'

'It's a sleeping draught. It helps with the pain.'

Dark brows bunched together. 'Was he injured in battle?'

'No. I mean, yes, but that healed weeks ago. It's not for that.'

'Then what are you doing to him?'

'Taking care of him!'

She shouted back at him this time, heedless of whoever might hear her now. How *dare* he ask her such a question, as if she'd do anything to hurt her own father, as if it didn't break her heart to nurse him every day and be powerless to do anything that might actually help!

'Then you have a strange definition of care, my lady.'

He looked around at the bleak stone walls and her heart sank. No wonder he thought it was a prison. Short of some chains, it could hardly have looked any more like one.

'Just let me explain.'

'Save it for the Empress.'

His expression was grim and she felt an ice-cold tremor of fear, the same as she'd felt the first time she'd seen him. She'd got to know him since, had almost been tempted to tell him the truth about her father, but now it was too late. He was the same granite warrior she'd first glimpsed from the battlements, unyielding, unwavering and dangerous, and yet, strangely enough, she wasn't frightened of *him*. As furious as he looked, somehow she knew he wouldn't hurt her. That was one consolation. As for turning her over to the Empress however...

'What do you mean?' she hardly dared ask.

'Your father was one of her most loyal supporters. She'll want to deal with you herself.'

'But I can't go to Devizes! Surely you wouldn't...' Her protest faded away as two of his soldiers appeared in the doorway.

'Take her to her chamber and lock her in.' Lothar turned his back as if he couldn't bear to look at her any longer, the ire in his voice sending shivers down her spine.

'Wait!' She dodged away from the soldiers and grabbed at his arm, ready to beg if necessary. She'd take whatever punishment he thought fit, just as long as he didn't separate her from her father—not now, not yet! She'd do anything to prevent that, though judging by the intractable look on his face *anything* might not be enough. 'He needs me.'

'He needs a proper bed in a warm room, not *this*!'

'This was only going to be for one night, I swear it. You heard him moaning in his chamber yesterday morning, didn't you? You know he was up there then. He isn't a prisoner.'

The tension around his eyes seemed to ease slightly. 'Then why did you bring him down here?'

'Because I thought it was the safest place. I didn't know what would happen when I surrendered.'

'I promised you that no one would get hurt.'

'I had to be certain.'

'And after I stopped Sir Guian's soldiers from ransacking the castle, why didn't you take him back to his chamber then?'

'Because you said you were leaving…' she grimaced, realising how bad it sounded '…and I thought that maybe I could still keep him secret. I don't know if Sir Guian ever met my father, but I doubted he'd look at a sick man too closely. Once you left, I was going to take him back to his chamber and say he was one of my soldiers.'

'But you knew that I'd recognise him?'

'Yes.'

An expression of something like hurt swept over his features. 'So you were just waiting for me to leave?'

A feeling of guilt assailed her, as if she'd actually taken advantage of his honourable behaviour. 'Yes.'

'So you *wanted* Sir Guian to stay instead of me?' His mouth twisted bitterly. 'And I thought I was protecting you.'

'It wasn't like that.' She shook her head vehemently. 'I didn't want Sir Guian, but I wanted to keep my promise to Stephen, as far as I could anyway. I gave him my oath.'

'As I gave mine to the Empress.' He shook her hand away from his arm brusquely. 'I don't know what this is, but I've heard enough. Take her away.'

'No!' She tried to back away from his men, but there was nowhere to go. 'You can't do this. I know how to look after him. I know what to do!'

'You've done enough.'

'No!' She kept on resisting, wrestling furiously with his soldiers as they half-led, half-carried her towards the door. *'Please!'*

She stopped struggling when they reached the stairwell, refusing to suffer the indignity of being carried upstairs. It was no use. Lothar wasn't going to listen, no matter how much she begged or pleaded with him, and by the look of things he wasn't going to forgive her either. She marched furiously up to her room, spinning around at the last moment to confront her captors, only to see the door close in her face instead. She gulped as the key turned in the lock. She'd exchanged places with Lothar completely now. He had her home and her father, and now somehow she'd become his prisoner, too. Her secret had been discovered in the worst possible way and she'd already been judged and condemned.

She sank down on to her bed, overwhelmed by a sense of her own helplessness. Her one consolation was that her father would soon be back in his old chamber, too, back in his own bed, but everything else about the situation was too upsetting to think about. What if he woke up surrounded by strangers? What if he woke up in pain? Ulf was the only other person who knew what to do—would Lothar let him?

She lay down on the mattress and closed her eyes. If Lothar was just going to ignore her, then there was nothing she could do for the moment except worry and she was too tired even for that. She hadn't slept for so long that she felt as if there were actual weights pressing down on her eyelids. Now that her secret was out, there was no need for her to think or to plan or to hide any more. That was almost a relief. She'd done her best to honour her promise to Stephen, but it was over. In the meantime her father was safe and not in pain. That was all that mattered now. As for the rest, she'd think about it later. It was all out of her hands finally...

On that thought, she fell asleep.

Chapter Fifteen

Lothar folded his arms, looking down at the emaciated, corpse-like shadow of his friend. William was sleeping deeply, too deeply for his liking. He hadn't even stirred when they'd carried him up two flights of winding stairs, probably due to whatever potion his daughter had given him. A sleeping draught she'd called it, though he had his own experience to know how powerful those could be.

He shook his head, still struggling to get over the shock he'd felt when he'd first walked into the taproom. If he'd found Stephen himself, he couldn't have felt any more surprised. He'd sent Lady Juliana away because he'd been too overwhelmed to take anything else in, certainly too angry to think straight and listen, though worse than that had been the feelings of betrayal and disappointment, as if she hadn't been the woman he'd thought she was.

Somehow he'd managed to restrain his temper. He would never have hurt her, but there had been men enough in the bailey that he could have vented his anger on. Still he hadn't done it, remembering what she'd said about not wanting violence, and, ironically, he hadn't wanted to let her down. No matter how much of a liar and deceiver she was, somehow her influence *still* had the power to calm him, even when she was the one making him angry.

Now that he'd had some time to think, however, the other things she'd said tugged at the edge of his consciousness. She'd said that her father was in pain, though not from an injury, which suggested an illness of some kind. That made sense. William was too thin, like everyone else in the castle, but he seemed to have aged twenty years since they'd last met as well. There was something unnatural about his appearance, too, his blue veins standing out against pale skin that looked almost translucent, as if he were wasting away to bone.

'Sergeant?'

He turned to find one of his men standing in the doorway.

'Have you brought him?'

'Yes, sir.'

'Good. Send him in and then leave us.'

He set his feet further apart, bracing himself

for another confrontation as Ulf stumbled unceremoniously into the chamber.

'Where's Lady Juliana?' The Constable's truculent expression was back with a vengeance.

'That's none of your concern. Did you know about this?'

He gestured at William, expecting some kind of denial, though Ulf answered at once.

'Yes.'

'What about your men?'

'Yes.'

He lifted an eyebrow. '*All* of them?'

'Yes.'

'Then how the hell could you go along with it?' His temper exploded at last. 'This is your master, the man you ought to serve, not hold captive! Give me one good reason why I shouldn't execute the lot of you for disloyalty.'

'Do whatever you want.'

'Your lady, too?'

'No!'

'And why shouldn't I?' He took a threatening step closer. 'Bad enough that she sided with her father's enemy, but then to keep him hidden away like a dog! I ought to leave and let Sir Guian deal with the lot of you.'

'Wait until he wakes up.'

'What?' He frowned. 'Why?'

A look of pain crossed the Constable's face. 'Just wait. It won't be long, it never is now. Then you'll understand.'

Wait! Lothar took a deep breath, tempted to tell Ulf exactly what he could do with that suggestion. The last thing he wanted to do was wait! He'd waited too long already, delayed his departure too many times. He'd almost left that morning, had only come back because he'd wanted to make peace with Lady Juliana. Now part of him wished that he'd left when he had the chance. This time he was well and truly trapped. No matter what he'd just told Ulf, he couldn't leave now. The thought of abandoning Lady Juliana with Sir Guian had been bad enough, but William, too? Not just his friend, but his sick friend? How could he possibly leave now?

A fit of coughing drew him to the bed.

'William?' He leaned over, alarmed to see the vacant expression on the face looking up at him.

'Who are you?' The voice was frail and wavering, nothing at all like the one he remembered.

'It's Lothar. From the Empress's court.'

'The Empress?' William's green eyes, so strikingly like his daughter's, darted wildly around the room as if he were searching for someone. 'Where's Ana?'

Ana? He felt a faint stirring of unease. He'd never heard William call his daughter by the short version of her name before.

'Lady Juliana's resting.'

'Not her—my wife! Tell her to come to me.' William closed his eyelids briefly, before opening them again with a fresh look of confusion. 'Who are you?'

'Lothar.' He tried again. 'I've been sent by the Empress.'

'Who?'

'Empress Matilda.'

'But she's a child! I thought she was in Francia. Why is she sending me a message?'

'He means the King, my lord,' Ulf interrupted hastily. 'King Henry.'

'Ah.' William looked relieved. 'Then what does the King want with me?'

'He sends his greetings, my lord, and Sergeant Lothar here. Do you remember him?'

The old man's face wrinkled in concentration. 'There's something familiar, but I don't know the name.'

'It doesn't matter.' Lothar took a discreet step backwards. He had the feeling his presence was only making William more distressed. 'We'll talk later. You ought to rest now.'

'I can't. It hurts.'

'My lady gives him some medicine for the pain.' Ulf lowered his voice. 'Will you allow it?'

'Yes.' This time he didn't hesitate. 'Do it.'

He didn't stay to watch, moving away from the bed with a fresh sense of despair, as if he'd lost his old friend all over again. The last time he'd seen William had been just over a year ago. Now that he thought of it, there had been something odd about his behaviour then, as if he was missing some of his usual alertness, but he'd put it down to the strains of war.

'Is he always like this?' He waited for Ulf to join him in the doorway.

'No. Sometimes he's aware of everything, though that doesn't happen often now. It's not just his mind either. There's some kind of sickness.'

'Did he ride out to fight Stephen like this?'

'Aye.' Ulf shook his head regretfully. 'Six months ago he still seemed to know what he was doing, but he was worse than we realised. My lady didn't want him to go, but she couldn't nay-say him either. We'd no idea that he intended to charge off all on his own. It happened so fast that I couldn't stop him. That's why he was knocked down and captured. Lady Juliana blames herself.'

'If he was captured, then how did he get back here?'

Ulf's face took on a look of pride. 'Because she rode into Stephen's camp to get him.'

'Lady Juliana?' Both his eyebrows shot up. 'On her own?'

'She wouldn't let anyone go with her.'

'Was there a ransom?'

'If there was, we couldn't have paid it. Every-thing he had was spent on supporting the Em-press.'

'Then how...?' Lothar let out a low whistle as the truth finally struck him. 'That's why she swore her allegiance to Stephen, to get him back?'

Ulf nodded. 'She came back an hour later with her father on a litter. He hasn't got up since.'

'*Taking care of him…*' Lothar murmured the words softly. 'Is that why she's always so tired, because she's been nursing him?'

'Ever since she brought him back, running herself into the ground doing it, too, no thanks to your lot.' Ulf's expression turned combative again. 'So what are you going to do now?'

Lothar folded his arms, knowing that he ought to rebuke the other man, but lacking the will to do so, glancing across to her chamber door instead. She'd stopped protesting once his men had dragged her away, though he'd been no less aware of her presence in the tower. Every thought he'd had seemed to come back to her, as if his mind were incapable of *not* thinking about her for long. Now it seemed that he'd misjudged her and badly. The fact that she'd been keeping secrets from him still rankled, but the sense of relief he felt was greater still. She hadn't been holding her father prisoner after all. She hadn't betrayed him simply because she wanted to be chatelaine. She'd been telling the truth when she'd said she was taking care of him. Which meant that he owed her an apology.

'Stay with him.'

He pulled the key to her chamber from his gambeson and crossed the gallery, knocking lightly on the door before pushing it open.

She was lying sprawled across the bed, her legs

dangling over the edge as if she'd simply tumbled backwards where she'd sat. Probably she had. At least now he knew the reason behind her exhaustion. Every time he'd thought he'd been sending her to bed she'd been nursing her father instead. No wonder his knock hadn't disturbed her. She was probably tired enough to sleep for a week.

He studied her face, half-obscured by a swirl of dark red hair. Her forehead was creased slightly, as if her cares were too ingrained to be forgotten in sleep, her lips slightly parted, as if just waiting to be kissed. He tensed at the thought, inappropriate as it was, surprised, too, by a rush of admiration. She was a better woman, not a worse one, than he'd realised. A woman who'd sided with Stephen to save her father, not to gain anything for herself. She hadn't even sided against Matilda, not really. In which case, they weren't on different sides any more. The thought made her even more tantalising. As if leaving her hadn't been hard enough in the first place...

He backed towards the door and closed it softly behind him. There was no need to wake her just yet. Questions could wait. The other things he had to do couldn't. He might have a difficult time explaining himself to the Empress when it came to it, but he had no choice. He couldn't leave Lady Juliana. Not yet anyway, but Sir Guian most definitely could.

Chapter Sixteen

∽⌒⌒⌒∽

Juliana stretched her arms above her head, perplexed and vaguely disorientated by the peculiar sensation of actually feeling well rested. She'd only intended to doze, but now her chamber was dark, the only light spilling in from a torch in the gallery outside.

She rolled over and propped herself up on one elbow, frowning at the yellow puddle of light on the floor. There was something out of place about it, as if it shouldn't be there, but what was so strange about torchlight? Nothing at all except... She sat up with a jolt. The door was open!

She sprang off the bed, hurtling out of her room and across the gallery before skidding to a surprised halt. Her father was sleeping peacefully in his bed with Lothar settled in a chair beside him, his stern features overshadowed by the hand resting on his forehead. She took a few cautious steps closer, wondering if there'd been some mistake and someone had left her door open by accident. Was Lothar asleep? He wasn't moving, though he didn't look particularly relaxed—not that she expected him to. It was almost impossible to imagine him without that air of dangerous, tightly leashed tension. She leaned forward. How would he react if he woke up and saw her?

'I owe you an apology, my lady.'

She jumped at the sound of his voice, embarrassed to have been caught looking at him. Peering closer, she could see shards of silver-grey shimmering between the gaps in his fingers, as if he'd been watching her as she'd been studying him. He must have known she was there the whole time.

'An apology?' It took her a moment to realise the significance of his words.

'Yes.'

He sat up, dropping his hand from his face wearily. He still looked stern, but his earlier anger seemed to have dissipated, replaced by an air of almost mournful sadness, as if... She glanced quickly towards the bed. There was only one thing that could have changed his mind so completely.

'He woke up?'

'A while ago.'

She was half-afraid to ask her next question. 'How was he?'

'He asked for your mother.'

'Oh.' Her vision blurred. 'He often thinks that I'm her. I used to correct him, but it only made him more upset. Now I just pretend.'

He nodded and glanced away, as if giving her a chance to control herself. 'Ulf gave him some of your remedy. At least now I know why you keep such powerful medicines to hand.'

She brushed a hand across her eyes. 'I don't want to give them to him. I want him to wake up and be himself again, but he's confused and in pain more and more. I can't bear to see that.' She paused. 'Do you think it's wrong of me?'

'No. You're taking care of him.'

'I'm trying to.'

'For what it's worth, I'm sorry I accused you of anything else.'

'Thank you.'

She took a chair on the opposite side of the bed, watching him from beneath her lashes. His eyes were hooded, though she could sense that he was still watching her, too. She had the impression that they were both seeing each other in a new light.

'I thought you were leaving.'

'So did I.' He leaned back in his chair and sighed. 'We seem to go around in circles, Lady Juliana. First you imprison me, then you release me, then I imprison you and now...' He blew air from between his teeth. 'Is there anything else you've neglected to tell me about? Is Stephen hiding in one of your stables?'

'No.' She smiled despite herself.

'Good. Because I don't want any more lies between us. We're in this together now.'

'What do you mean?' She looked up again hopefully. Had he changed his mind about sending her to Matilda for punishment then? Was he going to help her? He was regarding her levelly.

'I'm still here, aren't I?'

'What about Sir Guian?'

'He's gone.'

'Gone?'

His lips twitched. 'He was as surprised about it as you are. I sent him back to the Empress.'

'But won't he tell her about my father?'

'He can't tell her something he doesn't know. That's why I sent him away.'

'You mean…' She could hardly believe what she was hearing. 'You mean you're *not* telling her?'

'No, I'm just not telling her *yet*. Some news is best delivered in person. For the time being, this is our secret.'

She felt a flicker of something like triumph, as if she'd just won an important piece in a game of chess. She wasn't sure who she was playing against, but she'd won the piece all the same. He'd chosen to stay with *her* rather than rush back to Matilda. Not that she understood why…

'Surely you could have left me here with Sir Guian while you told her?' She tried to sound uninterested.

'I could have.' He gave her a look that she couldn't interpret. 'But I didn't. I owe your father better than that.'

'Oh. Yes.' A stab of guilt mingled with disappointment. Of course he'd stayed for her father—just as he should have. It was selfish of her to hope otherwise. Her father was what mattered after all, not this strange attraction, or whatever it was, she seemed to feel towards Lothar.

'Then I'm grateful. I know I don't deserve your help, but l thank you for it anyway.'

He leaned forward suddenly, resting his forearms on his knees as he fixed her with a hard stare.

'*Why* didn't you tell me? The rest I can understand, but not that. What was the point of still pretending your father was dead after you surrendered? I told you he was my friend. Why didn't you ask me for help?'

'Because I didn't need help.' The words came out by habit.

'You were half-killing yourself taking care of him. What use would you have been to anyone then?'

She stiffened defensively. 'I told you, I made a promise to Stephen. If people had found out he let my father go without a ransom, then it would have looked like weakness. I owed him for that. I'd already failed him in every other way by surrendering to you. I thought that I could still keep that part of my promise.'

'Even at your father's expense?'

She winced. 'I was with him almost the whole time in the taproom. I made him as comfortable as I could.'

'You still could have trusted me.'

'I couldn't take the risk! I know I've been holding the castle unlawfully. That's ten times worse than defying Sir Guian. Sick or not, my father's still alive. Haword should still be his to command.' She looked down at her hands. 'Besides, it wasn't that I didn't trust *you*, but I thought you'd tell the Empress. I was afraid that she'd punish my men for helping me.'

'She wouldn't.'

'How do you know?'

'Because I know *her*.' He shook his head remonstratively. 'You should have asked me for help. It's not a weakness to ask.'

'Maybe not for a man, but most men already think women are incapable of acting without their help. Asking for it only reinforces that.'

'I've never said you were incapable.'

'You didn't have to.'

A moan from the bed interrupted them and she bit her lip, waiting for her father to settle again before standing up and beckoning for Lothar to follow her to the window embrasure.

'You've made your opinion about my abilities perfectly obvious.' She swung round to hiss at him. 'You undermine me in front of my men, you refuse to fight me…'

'That wasn't intended as an insult.'

'You think that a woman ought to be delicate and refined like Matilda. If I were more of a *lady* then maybe you'd think I was fit to be chatelaine.'

'It's obvious that you've never met the Empress, my lady. No one has ever called her delicate before.'

She snorted derisively and he frowned.

'Why don't you like her?'

'I've never met her.' She tensed, caught off guard by the question. 'Why wouldn't I like her?'

'I don't know. Perhaps you resent her?'

'You mean for doing nothing to help my father when he needed her?'

'I told you, she had no men to spare.'

'Then perhaps I'm just sick of coming second!' She couldn't restrain the truth any longer. 'My father would have razed this castle to the ground rather than fail her. Is it any wonder that I resent her?'

'No.' He looked sombre. 'Your father was loyal by nature, but didn't you ever think that he was acting on your behalf, too? He believed that a woman was capable of ruling the country. Maybe he thought that if Matilda succeeded, then you could, too. You're very similar.'

'What?'

'You remind me of her. Maybe not in looks, but in spirit.'

She gaped in astonishment. What did *that* mean, that she reminded him of the woman he loved? Of course he had to qualify the statement by mentioning her appearance, but was that a good or a bad thing?

'You're brave like her, too. Not many men would have ridden into an enemy camp on their own.'

His gaze seemed smoky and she dropped her own quickly.

'I had to. I should never have let Father ride into battle, but I didn't know how to stop him either. Everything he said seemed to make sense, but when he charged off on his own I knew I'd made a terrible mistake. When he was knocked down he hit his head…' She shook hers at the memory. 'I had to try to get him back.'

'You met with Stephen?'

'Yes. It wasn't hard to convince him that Father was sick. After the way he'd behaved, it was obvious something was wrong.'

'So you gave your allegiance in exchange for your father?' He seemed to sway closer towards her. 'You know you can retract an oath given under duress. You can still rejoin the Empress.'

She gave him a barbed look. Typical that he'd think that way, as if her allegiance to Matilda were all that mattered.

'It wasn't given under duress.'

'You were in an impossible situation.'

'Yes, but Stephen was more generous than I expected. He could have refused my request, could have thrown the rest of us out of Haword, but he didn't. He let me bring Father home. I gave my oath willingly in exchange. I gave him my word and I won't go back on it. Father would never have done.'

'He wouldn't have wanted this.'

'I know that! I know he would rather have rotted away in a dungeon than have me take sides against Matilda, but I couldn't bear the thought of it. I have my own mind and I make my own decisions. I love him more than I care about your Empress. I couldn't abandon him to die like that.'

There was a heavy silence between them before Lothar jerked his head at the bed.

'Does he know?'

'That I swore allegiance to Stephen?' Her voice wavered slightly. 'No. He was unconscious when I brought him back to the castle and then...there were a few times when I thought I should tell him, but I couldn't bring myself to do it. He doesn't remember the battle and I couldn't bear it if...' She felt a sudden rush of panic. 'You wouldn't?'

'No. I wouldn't.' His gaze slid to the bed. 'I've no wish to upset him either.'

'So you'll still let me look after him?'

'No. *We'll* look after him. We may be on different sides of this war, but for the time being I suggest a truce.'

She felt a lump rise in her throat. For the time being... Until it was over, he meant. Which also meant that he didn't think it would be long. He was right. As much as she'd hoped for an im-

provement, her father's condition had only dete-
riorated in the months since she'd brought him
back from Stephen's camp. Now there was no
denying the fact that he was dying, fading away
before her very eyes. And when he was gone—
she felt as though an icy hand were clutching her
heart—when he was gone she'd be all alone in
the world, without a home or a position or purpose—because this man had taken them all away
from her. She swallowed, forcing the lump in her
throat back down again. She couldn't think about
any of that just yet. Better to have a truce for now
and think about everything she'd lost afterwards.
She could blame Lothar and the Empress then.

'Truce.'

'Good. Then tell me one more thing, my lady.
Have you had word from Stephen? Is he coming?'

She lifted her hand up as if to brush his question aside at the same moment as he moved
slightly towards her, so that her fingers pushed
inadvertently against his chest. She froze at the
contact, her pulse quickening at once. She could
feel his heartbeat through his tunic, accelerating
almost as quickly as hers was, though surely for
a different reason... She stared at her splayed
fingers, somehow unable to pull them away. He
felt warm and solid, the muscles of his chest flexing slightly beneath her fingertips. Every nerve
in her body seemed to vibrate in response. He'd
asked her a question, she remembered vaguely.
Something that had shocked her at the time,

though now she could barely remember it. Something about Stephen? What should she say? She couldn't lie, not when she'd just promised that she wouldn't, but her throat was so dry she didn't trust herself to say anything…

'Lady Juliana.' The way he said her name almost made her knees buckle. 'If you don't answer, then I'll be forced to assume the worst. We need to be ready, for your men's sake as well as your father's.'

She peeked up and let out a panting breath. His eyes were boring into hers, smoke-coloured and smouldering with white-hot intensity, as if he were feeling the same way she was. *Was he?* The thought made her stomach leap with excitement, but she still hadn't answered. She *had* to answer, but she couldn't, *shouldn't*, do this—whatever this was.

She tore her hands away, her fingers turning numb as she did so.

'He sent a message nine days ago saying that he'd be here in two weeks. That's why I tried to take you prisoner. I was trying to stall your attack until then.'

'Not a bad plan.' His voice seemed to have gravel in it.

'It might have worked if you hadn't already given the order.'

'You were still a worthy opponent, my lady.'

'Just not good enough to win.' Her heart misgave her. 'Not good enough for Stephen or my father either. I've failed both of them.'

'On the contrary, you did your best for them both. Sometimes our choices aren't as clear cut as one side or another.'

'Not just Stephen or Matilda, then?'

'Perhaps not.' He hesitated for a moment before clearing his throat with a husky sound. 'I ought to go and make preparations.'

'Yes.' She took a step backwards, willing her pulse to slow down. 'Of course.'

'I won't be long. From what Ulf tells me, you have four months' worth of sleep to catch up on.'

'There's no need—'

'There is,' he cut her off. 'From now on, we'll take turns to look after him. No arguments, my lady.'

He made for the door and then stopped, half-turning his head as if another thought had just occurred to him.

'For what it's worth, I never meant to imply you weren't a fit chatelaine. Under the circumstances, I'd say you were one of the best I've ever met.'

She stood rooted to the spot in silence, waiting until he left the room before letting the tears roll down her cheeks. Despite everything else he'd taken from her, somehow she felt as if he'd just given her the best present of all.

Chapter Seventeen

'We need more arrows.'

Lothar ran an experienced eye over the armoury, over the long rows of bows and crossbows, swords and slingshots, assorted knives and shields. It was a decent selection, not bad for such a small castle, in reasonable condition, too, without any traces of rust, but there was still no harm in being over-prepared.

'I'll see to it.' Ulf nodded curtly.

'More missiles, too.' He peered into a barrel filled to the brim with assorted shapes and sizes of stones. 'We have the space. We might as well fill it.'

'I'll send some men out.'

'Be sure to send lookouts with them. I don't want Stephen catching anyone by surprise.'

'Yes, sir.'

'Otherwise, I'm impressed.' He gave the Constable a nod of approval. 'I didn't expect your armoury to be so well maintained.'

'Lady Juliana insists on everything being kept in good order.'

'Then I'll be sure to compliment her on it later.'

He watched the Constable go with the ghost of a smile. He'd told him that Lady Juliana wasn't a prisoner, but Ulf and his men still seemed determined to heap as much praise upon her abilities as chatelaine as often and as loudly possible. At this point he wouldn't have been surprised to hear she'd built the castle herself. Not that he disagreed with them. She was clearly well suited to the role and certainly nothing if not organised. Now that he'd commandeered the bulk of Sir Guian's provisions—a fact that the Baron would no doubt be reporting to Matilda within days—there was very little for him to do. Which was probably the way Lady Juliana would want it.

He picked up a sword and ran his finger down the flat side of the blade. After a long night spent thinking about their predicament he'd decided to focus on practical matters that morning instead, though the fact that he'd countermanded the Empress's orders still lay heavy on his mind. He'd had no choice, but he could only hope Matilda would understand that. If she didn't—if she sent Sir Guian back and summoned *him* to Devizes instead—what then? He hoped it wouldn't come to that. The earlier message he'd sent her warning about Stephen's possible return into Herefordshire ought to explain his remaining there, and she'd always trusted his judgement before. William wouldn't last much longer, that was obvious, and after that...

He swore vehemently. If Lady Juliana would only renounce her allegiance to Stephen then it would help her cause with the Empress a little, but she refused to consider it, and he could tell it was useless to argue. The stubborn glint in those green eyes was exactly the same as her father's when he'd made up his mind about something and there had never been any chance of budging him either. The last thing he needed was another stubborn woman in his life, yet he couldn't help but admire her as well. Amidst all the self-seeking opportunists in this war, she'd sided with Stephen simply to protect her father. She'd even been willing to tolerate Sir Guian if it had meant keeping her word. Under the circumstances, it was hard to see what else she *could* have done. The only question was whether Matilda would forgive her refusal to switch sides again...

He sighed. It wasn't his job to defend or protect her. She'd made her own bed. He ought to let her lie in it, though he already knew that he couldn't. He hadn't even been able to leave. He'd told her that he'd stayed for her father, though in truth it had been just as much for her. He couldn't abandon her, even if he had no idea what to do with her either. If she wouldn't renounce her allegiance, then there was no way he could let her remain at Haword once the crisis was over. He could still send her to Stephen, though now that she'd revealed the truth about her father as well as surrendered the castle, there was no knowing what he'd do with her. Besides the fact that he'd *have* to tell Matilda about William eventually—and once he did that, he knew that she'd want to confront Lady Juliana herself. Neither option was very appealing. He doubted either side would be sympathetic, which left Lady Juliana trapped in a precarious position somewhere between the two. Not to mention him stuck in the middle defending her. Hell's teeth!

Distracted, he sliced his finger along the edge of the blade, grimacing as blood dripped into the rushes below. Damn it, this was what came of thinking and not acting. He ought to stick to what he was good at, not waste his time in useless speculation. There was nothing he could do for now except defend the castle against Stephen and help take care of William as best he could. Lady Juliana's fate, uncertain as it was, would have to wait. He tossed the sword back on to its pile and strode out of the armoury, slamming the door behind him as he made his way back to the keep and up to her father's chamber. There was no need for him to return there so soon, but he seemed unable to stay away, as if his feet were moving of their own accord. As he'd expected, she was sitting just where he'd left her, folding squares of material on her lap as she murmured the words of a poem. He stopped in the doorframe to listen, surprised by the melodious timbre of her voice, so different to the defensive tone she usually adopted around him. It sounded natural, relaxed, and so soothing that he wanted to sit down and listen…

'I thought you didn't know any poetry?' He clapped his hands as she finished.

'Poetry?' She looked faintly embarrassed, though her voice had a smile behind it. 'No, that's an old Saxon ballad. Father taught it to me as a child. I thought the words might comfort him.'

He glanced down at the bed and wondered if she was right. The lines around William's mouth seemed to have eased slightly. He even had more colour than before.

'What's all that?' He gestured at the pile of material in her lap.

'Bandages.'

'Are you preparing for battle?'

She shrugged. 'Just in case we need them.'

'We?' He lifted an eyebrow. 'I thought you were on Stephen's side.'

'It's not a question of sides. Just because I've sworn allegiance to Stephen doesn't mean I *want* him to attack us.'

'It might mean you get your castle back.'

'Until the next siege, you mean.'

He sat down in a chair and stretched his legs

out in front of him. There was no answer to that. The way the fortunes of this seemingly endless war veered back and forth he couldn't exactly argue.

'Finished in the armoury already?'

She tipped her head to one side and he smiled. He was starting to recognise her mannerisms.

'There wasn't much for me to do. You put the Empress's armourers to shame, my lady.'

'Is that permitted?' Her tone sharpened like a dagger itself. 'Since I'm not allowed to fight, am I allowed to keep and clean weapons instead?'

He made a face. 'I told you, my refusal to fight wasn't meant as an insult.'

'It still felt like one.'

'I don't fight women.'

'Not even if they ask you to?'

'Not even then.'

Her eyes flashed. 'What if the Empress asked you to?'

'For a start, she'd have to order me. Then I suppose I'd have to let her attack me.'

'You wouldn't defend yourself?'

'No.'

She put down the piece of material she was folding. 'You didn't object to your soldier sparring with me.'

'I didn't like it, but I'd no right to stop you.'

She frowned slightly, as if trying to gauge whether or not he was telling the truth. 'In that case…what did you think?'

'About?'

'About my sword skills? Was I any good?'

'Better than that.'

Her frown lifted and her lips twitched before she broke into a broad smile. 'So if *we* fought—not that *we* would—do you think I might win?'

'I didn't say *that*.'

She laughed before her expression clouded suddenly.

'What happened to your hand?'

'What?' It took him a moment to understand the question. The sound of her laughter seemed to have actually stunned him. 'Oh, nothing. Just a scratch.'

'Let me see.' She put the pile of folding aside and hurried towards him. 'You should let me bind it at least.'

'It looks worse than it is.' He glanced down at his hand. That was true. There was a lot more blood than he would have expected from such a small cut.

'I'll be the judge of that.' She crouched down and took hold of his hand, turning it over and studying the wound with a look of such intense concentration that he couldn't drag his eyes away from her either. Her fingers were so velvety smooth that he felt a strange compulsion to wrap his own around them. Her very touch seemed to make him feel better.

'What happened?'

'I cut myself on a sword when I was inspecting the armoury.'

Her eyes leapt to his face with a look of amusement. 'How long did you say you've been a soldier?'

'Too long and, yes, I should have been paying attention.'

'Well, just so you know what you did wrong.'

She laughed again and he felt a powerful impulse to wrap his arms around her and scoop her up into his lap. When she laughed she looked radiant, as if there were actually a light shining behind her eyes. The effect was so mesmerising that she was already back on her feet before he could do anything about it, fetching a bowl of water and two of her newly folded bandages from the other side of the room.

'I didn't think these would come in handy quite so soon.' She crouched down again, dabbing one of the cloths into the water and gently wiping the blood from his hand before tying the other around it.

'There. Now don't take it off for a few hours and no playing with swords in the meantime.'

'Playing?'

'Yes.' Her eyes glinted with humour. 'But if you must, remember the sharp end is the one to avoid.'

'I'll try to remember that. Now have you finished laughing at my misfortune?'

'Almost.' She sat back on her haunches though

she still didn't release his hand. 'You can't blame me for enjoying one small victory. I haven't won many of late.'

He gave a low chuckle. 'Then I'm glad I've made you feel better.'

'You have.' She tilted her head to the side again. 'You know, I've never heard you laugh before.'

'It happens. Not very often. Though I could say the same about you.'

'There isn't much to laugh about.' She ran her fingers absently along the inside of his wrist. 'But maybe one day, when the war's over... Did you get your scar with a blade, too?'

'*This?*' He touched his forehead incredulously. 'How careless do you think I am?'

'That's what I'm trying to work out. What happened?'

He took a deep breath. His scar wasn't something he talked about. It had been part of him for so long that he barely noticed it himself any more and nobody else usually dared to ask questions. He'd never really considered the effect on his appearance either, but now for the first time in his life he felt self-conscious. What did *she* think of it? he wondered.

'Lothar?'

She said his name softly and he sighed, feeling as though those green eyes were somehow drawing the truth out of him.

'My father kicked me into a table.'

She clamped a hand over her mouth in shock. 'But that's terrible!'

He smiled mirthlessly. 'He *was* terrible. Everyone who knew him thought so. Though most of the time he was just drunk.'

'You mean he did it more than once?'

'Let's just say it wasn't unusual. My mother took the brunt of it.'

'So when you said her death wasn't an accident, you meant…' Her voice trailed away to a whisper.

'My father, yes.' He felt an uncomfortable tightness in his throat. 'He might not have known what he was doing at the time, but he still did it. It was no accident.'

'Was he punished?'

'No.' The tightness seemed to be strangling him. 'Nobody with any authority cared enough to punish him and those who did care were too scared. It was just hushed up and forgotten. *She* was forgotten.'

'Not by you.'

'No.' His voice sounded rough even to his own ears. 'Never by me.'

'I'm sorry.'

'It was a long time ago.'

'But something like that never goes away. Is that why you don't fight women?'

He rubbed a hand across his throat. The tightness was getting worse the longer he talked, but he didn't want to stop either. Now that he'd started, he actually wanted to keep going. He *wanted* to tell her everything. How could he feel so close to a woman he'd known for such a short space of time? he wondered. He liked her. He admired her. He even trusted her. Ironically, given how much of the time she'd spent deceiving him, she seemed more real, more her*self* than any other woman he'd ever met.

'I won't raise a hand to any woman in violence. Real or pretend.'

'Is that the reason you don't drink wine either?'

He snorted. 'My father rarely had wine, but he drank everything else he could find. That's why I don't drink anything stronger than ale. Usually.'

'Then I'm sorry I asked you to drink it…' her cheeks flushed slightly '…on that first day.'

'When you kissed me?'

He hadn't known he intended to say the words until he said them. He only knew that he didn't want to pretend that it hadn't happened any longer. More than that, he wanted to kiss her again, so much that it hurt, as if only the touch of her lips could banish the darkness of his past.

'I don't know what you mean.' Her voice trembled unconvincingly.

'Don't you?' He lifted a coil of stray hair away from her cheek and tucked it behind her ear, brushing his fingers lightly along the line of her jaw. 'Then why do I remember this?'

He closed the space between them, grazing her lips with the softest of pressures before pulling away again, surprised by a stirring sensation deep in his chest, as if some long-dormant part of him were waking up again. It wasn't like him to act on impulse, to do anything without analysing all the risks first, but this time he hadn't been able to resist. Two decades of learning how to guard his behaviour and every technique had seemed to fail him at once. Now he felt as if his head were spinning. Somehow, the very lightest of kisses felt more powerful than the most passionate embrace.

'I thought you didn't remember...'

She must have closed her eyes because she opened them again as she spoke, her breathing fast and unsteady, as if she'd just run up the keep steps.

'I wasn't certain until now.'

'It wasn't... I didn't...'

Her voice faltered and he sat perfectly still, waiting for her to say that it had all been a pretence, a means of entrapping him, nothing more. She didn't. Instead she bit her lower lip, frowning slightly as if she were trying to make sense of something, though the effect was to bring his attention back to her mouth. It looked even more tempting than it had before, moist and pink and apparently not out of bounds either. The thought led to other, more dangerous ideas.

'Apologies, my lady.' He shifted uncomfortably, feeling as though they were on perilous ground suddenly. 'I shouldn't have done that.'

Her lips parted, though she still didn't speak. Did she want him to kiss her again? His hose became painfully tight at the thought. He would, given the slightest encouragement, though he knew that he shouldn't. It was wrong. No matter how close he felt to her, or how much he wanted to pull her into his arms and kiss her breathless, he was still a low-born blacksmith's son. Not to mention incapable of feeling anything other than a physical reaction. Even if the stirring sensation in his chest felt like something more—like one of the real emotions he'd banished a long time ago. But no good could come of those—no good, only pain—and he'd felt enough of that to last a lifetime.

He forced himself to smile, knowing that he had to push her away, had to antagonise her again somehow. If he didn't, then he was in danger of wanting more than just a kiss. Much more. And then he'd be well and truly lost…

'At least now we're even. As I recall, you were the one who kissed me first last time.'

The flash of temper was instantaneous. 'And as *I* recall, I only did it to trick you!'

She jumped to her feet with a look of something like hurt. *Hurt?* He felt a pang of guilt. Had he hurt her? He hadn't intended to do that, had to dig his boots into the rushes to stop from following her as she swept furiously past him and out of the chamber.

Then he sat back in his chair, inhaling the delicate scent of honeysuckle that still clung to the air, feeling as though he'd done something wrong and taken a step forward at the same time—and now that he'd taken it, he had a feeling there was no way he'd ever be able to go back.

Chapter Eighteen

Lothar waited until the sound of Juliana's footsteps faded away before dropping his head into his hands with a groan. What the hell had just happened? Definitely not what he'd intended to happen when he'd come up to her father's chamber. He felt as though he'd just been shaken to his core. He'd tried to do the honourable thing in pushing her away, but in truth, he'd been protecting himself, too. The way their kiss had made him feel had been terrifying and bewildering in equal measure.

The sound of his name being whispered gave him a visceral jolt, shocking him out of his reverie *and* his chair.

'William?' He leaned over the bed at once.

'Lothar the Frank.' A familiar face smiled up at him. 'I thought it was you.'

'You're awake?' He shook his head at the inanity of his own question. Of course William was awake. Judging by the look in his eyes, he was lucid, too. But how *long* had he been awake? What had he seen?

'I thought perhaps I was dreaming.' William started to smile and then winced.

'Are you in pain?'

'Nothing I can't bear. It's good to see you, my friend, but what are you doing here? How did you get through the siege?'

He hesitated. If William didn't remember the battle with Stephen, then the less *he* said about it the better. The thought of lying made him distinctly uneasy, though telling the truth didn't seem a much better idea...

'The Empress sent me.' That was true anyway.

'Ah...reinforcements.' William gave a relieved-sounding sigh. 'At last. I knew she would.'

'Stephen's gone and the castle holds for Matilda.' That was true, too.

'And Juliana? Is she all right?'

'Your daughter?'

William looked surprised. 'Who else?'

'Of course. Forgive me, I'll fetch her.'

'Wait!' The other man's hand shot out, clutching his arm in a surprisingly firm grip. 'I need to speak with you first.'

'Very well.' Lothar nodded reluctantly. If William had just seen him kiss his daughter, then doubtless he was about to rebuke him for it. There was equally no doubt that he deserved it. He only hoped William didn't ask him to explain himself, because he truly didn't think he could.

'I've made a mistake, Lothar.'

He blinked in surprise. Those definitely weren't the words he'd been expecting, but William looked more sombre than accusing.

'What do you mean?'

'With Juliana. I thought I was doing the right thing, raising her to be a free woman, to act on her own, but now I'm afraid it was wrong of me.'

'She's a strong woman.' Lothar felt oddly defensive about her. 'How is that wrong?'

'Because it's not enough. I thought it would be, but if the Empress can't win what's rightfully hers, then what hope is there for Juliana? If this war were over, she might stand a chance, but the way things are, she isn't safe. I can't protect her any more. I won't be here much longer, we both know that, and I don't want to leave her alone.' He looked up at him with a half-pleading, half-resolute expression. 'I need you to take care of her, Lothar. You're an honourable man. I've seen how well you protect the Empress and I know why you do it, too. If you promise to take care of Juliana, then I know that you will.'

'I'll do what I can.'

'No!' William shook his head vehemently. 'I need more than that. I'll give you everything. My castle, my lands, my title, just as long as you keep her safe.' He dragged in a breath, as if he were building to something. 'I need you to marry her.'

'*Marry?*' For a moment Lothar wondered if the other man *had* seen him kiss her after all. Either that or he was delirious. 'William, you know where I come from. There are better men, worthier men.'

'You're better than you think. I wouldn't ask you if I didn't think you were the right man.'

'But you know my past. You know I'm not suited to marriage.'

'I also know that you're not your father. You would never do what he did.'

He drew in a sharp breath. No, he would never do that, not when the very thought made him feel physically sick, though the idea of marriage terrified him almost as much. A husband was supposed to care, to feel, to *love* his wife, wasn't he? Whereas he... He'd closed his heart to that particular emotion a long time ago—had no intention of opening it again, even if he knew how. He didn't have emotional attachments. He wasn't capable of such things. The very idea was madness!

'You don't like her?' William's brow furrowed.

'It's not that.'

'She can be a little stubborn, I grant you.'

He had to stifle a laugh. 'A little.'

'But she'll be a good wife. Once she's come to terms with the idea, that is.'

'She won't like it.'

'No.' William conceded. 'I raised her to think that marriage wasn't necessary, that she could find her own way, but I've run out of time. I need you to take care of her for me now.'

He raised a hand, about to run it through his hair when he saw the bandage she'd wrapped there so tenderly half an hour before. *Would* he marry her? *Yes.* If she needed his protection then how could he refuse his old friend? As long as protection was all William asked of him... And he *did* like her, stubborn temper and all. A lot of marriages were based on less. The impulse that had led to their kiss had been unnerving, but surely he could control his desire for her. Perhaps they could be friends, though he had a feeling her *coming to terms with the idea*, as William had put it, might take a while. Maybe if he hadn't just kissed and then pushed her away he might have stood a chance of convincing her, but the look on her face as she'd stormed out of the chamber didn't offer much hope.

'I'll need to ask the Empress for her consent.'

'There's no time. Tell her it was my last wish. She'll understand.'

Lothar clenched his jaw. That was probably true. Not to mention the fact that she was unlikely to arrest his wife. Even if Matilda didn't approve of the marriage, Juliana would be in a far safer position married to him than otherwise. And if he vouched for her, he might even be able to persuade Matilda to let Juliana remain as chatelaine. It would be the perfect way of protecting her, even better than William realised. Not that *she* was likely to think so.

'What about your daughter's consent? She might not give it willingly.'

The words were barely out of his mouth before he heard an exclamation and the lady herself came running across the room. 'Father, you're awake!'

'Juliana.' William's voice was weak, though his expression was utterly transformed at the sight of her. So was hers, Lothar noticed with a pang. She was smiling with a look of such pure love that he felt his chest clench with an unwonted feeling of longing.

Clearly she hadn't heard what her father had just said. If she had, then he had a feeling she wouldn't be smiling.

Juliana clutched at her father's hand, pressing a kiss to the fingertips as she saw the skin around his eyes crinkle with his old familiar smile. It had been so long since she'd seen it, since he'd looked at her with anything besides confusion.

'Why didn't you summon me?' She threw an accusing look towards Lothar.

'Because I wanted to talk with him first.' Her father's voice was faintly admonishing. 'Lothar and I are old friends. He tells me that Stephen's gone.'

'Ye-es.' She felt a flutter of panic at the thought of what *else* he might have told him.

'I told him that Haword's still loyal to the Empress.' Lothar's voice was reassuring, as if he guessed what she was thinking.

'But it's not safe for you any more, Daughter.'

'Don't worry about me.' She shook her head dismissively.

'I can't help it. If the Empress can have her country stolen from her, what's to stop someone from taking Haword from you? There's precious little honour or justice left in the world. I can't rest until I know you're safe.'

'You raised me to take care of myself.'

'That's not enough, not any more. You need to marry.'

'What?' She found it difficult to breathe suddenly, as if all the air had been sucked from the room. 'You don't mean that, Father. You're not well.'

'It's the only way you'll be safe.'

'We'll talk about it later.'

'No.' An edge of stubbornness crept into his voice. 'I might not be able to talk about it later. I need you to marry now. Promise me, Daughter. Marry Lothar.'

'Lothar?' She dropped her father's hand in shock.

'He's a good man and I trust him.'

'Lothar?' She repeated the name as she stared, thunderstruck, at its owner. Her emotions were still in turmoil after their kiss, but now she felt as if he'd tricked her, too. Was that *why* he'd kissed her, because he'd been scheming to find a way of keeping Haword for himself? The thought was appalling, and yet wasn't it also the most likely explanation? Everything he'd done over the past few days seemed to take on a new, more sinister aspect. He hadn't stayed to protect her father. He'd stayed because he'd seen an opportunity for his own advancement. Kissing her had just been a part of it. The rest of the time he'd been waiting to put the idea of marriage into her father's head, *using* both of them! And if he thought she was going to consent, then he could think again!

'I know I'm not noble, Lady Juliana.' Lothar's face was stonier than ever. 'But I'll take care of you, I promise.'

'And my inheritance, too?' She glared at him. 'Not bad for a blacksmith's son!'

She regretted the words the moment they were out of her mouth. Not the gist of them—after all, what other reason could he have to marry her than to claim her inheritance?—but to mention his father after what he'd just told her about him caused a twinge of remorse. Fortunately, his expression didn't waver.

'Have I failed you, Father?' She leaned back over the bed again. 'Have I let you down?'

'Never.'

'Then why would you ask this of me? You used to say that I was as good as any man. Was that a lie?'

'No. You *are* as good as any man, Juliana. I believe that, but the rest of the world doesn't know it, not yet. Forgive me, but I need to know that you're safe. I'll never be at peace otherwise. You need to give your consent to each other. Now, so I know it's done.'

'*Now?*'

She caught her breath, feeling as though the floorboards had just given way and she was falling, flailing in mid-air as she tried to find her feet again. If they both gave their consent, then their marriage would be legal. An official ceremony could be performed later, but to all intents and purposes, the contract would be binding. Just saying the words aloud would make her a married woman.

'I'm tired.' William looked between them with a beseeching expression. 'Please. Let me see it done.'

'I consent.' Lothar pulled a ring off his little finger as he uttered the words, his voice strong and clear, as if there were no doubt in his mind.

'Ah.' Her father gave a nod of recognition. 'I remember when the Empress gave that to you. After Oxford, as I recall.'

'The *Empress*?' Juliana clenched her fingers, staring at the ring with distaste. It was a plain gold band set with a single shimmering ruby. Beautiful, valuable and tainted. She didn't want anything that had ever belonged to Matilda.

'Juliana?'

She unfurled her fists at her father's prompting and reached her hand out, averting her face as Lothar slipped the band over her finger.

'I consent to this marriage.'

He repeated the vow as if to emphasise her own lack of an answer and she sucked in a breath, stung by the irony. How long had she waited for her father to regain his senses and be himself again? For weeks and weeks she'd sat by his bedside, wishing that he'd show some sign of awareness again, but now she almost wished she hadn't been there to see it, that she hadn't followed the impulse to check on him one last time tonight before retiring to her own chamber. She could hardly believe what was happening—that he could ask this thing of her. Even though she knew he was trying to protect her, it still felt like a betrayal, as if everything he'd raised her for had meant nothing. And after she'd actually *gloated* to Lothar about Matilda's chances of wearing the crown, about her chances of succeeding in a man's world! Now the words seemed to be coming back to haunt her, as if Matilda herself were taking revenge. Her father had asked of her the one thing she'd never expected and now she had no choice. She couldn't say no. She was trapped—and all three of them knew it.

The words almost stuck in her throat. 'I consent.'

Chapter Nineteen

Juliana charged down the stairwell, almost tripping over her skirts in her haste to reach the bottom. *Where was he?* She was clutching the ring that he'd given her—*the Empress's ring*—so tightly in her hand that the jewelled edges bit into her skin, but she didn't care. All she wanted was to find her *husband* and throw it back in his face as violently and painfully as possible!

He'd left the chamber immediately after she'd given her consent to their marriage, though he'd sent Ulf up to relieve her soon after, as if he'd guessed that she'd want to confront him as soon as possible. Still, she'd tarried a while, holding her father's hand and talking about the past— the present was too confusing—until he'd finally closed his eyes and drifted off to sleep again. *Then* she'd allowed herself to acknowledge all of the grief and rage and feelings of utter powerlessness inside her until she'd wanted to rail and scream at the top of her lungs—and she'd known exactly who she wanted to vent her anger on!

Lothar was standing by the fireplace talking to a group of his soldiers when she entered, though he looked round the instant she emerged from the stairwell.

'How could you!' She stormed across the flagstones, not even waiting for him to dismiss his men before launching into her attack. 'How could you do it?'

'My lady.' He folded his arms as his soldiers hastened towards the door. 'Do what exactly?'

'What do you think?' She pulled up short in front of him. *'How could you marry me?'*

'Your father asked me to.'

'You could have said no!'

'So could you. You're always telling me you have a mind of your own. I expected you to use it.'

'How could I have refused? He's my father and he's dying! How could I refuse his last wish?'

'He's my friend, too. I could make the same argument.'

'It's different and you know it! You already had Haword. You didn't have to humiliate me as well!'

The muscles in his neck and jaw all seemed to tighten at once. 'I had no intention of humiliating you.'

'Well, you have! You as good as said so yourself!'

'When?'

'After you kissed me! You admitted this is all just some game to you.'

'That wasn't what I meant.'

'You said we were even and now you do *this*?'

'Juliana…'

'I don't *want* to be married!'

His gaze darkened this time. 'Especially to a blacksmith's son?'

She narrowed her eyes, too angry to contradict him. Let him think that she despised him for his low birth. She despised him for enough other reasons now.

'Especially to someone who uses his friendship with a dying man to secure his own future. You must have worked quickly, too. Tell me, how *did* you persuade my father to hand over my inheritance?'

'I persuaded him of nothing.' Lothar's voice deepened dangerously.

'He's never even mentioned the idea of marriage before!'

'By your own admission, he had doubts about a woman being allowed to hold a position of authority.'

'Those were about Matilda, not me!'

'They were about both of you. Your father asked me to marry you because he thought you needed protection.'

'I don't need anything from you! I was managing perfectly well until you came along.'

'Managing?' A ripple seemed to pass over his

face, as if all his facial muscles were clenching at once. 'You were starving yourself and your men to death for a cause you didn't even believe in. If that's what you call managing, then perhaps you *aren't* fit to command after all.'

'How dare you!'

'As my wife, you'll hopefully be able to keep your position as chatelaine without your father ever knowing you lost it. I would have thought you'd be pleased by that.'

'You expect me to be grateful to be married to you?'

The ripple turned into a crack, as if his stony expression had just been a mask that was splintering apart to reveal the real face underneath— one that was working with so many emotions she didn't know which was dominant, though she suspected it was anger.

'Then you're fortunate that I've no desire for a wife either. Especially one who looks more like a stablehand than a woman!'

She reacted instinctively, swinging her arm back and throwing her fist square at his jaw, gratified to hear a sharp thwacking sound as his head snapped to the left.

There was a prolonged silence before he turned back to face her, his expression a blank again, as if her fist had actually rammed the mask back into place.

'Then it seems we understand each other, *Wife.*'

'We do. And you can keep this!' She unclenched

her fist and hurled Matilda's ring at his chest. 'I wouldn't want the *Empress* to miss it!'

Lothar rubbed his jaw gingerly with his knuckles as she stormed away. He'd guessed that she'd been about to hit him. He'd even been ready, braced for the sting of a womanly slap across his cheek, so that getting her fist in the jaw instead had caught him by surprise. His wife had an impressive right hook, it seemed. Something else her father must have taught her.

In retrospect, he supposed he could have handled the situation better. She was right, their marriage was a greater advancement than any he could have expected, but her accusations had undermined his self-control to the extent that he'd finally lost his temper as well. He'd *meant* to say that he'd accepted her father's offer because he wanted to help her keep her inheritance, not to steal it for himself. He'd *meant* to say that he was a soldier, that when it came to managing a castle, she was a far better person for the job. He'd *meant* to reassure her that it would be a marriage in name only, or at least insofar as she wanted it to be one. Most of all, he'd *meant* to tell her that nothing about this was a game. Instead he'd told her she looked like a stablehand. *That* had definitely been a mistake. One of many. Overall it couldn't have gone much worse.

He bent down to retrieve Matilda's ring. Her reaction to that had been the most confusing thing of all. He understood why she objected to their marriage, but the band itself seemed to have enraged her, as if she were actually jealous of the Empress, though the very idea was ludicrous. It would have been ludicrous even if she cared about him, which she obviously didn't. He'd never given a present to any woman before, but he'd been led to believe that such gestures were generally appreciated. Apparently not, but he'd still wanted her to have the ruby. He couldn't think of a stone that would suit her better.

'Sergeant?'

'What is it?' He turned to find one of his soldiers standing in the doorway.

'It's Mattias, sir. He's back from Devizes.'

'Already?'

He felt a prickle of unease. He'd sent Mattias to report to the Empress as soon as Juliana had surrendered the castle. Riding as hard as he could, it would still have taken him a day and a half to get there and the same again to get back. In which case, Matilda must have turned him around almost at once. He frowned, his soldier's instincts warning him something was wrong—something that had nothing to do with his remaining in Haword either. When Mattias had left he'd still been intending to leave. Which meant that something else must have happened...

'Send him in.'

He rested a hand on one of the table-tops, tapping his fingers impatiently until an exhausted-looking rider entered the hall.

'What's happened?' He didn't waste any time.

'It's the Earl of Gloucester, sir. He's dead.'

'What?' He felt a jolt of surprise. 'How?'

'They say natural causes. He was at home in Bristol Castle.'

'And the Empress?'

'She's very upset, sir.'

Upset. He slammed the flat of his hand down hard upon the table. Upset wouldn't even begin to describe it. Robert FitzRoy had been Matilda's greatest supporter and ally, the most powerful man in the south-west of the country, not to mention her illegitimate half-brother. His loss would be a devastating blow in more ways than one.

'She asked that you return to Devizes at once.'

He stiffened. He ought to have expected that, he supposed, but his own immediate reaction was something far less expected. He'd never questioned any of the Empress's orders before, but now he felt a tug of resentment. For the first time in his life he actually wanted to say no. Despite the swelling in his jaw, he didn't want to leave Haword. What did *that* mean?

'Was it an order or a request?'

'Sir?' Mattias sounded confused.

'What did she say exactly?'

'I don't recall the exact words, sir. She just said for you to hurry.'

'Did you give her my message about Stephen?'

'Yes, sir, but she already knew. The usurper was called back to Winchester. His army isn't coming now.'

'I see.' He tried not to sound disappointed. 'What about Sir Guian?'

'He hadn't reached Devizes by the time I left, sir.'

'Good.' That was one consolation at least. If he rode hard then he could hopefully get there around the same time, or just after. 'Go and get some rest.'

He curled his hands into fists. That was that, then. If there was no chance of Stephen returning to Herefordshire, then there was no need for him to remain there either. No reason that he could explain to the Empress anyway. None at all except for his marriage—and he still had to ask Matilda's permission for that. Not that she could do anything about it, he reassured himself. She didn't have the authority to annul their union, although she could still show her displeasure in other ways if she chose. Sending Sir Guian back and taking Juliana's home away from her for a start… In which case, he *really* ought to go and explain.

'Tell the stables to get my horse ready,' he called after Mattias as an afterthought. 'Tell Gervase and Jan to prepare, too.'

'Just the two of them, sir?'

'Just them.'

He looked pensively towards the stairwell,

wondering what to do next. Matilda, his Empress, needed him—but so did the woman upstairs, from a practical perspective with her father at least. Hadn't he just sworn an oath to her, too? But Matilda needed him now *and* she'd asked for him, whereas Juliana… She'd said that she didn't want him at all. He doubted she'd want comfort from him even when the time came and, in any case, that might not be for a while. William was definitely failing, but it might still be possible to ride to Devizes and back before any crisis occurred.

Matilda's crisis, on the other hand, was upon her now. As much as he hated to admit it, Robert of Gloucester's death dragged the battle for the crown even further into the mire. Matilda would need his support more than ever as she decided on her next move. One that would be potentially even more dangerous now than it had been a month ago.

He started reluctantly towards the stairwell, heading after his wife. The last thing he wanted was another confrontation so soon, before either of them had had a proper chance to calm down, but there were things they needed to discuss. He had to tell her where he was going and why. His *wife* had a right to know, whether she gave a damn about it or not.

Juliana paced up and down the gallery, trying to walk out her anger. Her whole body was trembling after their argument, her knuckles throbbing from the force of her punch, too. She didn't feel guilty about that, not after what he'd said about her resembling a stablehand, but she did regret it. After everything Lothar had told her about his parents, she shouldn't have started their marriage with violence, no matter how furious she'd been, or how much he'd deserved it. As for their marriage itself, she was still in too much shock to make any sense of that. If her father had known of her treachery with Stephen, he could hardly have punished her any more effectively. *Marriage!* To a man who loved someone else, who saw her simply as part of some game! Even if he didn't strike her as a man who played games. Even if the other things he'd said had made sense, as if he hadn't just married her for her inheritance—as if he really *were* trying to protect her. *Was it possible?*

A footstep in the stairwell made her swing round at once.

'Peace!' Lothar raised both hands when he saw her. 'I'm not here to argue. I've only come to tell you I'm leaving.'

'Leaving?' She didn't know which shocked her more, the words or the violent lurch in her stomach as he said them. Despite their argument she hadn't expected him to do anything quite so extreme. Nor to give up so easily. She must have been more convincing than she'd thought if he was just going to walk away so soon. Strange that she didn't feel more relieved about it.

'Matilda's summoned me back to Devizes. The Earl of Gloucester is dead.'

'Oh!' She froze instantly. 'I'm sorry. My father said he was a great man.'

'He was. I'll pass on your condolences, but I have to go to her.'

'To comfort her?' She winced at the note of bitterness in her own voice. She hadn't meant to say it quite like that.

He frowned slightly. 'To offer my support.'

'Of course. It's never easy to lose someone.'

'I'll come back as soon as I can. In the meantime, let Ulf help you.'

She shook her head. 'He finds it too distressing.'

'And you don't?' He made a movement towards her, slowly as if she were some kind of wild animal. 'I wish the timing were better, but I have a duty to the Empress. Besides, I need to explain about your father, as well as everything else.'

'Are you going to tell her about...us?' She didn't know quite how to phrase it. 'Will she object?'

'That might depend upon how I explain your allegiance to Stephen.'

'Which I won't surrender.' She jutted her chin out stubbornly.

'It would make things a lot easier if you did.'

'I don't care what she thinks of me.'

'She has the power to let you stay in your home or cast you out of it. You might consider that.'

'You'd *let* her cast your wife out?'

'I might if she were behaving like a stubborn shrew.'

'Shrew?'

'In any case, I'm leaving you in command.'

'Me?' She started in surprise.

He nodded. 'Despite what you think, I've no wish to take anything from you. I've already told you, you're an excellent chatelaine. I can't think of anyone I'd trust more.'

She swallowed, fighting back a swell of emotion. Did he truly mean it? He seemed to, standing so close to her now that she could feel the warmth of his body against hers. Despite everything, she found herself wanting to move closer still, to lean her head against his chest and wrap her arms around him...

'What about Stephen?' She pushed the temptation away. 'What if he comes back when you're away?'

'He won't. He's gone back to Winchester.'

'Oh.' She was surprised by her own lack of reaction. In truth, the news didn't bother her half as much as she would have expected. If Stephen wasn't coming, then she wouldn't be forced to make any difficult decisions about her allegiance. That was a relief more than anything. She might not want to be married, but she didn't want to side against her new husband either.

'My men will be under your command while I'm gone.'

She blinked. 'They're not going with you?'

'Only two of them. The rest will stay here to protect you.'

'But only two? Is that safe?'

He looked faintly amused. 'I've accomplished far more perilous feats on my own, I assure you.'

'So...' her stomach lurched again '...you're coming back?'

'I intend to. I apologise if that's not the answer you were hoping for, but I made a promise to your father.'

Her heart lifted briefly and then plummeted again. He was coming back, but only because of the promise he'd made to her father. That was the only reason he'd come back—nothing to do with *her*. Not that she wanted it to be for her, she reminded herself, but he'd made a promise to her, too! He'd said that they'd look after her father together. She'd told him that she didn't want his help, but that last day had still felt like a respite. Knowing that there was someone to help her, someone to share the burden with, she'd felt some of the weight of the past few months lift from her shoulders. She'd actually started to rely on him and now he was leaving. Barely an hour since they'd uttered their marriage vows and he was leaving. Had he meant any of it? She hadn't wanted to marry him, but at least she'd gone through with it for the right reasons, to fulfil her father's last wishes. If Lothar could leave her so easily, then surely that *proved* he'd only married her for Haword. Now that he'd received word Stephen wasn't coming, he had no qualms about abandoning her *and* her father. He was more than happy to go running back to Matilda.

'I've been summoned.' He seemed to sense her resentment. 'I can't refuse, especially now.'

'No.' She supposed that was true…

'I only have one request while I'm gone.' He drew Matilda's ring off his little finger again. 'You might not wish to wear it, but men know that it's mine. It might come in useful if you ever have to vouch for yourself.'

'Why would I need to do that?' She narrowed her eyes suspiciously.

'Because truthfully, I don't know what's going to happen. There's rarely fighting during the winter, but given the circumstances, there's a chance.'

She frowned, remembering what her father had taught her about politics. 'Because the Empress won't want to appear weakened by the Earl's death. She might feel the need to assert her power.'

He looked impressed. 'It's possible. If she does, then there'll be risks.'

She nodded fearfully. Bad enough that he was only taking two guards with him on the dangerous road to Devizes. The thought of him being in a battle made her feel ill. No matter how angry she was with him, she didn't want him to get hurt. Now that it came to it, she didn't want him to leave either.

'All right.' She held her hand out, bending her head to hide her expression as he slid the band gently back over her finger.

'Won't the Empress miss her ring?' She tried to keep her voice even.

'I doubt she'll notice. She'll have bigger things on her mind.'

'Yes, of course.' She stared down at her hand, pressing her lips together to stop them from quivering. This was ridiculous. Ten minutes ago she'd been furious with him and now she was tearing up at the thought of his departure. She must be overtired again. Why else would she want him to stay? It wasn't as if he cared for her... Then she felt his fingers, light on her chin, tilting her face up towards him.

'It wasn't a game.'

'What?' She felt breathless suddenly.

'The reason I kissed you. It wasn't a game. I wasn't plotting to steal your inheritance either.'

'Then why?'

He shook his head as if he didn't know the answer. 'Maybe because I've never met anyone like you before, Juliana.'

'Oh.' She didn't know what else to say. Was that a compliment? It was what people usually said about her, though rarely in a good way.

'I just never thought, never imagined, that your father would ask me...' He cleared his throat, pulling his fingers away again. 'I have to go. In the meantime, if you need me, send word and I'll do my best to come. I promise you that much. I wish it could be more.'

She stared into his eyes. They seemed to be blazing with some emotion she couldn't read on his face. The mask was firmly back in place again, like a wall between them, but his eyes... surely his eyes said he didn't want to leave her either?

'Take care of yourself, Juliana.'

'You, too.' She tore her gaze away finally. 'Ride safely.'

He turned and walked away then, leaving her staring into the empty blackness of the stairwell, wondering at how anger could turn into confusion and pain so quickly. He'd just said—implied, anyway—that he'd actually *wanted* to kiss her that morning, that what had happened between them hadn't just been a game, that he really *was* attracted to her, and yet he was still leaving, still going back to the Empress. She didn't know what the hollow feeling in her chest meant, but she ran across to the window anyway, watching as his horse was led round to the steps below, ready to take him back to Devizes. Surely Matilda had dozens of supporters to turn to! Whereas she... She glanced across to her father's chamber. Soon she'd have no one. No one except a husband whose heart belonged to another woman.

She looked down at the ruby he'd given her, admiring the vibrant shine of the jewel. Matilda's jewel, so much like the Empress herself, exquisite, remote and magnificent. If she hadn't recognised the hollow feeling for what it was before, she recognised it now. She'd never felt more jealous of anyone in her life.

Chapter Twenty

Lothar strode down the centre of Devizes's great hall in the foulest of foul tempers. He had a ferocious headache—one that seemed to have descended the moment he'd ridden out of sight of Haword and seemed to get worse with every furlong since, accompanied by the same constricting sensation in his chest that he'd felt the last time he'd tried to leave. Riding away had been even more of a wrench than he'd expected, as if he'd actually left a part of himself behind. His usual single-minded clarity of focus was gone. Instead, he'd spent the entire journey reliving every conversation he'd ever had with his wife and regretting half of them.

At least he'd made an attempt to patch things up with her before he left. She hadn't made any fresh accusations, had even agreed to wear his ring without attacking him again, though she'd made no further comment on their marriage. He had no idea how he felt about their situation either. He'd meant it when he'd said that he'd never met anyone like her before, though as to why he'd said it, he had no idea. He'd only wanted to say something, to make her understand that it hadn't all been a game, even if it wasn't a real marriage either. He was still a blacksmith's son and she was still a lady. Her father had chosen him because he'd known that protecting people was what he did, was what he was good at. Deeper feelings were beyond him. So why did he now feel as if he were protecting both of them? Her from both Stephen *and* Matilda, himself from the compelling desire to turn around and ride back the way that he'd come.

He dragged his attention back to his surroundings. The season of Yuletide was approaching, but there was no sign of it yet here. The vast hall was less crowded than it had been in recent months and the mood was sombre. Hardly surprising given the circumstances, though he could see that Sir Guian had been busy spreading poison about *him*, too. Some of the faces watching him were openly antagonistic, some curious, but all kept their distance. He was too close to the Empress for anyone to dare criticise him openly, but if she fell then it wouldn't take long for the buzzards to start circling.

'Brian.' He found a friendly face at last, that of a stocky, dark-haired man standing close to the fireplace. Brian Fitzcount was one of the Empress's oldest supporters, a man who'd been raised by her father and one of the few she implicitly trusted. The number of those was dwindling by the day.

'Lothar!' Brian clapped a hand on his shoulder in greeting. 'It's good to have you back. We've been hearing strange rumours about you.'

'Really?' He presented his usual inscrutable façade and Brian smiled.

'Don't worry, no one gives credence to anything de Ravenell says, no matter what he thinks. The Empress will be glad to see you. You've heard about Robert Fitzroy?'

'Yes. Where is she?'

'In her private apartments.' Brian lowered his voice. 'See if you can get her to come out. I know she's grieving, but people need reassurance. They need to see her.'

'Haven't you told her that?'

'I've tried, but she doesn't listen to anyone else the way she listens to you. The rest of us have too many vested interests. You're the only one she trusts to have purely her interests at heart.'

He felt a twinge of guilt at the words. A week ago that would have been true, but now...now he had a castle of his own to protect, not to mention a wife.

He gave a terse nod and walked past the guards at the entrance to Matilda's apartments, dropping on to one knee in the doorway.

'Empress.'

'Come in, Lothar.' A tall, striking-looking woman turned from where she stood by the window, favouring him with a sad smile. She looked every inch the Empress in a fine azuline-blue gown and matching headdress, yet something about her seemed different somehow, in some subtle way he couldn't quite put his finger on. 'You got my message about Robert?'

'Yes, my lady. Do they know what happened?'

'It wasn't Stephen's doing. What else matters?' She held out her hand for him to kiss. 'He's gone, Lothar, and I'm so tired.'

'Shall I fetch your ladies?'

'Not tired like that. I mean tired of all of this. This *war*.' She waved a hand in the air before rounding on him accusingly. 'I've been hearing rumours about you, too. Tell me what happened at Haword.'

'It was just as my messenger informed you, Empress. Lady Juliana surrendered the castle without any bloodshed.'

'Yet now I hear that you sent Sir Guian away. Those weren't my orders.'

'I'd heard that Stephen was on his way back into Herefordshire. I didn't think Sir Guian capable of holding the castle against an attack.'

'None the less, he was the man I chose.' Matilda's nostrils flared slightly. 'You've never questioned my judgement before.'

'I would never presume to do so, Empress, but

there was another situation at Haword Sir Guian wasn't aware of.'

'*Situation?*' A thin, delicately arched eyebrow drew upwards. 'Is that what you call it? I've heard that she's a very attractive young lady.'

'Sir Guian seemed to think so.'

'Ah.' The eyebrow dropped again. 'I should have remembered that weakness in you. You've never been able to walk away from a damsel in distress, Lothar. Even one who betrays me, apparently.'

'She didn't betray you, my lady, at least not in the way that we thought. Stephen was holding her father captive.'

'William? I thought he was killed in battle?'

'That's what we were supposed to think, but he survived. He was still alive when I left, though he's failing. Lady Juliana surrendered Haword to Stephen in order to get him back.'

'She made a bargain?'

'Yes, my lady. She didn't want to betray you.'

Matilda was silent for a moment, as if considering all the ramifications of his words. 'She must have been very convincing for Stephen to let her stay at Haword.'

'She couldn't have moved William anywhere else in his condition.'

'But still, for Stephen to trust her to hold the castle…' She frowned. 'She'd no right to assume the position of chatelaine at all whilst her father was alive.'

'I believe she had no choice. Keeping her father a secret was part of her agreement with Stephen.'

'Indeed?' Matilda looked sceptical and he felt an uneasy sense of foreboding. This was exactly the situation that Juliana had feared. He'd assured her that the Empress would understand, though now he wasn't so sure. She didn't seem in a particularly forgiving mood.

'If she swore allegiance against her will, why didn't she simply cede Haword to Guian once Stephen had gone?'

'Because she'd sworn an oath to him. She felt honour-bound to keep it.'

'Yet she surrendered to *you*?'

'Eventually, yes, for the sake of her men.'

'Or perhaps she's just a clever woman?'

'Empress?'

Matilda's blue gaze honed in on him thoughtfully. 'How long have we been in England now, Lothar?'

'Nine years, Empress.' What did that have to do with Juliana?

'And yet my cause has advanced hardly any further than it did in the first year. Stephen still holds most of the country.'

'You're still the rightful Queen.'

'A queen without a country. Is it all worth it, I wonder?'

He didn't answer, hearing Juliana's voice in his head, telling him that there had been too much violence already...

Matilda narrowed her eyes, as if surprised by his lack of response. 'In any case, I wonder if your Lady Juliana doesn't have the right idea. So many of the Barons are making private treaties, with both myself and Stephen. They don't know which of us will eventually win so they feel they have to appease us both. Maybe I ought to think about making a treaty, too.'

He blinked in surprise. She really *had* changed if she were considering such a thing! 'Surely you aren't thinking of surrendering, my lady?'

'Never.' She gave a curt laugh. 'England is my sons' inheritance. I would never surrender that, but perhaps it's time I ceded the fight to them. Henry's a young man and eager to prove himself. He's intelligent, too, like his grandfather, and a better military commander than Stephen's son Eustace will ever be. Men will support him who would never countenance a woman as their leader. If Stephen would agree to let Henry succeed him as King, it would be a kind of victory for us both.'

'Do you think Henry's ready?'

'He has to be. It's what he was raised for, and, now Robert's gone, I find I haven't the heart for fighting any more.' She heaved a weary-sounding sigh. 'I want to go home, Lothar.'

'Back to Anjou?'

'No. Anjou is Geoffrey's home, but thanks to him we now rule Normandy as well.' Her lips twisted into something like, and yet unlike, a smile. 'He's been far more successful than I have.'

Lothar held his tongue. That was true. Matilda's husband had seized the entirety of Normandy in the time it had taken her to claim one small corner of England. Given the volatile state of their marriage, he knew that must rankle.

'We'll cross the Channel to Normandy as soon as the weather improves. It will be good to see my sons again.'

He barely heard the last few words, distracted by the heavy thundering sound in his ears. *We? We'll cross the Channel…?* The words seemed to be echoing in his head. But of course it was *we*. It had been *we* for almost as long as he could remember. It was only natural that she would assume he'd go with her. A week ago it would never have crossed his mind to object either, but now he felt winded, as if she'd just knocked the very air from his lungs. He couldn't even bring himself to speak. Never in his wildest imaginings had he thought she'd do this—quit the field just as soon as he found a reason to stay.

'Lothar?' Matilda gave him a shrewd look. 'Is something the matter?'

'No, Empress, only… I thought you'd want me to stay and serve Prince Henry.'

'He has plenty of other men to serve him. I won't give up my best soldier, not even for England. You're one of the few people I can count on.'

The winded feeling turned into a cramped

tightness. He'd been so busy thinking about Juliana on the journey that he hadn't prepared what he was going to say about the marriage itself. Now it seemed that breaking the news was going to be even harder than he'd anticipated.

'I appreciate the compliment, Empress, but there's something else about Haword I need to tell you.'

A look of displeasure flitted across Matilda's face. 'Yes?'

'Before I left William asked me to protect his daughter. He was afraid of what might happen to her in the future. I couldn't refuse him.'

'Refuse *what* exactly?'

He took a deep breath, as if preparing himself for battle. 'Marriage, my lady. He asked me to marry her.'

He thought he heard a muffled gasp. 'And you said…?'

'I agreed. We made vows to each other, then I came here to ask your permission.'

'If you've already made vows, then it's a little late for *that*, don't you think?'

'William wanted to witness the ceremony. He won't survive much longer.'

'And you took this step simply as a favour?' Matilda's tone became scathing. 'If you'd wanted a castle, Lothar, you could simply have asked me.'

He stiffened at the suggestion. 'I didn't do it for the castle, my lady. I did it for William.'

'What about his daughter? Wasn't *she* in on

the scheme, too? She seems to have a gift for persuading men to do what she wants. First Stephen, then you.'

'There was no scheme.' He felt a faint stirring of temper. 'She was against the idea.'

'Yet you went ahead anyway.' Matilda's blue gaze sharpened. 'Do you care for the girl then?'

He baulked at the question. *Did* he care for her? It wasn't something he'd let himself consciously consider, simply assuming that he wasn't capable of such an emotion. But confronted with the question directly, he realised that he *had* been considering it. He'd done nothing *but* consider it all the way to Devizes. In which case, the answer was obvious—wasn't it?

No! His brain rebelled against the idea. He'd married her out of respect for William, not because he cared for her. He *couldn't* care for her.

'She's a brave woman. I admire her.'

'That's a different question,' Matilda snapped. 'I asked if you care for her, Lothar, this woman who sides with Stephen against me?'

'I hardly know her, Empress.'

'Then tell me who you've left in charge back in Haword?'

He paused for the space of a heartbeat. 'Her.'

There was a silence so heavy it was deafening, before Matilda gave a harsh-sounding laugh. 'Then it's true what they say, a woman can make a fool of any man.'

'I left my soldiers there, too.'

'Under *her* command. Do you think you can trust her not to betray me again?'

'Yes, my lady.'

'And if Stephen were to lead an army back into Herefordshire, what then? What if he marched up to Haword and demanded entry? Would she let him in?'

Yes. He clenched his jaw, knowing the answer just as well as he knew what would happen if he gave it.

'No.' He lied. 'She would not.'

Matilda seemed to freeze for a moment, her voice dropping to a lower register. 'You must truly care for her.'

'I want to keep my word to William, Empress. I want Lady Juliana to keep her home, too.'

'*Her* home? If you're married to her, then it's yours. Don't you want to stay here and claim it?'

He tensed, unable at that moment to frame an answer. 'I never thought that you'd want to leave England, Empress. I didn't think it would come to this.'

'Yet it has.'

'I made a vow to her, my lady.'

'You made one to me first.' Matilda's tone was reproachful. 'Will you abandon me now after I've just lost Robert?'

'No.' He ground his teeth. She was right. He *had* made an oath to her first. He'd made it as a boy and meant it because she'd saved him. Everything he was, he owed to her. He couldn't abandon her now, no matter how conflicted he felt about it, no matter what his promise to William. He'd think of another way to protect Juliana—he could leave his soldiers in Haword, for a start—even if the thought of sailing away to a different country caused an ache in the place where his heart ought to be, as if it were a real beating organ and not simply a stone. Then again, it was probably for the best. His wife didn't want to be married and he was hardly a fit husband for anyone. If he left, then Juliana could lead the life she wanted, without any man to tell her what to do...

'I'll do whatever you command, Empress.'

'Good.' Matilda gave a satisfied nod. 'In any case, we can't cross the Channel until the spring. You can go back and keep your word to William in the meantime.'

'As you wish, Empress. What about Haword?'

'You and your *wife* can keep it until then. After that...' she fixed him with a look that was both a challenge and a threat at the same time '...you can bring her to me.'

Chapter Twenty-One

~~~~~~~~~~~~~~~~~~~~~

Lothar peered down at the white carpet beneath his horse's hooves and knew that he'd arrived just in time. One week away from Haword and winter seemed to have arrived with a vengeance. Looking out at the snow-filled clouds from his room in Devizes Castle two mornings before, he'd known that he'd had to leave then or not at all. Once the cold weather set in, the roads could easily become impassable, and the last thing he'd wanted was to get cut off from his new wife.

He'd already stayed away longer than he'd intended. Despite what she'd said, Matilda had seemed in no hurry to dismiss him, wanting to talk about her plans for her son Henry instead. He'd had the uneasy feeling that she'd been watching him, too, trying to gauge his behaviour. He'd striven to maintain his usual impenetrable façade, but inside he'd been restless, anxiously counting the hours of his absence. The idea of Juliana looking after her father on her own set his teeth on edge every time he thought of it. What if she needed him? What if she wasn't sleeping again? Whether she wanted him there or not, surely a *husband's* place was at her side?

At last he'd been unable to stand the tension any longer. He'd finally asked permission to leave, though it had taken Matilda another full day to give him an answer. He'd actually thought she'd been going to refuse, though for the life of him, he hadn't been able to understand why. She'd already admitted that she'd no more stomach for fighting and she hardly needed a bodyguard in Devizes Castle, so what could it possibly matter to her where he spent the winter? Ultimately, he was left with the same strange suspicion of jealousy he'd felt on his way to Devizes, only this time from a different source, as if both the women in his life were jealous of each other when neither had any cause to be. He had a strong attachment to both of them, but the feelings—no, he corrected himself—the *way* he thought about each of them was completely different.

At last, the ramshackle tower of Castle Haword rose up out of the snowy twilight ahead of them and he felt a swell of relief. If it had been safe, he would have taken the last part of the journey at a gallop, but instead he had to control himself as much as his stallion, reining in his anticipation until he thundered across the drawbridge.

'Sergeant?'

He heard Ulf call out the moment he entered the bailey.

'What's happened?' One look at the Constable's face told him something was wrong. 'He's dead?'

'The evening you left.'

He swung out of his saddle at once. 'The *same* evening?'

'Yes, sir. There was no pain. He just slipped away in his sleep, but Lady Juliana… She took it badly, sir.'

He swore violently. 'Where is she?'

'Up on the roof.' Ulf gestured up at the gatehouse. 'She's been there every day since.'

'Outside? In this weather?'

'She won't come down, sir. I've tried everything.'

'It's all right.' He put a reassuring hand on the Constable's shoulder. 'See to my horse. I'll fetch her.'

He ran up the gatehouse steps, wishing now that he'd insisted on leaving Devizes earlier. He seemed to have done nothing but comfort women for the past few weeks, but this time he felt as if the pain were his, too. He hadn't felt even half so worried when he'd gone to Matilda.

'Juliana?' He flung open the trapdoor at the top of the stairwell, holding an arm over his head to peer through the gathering snowflakes, but there was no sign of her.

'You came back.'

The voice was faint, but he honed in on it at
once, feeling a strange, cracking sensation in his
chest as he did so. She was sitting in the far corner, wrapped up in a woollen cloak the same grey
shade as the stone around her, as if she were trying to blend in with the wall.

'I said I would.' He crossed the roof in two
strides and crouched down beside her, gently lifting the hood from her face. 'Ulf told me what
happened.'

'He was sleeping.' Her voice was so quiet that
he had to lean closer to hear it. 'When you left, he
was sleeping, but then…he just never woke up.'

'I'm sorry.' He reached out for her hand. It felt
like a block of ice. 'If I'd known… Forgive me.'

'It wasn't your fault.' She looked up at last with
eyes that seemed alarmingly blank, as if the spark
in them had gone out. 'It just happened.'

He tightened his grip on her hand convulsively.
Her very calmness was unnerving, so unlike her
that he felt almost afraid. He would have rather
she attacked him than this.

'Come inside.'

'No.' She shook her head slowly, but firmly.
'I like it up here. I feel as if I've been inside for
months. I want air.'

'You've had enough. You'll catch your death
if you stay up here. That's not what your father
would have wanted.'

'I've done a lot of things he wouldn't have wanted. What's one more?'

He frowned at the note of despondency in her voice. This was more than just grief. It sounded like guilt, too, though he had no idea what to do about that. A man of words might have been able to comfort her, but he wasn't one of those. Actions were all he knew.

'Enough.' He tugged on her hand, pulling her to her feet.

'What are you doing?' She sounded more bewildered than angry. 'I said I didn't want to go in.'

'And I made a promise to your father to take care of you. Now come on.'

'I said I don't want to!' There was an edge to her voice this time.

'Too bad.' He wrapped his arms around her, scooping her up off her feet and carrying her along the ramparts.

'Put me down!'

'Not if you won't see sense. I wouldn't wriggle like that either, not in these conditions, or you'll knock us both into the moat.'

She stopped resisting and glared at him instead, all along the walkway until they reached the side entrance to the keep.

'Have you eaten?' He kicked the door shut behind them, turning his head just in time to see her roll her eyes.

'Is something amusing?'

'No, you're just always asking me that. Next you'll be telling me to go to bed again.'

'You're right, I will.'

'Lothar…'

'No argument.' He pushed her chamber door open with his shoulder and lowered her back to her feet. 'Wait here.'

He went back to the gallery briefly and came back with a candle, putting it down beside the bed before wrenching the covers away.

'I'm not tired.'

'That's what you always say as well. It's never convinced me before and it's not going to convince me now. Now take off your cloak.'

'I can't.' Her voice was quiet again. 'My hands are too cold.'

'Here.' He reached up and unfastened the clasp for her, unwrapping the woollen garment as gently as he could and resisting the urge to wrap his arms around her instead. 'Now get into bed.'

'There's no point. I won't be able to sleep.'

'You can rest.'

'I don't want to.'

'But you can sit on top of a gatehouse in the freezing cold?'

'That's different.'

'Why?'

'I don't know.'

'Then tell me why you can't sleep.'

'I just can't.'

'Because?'

'I said I don't know!' She tried to put her hands over her face, but he pulled them away, grasping her wrists firmly in front of him. She looked overwrought and exhausted, more than he'd ever seen her, which was saying something, but temper was a good sign. If he could rouse that then maybe he could shake her out of her lethargy, too. She was starting to sound again like the Juliana he'd married. He wanted to see *her*...

'Tell me, Juliana.'

'Let me go!'

'Tell me why.'

'Because he's gone!' The words seemed to burst out of her suddenly. 'My father's gone and I never told him what I did! I was too afraid to tell him about Stephen and now it's too late!'

He frowned, confused by her words. 'We agreed that it was best if you didn't say anything. The truth would only have upset him.'

'I know.' She shook her head with an expression of pure anguish. 'I know it was for the best, but don't you see? Now I'll never know what he would have said! I'll never know if he would have forgiven me.'

'He would have forgiven you.'

He drew her gently towards the bed, sitting down on the mattress beside her. He was still holding her wrists, but he wasn't holding *her* any more. She wasn't trying to get away, but he didn't want to let go either.

'How do you know?' She was facing in the other direction so that her voice sounded muffled.

'Because I knew *him*. He was proud of you. That was obvious every time he spoke about you. He loved you, Juliana. He would have forgiven you anything.'

She turned her head slightly, though she still didn't look at him. 'Did he mention me often?'

'Every chance he could get. *Too* often for a soldier like me. Of course, now I've met you, I understand why.'

Her hand trembled slightly and he fought the urge to rub his thumb against the inside of her wrist.

'He didn't regret anything?'

'Like what?' He could barely concentrate, distracted by how silky soft her skin felt beneath his fingertips.

'I thought he might have regretted the way he raised me. Sometimes, when we spoke of the future, he looked worried. I thought perhaps he was disappointed with me.'

'You?' He was genuinely taken aback. 'Why would he have been disappointed?'

'Because of the way I am.'

'What's wrong with the way you are?'

She threw him a look that was part-accusing, part-exasperated. 'Because I'm not a lady, not a real one anyway. I'm not good at the things I ought to be good at. I can't sew or recite poetry, remember?'

'I doubt either of those skills would be much use in a siege.'

'No, but sometimes I feel as if I'm neither one thing nor the other. Neither a lady nor a soldier, just someone in between.'

'Maybe you're both.'

Her head dropped even lower. 'Then why did he force me to marry you? I don't understand.'

He felt a dull ache in his chest. 'Because he knew the war wasn't over and he wanted you to be safe. He wanted me to protect you, Juliana. It's what I'm good at.' He tightened his grip on her hand. 'Let me protect you.'

She drew in a breath. 'Do you really think he would have forgiven me?'

'I *know* that he would have. He might not have been happy about it, but he would have understood.'

'You're not just saying that?'

He arched an eyebrow. 'I never just say things. You ought to know that by now.'

'True.' Her lips curved slightly. 'I just wish I could be sure.'

'You can. Trust me, Juliana, you don't have to feel guilty. Sitting in the freezing cold punishing yourself won't do any good. You can't punish yourself for doing what you thought was right. It *was* right at the time. He would have done the same thing for you.'

'Choose *me* over the Empress?' She made a sceptical sound.

'Of course he would have. He loved you. Anyone who loved you…'

He faltered, unsure about how to finish the
sentence. What was he trying to say, that anyone who loved her would make the same choice?
The words cut too close to the bone for comfort.
Besides, it didn't sound like something he would
say. Love wasn't a word he ever used at all.

'What did the Empress say?' Her voice had a
slight tremor in it. 'About what I did?'

'She understood.'

'And our marriage?'

He stood up, letting go of her wrists finally.
'What the Empress said can wait until the morning. Now lie down.'

She gave him a look as if she were about to
protest and then seemed to change her mind,
clambering under the bedcovers and curling up
on her side.

'Close your eyes.'

'I know how to sleep.'

'Then you know you have to start by closing
your eyes. I'm not going anywhere until you do.'

'You're just going to stand there?'

'If that's what it takes.'

'Until I'm asleep?'

He folded his arms.

'But that's ridiculous!' She sat up again. 'You
can't just watch me all night.'

'Then go to sleep.'

'Aren't you tired, too?'

'A little.'

She hesitated briefly and then shuffled across the bed, making space beside her. 'Well, if you're going to wait, you might at least do it in comfort.'

He didn't move at first, considering all the options before him. He'd been in the saddle since daybreak that morning, hell-bent on reaching Haword by nightfall. The thought of lying down and stretching out his tired muscles was certainly tempting—though, next to his wife, perhaps a little too tempting…

'Don't worry.' Her expression was faintly challenging, 'I won't tie you up again.'

He stiffened involuntarily. There were worse things he could think of, though now definitely wasn't the time for imagining any of them. Now was the time to keep his mind focused on sleep. Just sleep, nothing more. Certainly not the fact that she was his wife and offering to share her bed with him.

'Are you coming?' She rolled away, turning her back as if whatever he decided didn't matter to her.

Slowly he removed his cloak and gambeson, wincing at the smell of horsehair. If he were really going to share a bed with her, then he'd prefer a bath first. But he *was* tired—and so was she, if the dark shadows under her eyes were anything to judge by. If he achieved nothing else this winter, he intended to banish those. Before he left, he wanted to make her feel better again, to restore her to health and something, hopefully, resembling happiness. With any luck, he might even make her smile—and if he could do that, then maybe their marriage, however brief it was destined to be, might be called a success after all.

He drew in a deep breath and lay down.

Chapter Twenty-Two

Juliana rolled on to her side and opened her eyes with a start, alarmed to find herself lying face-to-face with her new husband. Not just face-to-face either. Their chests were actually touching, her breasts pressed up against the thin linen of the undertunic he was mercifully still wearing. Somehow they must have rolled together in sleep, the mattress dipping in the middle to form a U-shape around them, the blankets wrapped tight around their bodies like a cocoon.

She held her breath, wondering how to extricate herself from her current position, before deciding against it. She'd never shared a bed with anyone before, but she had the distinct impression that if she tried to roll away then the movement would disturb him. For a horrifying moment she'd thought she'd seen his eyelids flicker, but then they'd stilled again, his breathing just as deep and regular as ever. She wanted to keep it that way. Bad enough that she'd actually invited him into her bed. How much worse would it look if he woke up and found them like this? Not to mention that she was his wife and in bed with him. What might he expect from her? Nothing, in all likelihood, given that he'd just come back from Matilda and thought she looked like a stablehand, but they'd never discussed *that* particular aspect of marriage. No, she definitely didn't want to wake him. With any luck, he'd roll away by himself soon enough, none the wiser about how close they'd been, and in the meantime the warmth from his body was surprisingly comforting. His chest felt sturdy and strong, just like the rest of him. She hadn't expected to sleep at all, but she must have and for a while, too. The last thing she remembered was him lying down beside her, but now, for the first time in as long as she could remember, she felt rested.

Slowly, she let herself breathe again. She hadn't used her chamber at all since the night her father had slipped away in his sleep, roaming aimlessly around the castle instead, sinking ever further and deeper into a morass of grief and despair. Despite Lothar's assurances, she hadn't expected to see *him* again either. After everything she'd said and accused him of, she'd doubted that he'd want to come back, yet she'd found herself wishing he would. Her father's death had put their quarrel into perspective. As much as she'd still resented their marriage, ironically she'd *wanted* her husband. Wasn't that why she'd gone up to the battlements every day? She'd told herself that she'd been looking for solitude, but deep down she knew that she'd been looking for him, too, as if he were the only one she could talk to about her loss, the only one who might understand...

And he *had* understood. The things he'd said about her father had made her feel better in one evening than she had in a whole week of her own tortured self-recriminations. Once he'd said them, it had all seemed so obvious, as if he were actually lifting the burden of guilt away from her shoulders. He'd seemed to care about how she felt, too, as if their marriage were more than just a promise he'd made to her father, or a means of getting a castle. She'd been scared to be left alone again afterwards, afraid that if he went then the feeling of relief might go with him, asking him to lie down beside her because she'd had the bizarre notion that she wouldn't be able to sleep without him. She certainly hadn't thought of the other implications, though now she was acutely aware of the fact that they were married and lying in bed together.

On the other hand, being in such close proximity gave her a chance to look at him properly for once. They'd barely had a pause to draw breath since they'd met, lurching from one crisis to another—Sir Guian, her father, Matilda. Now there was only the two of them, she could finally look at *him*. Not that she could see a great deal. Her eyes had adjusted to the darkness, but his face was still cast deep in shadow. Only the jagged white line over the left side of his face stood out in the blackness, like the streak of lightning she'd first imagined it to be. What had he said, that his father had kicked him? She shuddered at the thought, seized with a powerful urge to reach out and touch it, to stroke the sides of his face, to press her lips against the damaged skin... She half-lifted a hand, yelping in surprise as his eyelids sprang open.

'Juliana.' His voice sounded perfectly neutral, as if he found nothing unusual in their intimate position.

She pulled her hand back at once. 'You scared me! I thought you were asleep.'

'Your eyes woke me up.'

'My eyes?'

'I could feel them burrowing into my skull.' The corners of his mouth twitched upwards. 'I never realised I was so fascinating.'

'Just because my eyes were open doesn't mean I was looking at you!' Suddenly she was glad of the darkness concealing the scarlet tincture of her cheeks. They were probably redder than her hair. 'I was just thinking, that's all.'

'Might a husband ask what about?'

Husband? Her heartbeat started to flutter erratically, reminding her of the fact that their bodies were still pressed close together under the covers. Now that he was awake she *really* ought to pull away, but the blankets were wrapped so tightly around her they seemed to be holding her in place. His body was having a strange effect on hers, too, as if it were taking on an independent life of its own, her breasts straining through her gown as if she were cold, which she definitely wasn't. Quite the opposite—her skin felt red-hot, yet something about him made her want to press even closer.

'Your scar.' She said the first thing that popped into her head.

'What about it?'

'Does it hurt?'

'Sometimes.'

'Can I touch it?'

He hesitated for a moment. 'If you wish.'

She lifted her hand and trailed her fingers delicately along the barbed line of his scar. It felt surprisingly smooth, as if it were an ingrained part of him.

'It's not very pleasant to look at.' He sounded almost apologetic.

'I don't care about that.' She cradled her hand against the damaged side of his face. 'It's part of who you are.'

She met his gaze and her stomach flipped over. Even in the darkness, his eyes were burning with an intensity that made her temperature soar and her insides quiver with excitement. She felt as if she'd just been scorched. His whole body seemed to have tensed, too, the lower part in particular behaving in a way she'd never expected...

'Are you hungry?' His voice sounded strange.

'Hungry?' She had to repeat the word to make sense of it. *Was* she hungry? What did that have to do with anything? 'Yes, I suppose so.'

'Wait here.'

He rolled away suddenly and she gasped, feeling cold and bereft as he sat for a few moments on the edge of the bed before standing up.

'It's the middle of the night!'

'True.' He tugged his boots on.

'Everyone's asleep!'

'Also true. Except for the guards, I hope.'

'Then what are you doing?'

He picked up his cloak and flung it loosely around his shoulders. 'Taking care of you. Wait here.'

She lay down again, curling up in the warm space left by his body, hardly knowing whether to feel relieved or disappointed or both. For a moment, she'd had the impression that something was about to happen between them. She definitely hadn't imagined the way certain parts of his body had pressed so insistently against hers, but then he'd pulled away as if he couldn't wait to get out of the room quickly enough. Because of Matilda? The idea was mortifying, though it still didn't quell the ache in the pit of her stomach. Even the lingering scent of his musk on the pillow gave her a thrill of something, some new shivering sensation she didn't recognise, but that made her want to stretch out on the bed like a cat.

She trailed her hands over her body, from her breasts all the way down to her navel, then pushed her arms out to the sides, tipping her head back and arching her back to ease the feeling of tension in her limbs. Strangely enough, that *did* make her feel better, though there was something shameless about it, too. She was writhing on the bed like a... well, perhaps not quite like a cat any more. Not that she knew what else she could be. She tilted her hips up, lifting her body...

'Ready for a midnight feast?'

She shot up to a sitting position, clutching the covers to her chin in embarrassment. She hadn't expected Lothar to return so quickly, but he was already standing in the doorway, a dark shadow holding a heaped trencher in one hand and a candle in the other.

'No! I mean, yes... I mean, that was quick.'

'You said you were hungry.' His voice sounded deeper than before, almost guttural, and she bit her lip with mortification. Was he angry with her? Her behaviour must have been truly shameless if he was...

'Where did you find all that food?' She tried her best to sound nonchalant as he approached the bed.

'In the kitchens.'

'You woke up the cooks?'

He looked mildly offended. 'If I can climb over

the walls of Oxford Castle and escape past Stephen's army in the middle of the night, I think I can break into a kitchen without waking anyone.'

'They'll think we have some very large mice.'

'Probably.' He sat down on the edge of the bed and set the trencher in front of her. 'Now I want to see you eat.'

She didn't argue, tearing off a chunk of bread and popping it eagerly into her mouth. It tasted fresh and delicious and she instantly reached for more.

'Stop watching me.' She peeped up at him, acutely aware of his eyes on her face. 'It was bad enough when I was trying to sleep.'

'Says the woman who woke me up by staring.'

'That didn't wake you up.' She paused with another piece of bread halfway to her mouth. 'How long were you awake?'

'About the same amount of time as you, I imagine. You rolled into me.'

She lifted her chin up defensively. 'By accident and, if you were asleep, how do you know you didn't roll into me?'

'Good point. Shall we say we rolled into each other?'

'I'm surprised I slept at all, but I feel better.' She smiled, feeling shy all of a sudden. 'Thank you for everything you said last night. I needed to hear it.'

'I'm glad. I'm only sorry it took me so long to come back.'

'It wasn't your fault. You couldn't have known what would happen.'

'No, but your father asked me to take care of you. I wanted to take care of you.'

'You did?' She opened her eyes wide, caught off guard by the tender note in his voice, though judging by the suddenly quizzical expression on his face, so was he.

'Of course. You're my wife.'

'Still?' She asked the question hesitantly. 'I thought the Empress might have had our marriage annulled.'

'Is that what you want?' His voice sounded tense again.

'I…' She faltered. She didn't know what she wanted. She knew she didn't want to be married, though that didn't necessarily mean that she didn't want him…did it?

'In any case, she doesn't have the power.' His expression turned to a scowl. 'Do you think I'd be sharing a bed with you if she did?'

'No, I suppose not.' She caught her breath unsteadily. That was true. Everyone in the castle must know where they were now, not to mention the fact that they were alone. In which case, there was no turning back. They were definitely, irrevocably married. 'So Haword is yours.'

'No, it's *ours*.' He sighed. 'Do I really need to tell you again, Juliana? I don't want to take anything away from you. To all intents and purposes, the castle is still yours to command. I won't interfere. I only hold it for the Empress.'

She stared at him in astonishment. 'So you don't want to take over? Not at all?'

'Only in name. That way you're protected against retribution from Stephen.'

'What do you mean?'

'I mean in case he ever comes back. In the unlikely event of my losing a battle against him, you can tell him you were forced to marry me against your will.'

'But that's…'

'The truth?'

She held his gaze uneasily. That *was* the truth, though the thought of him fighting Stephen made her feel wretched. She'd given her allegiance to Stephen over Matilda, not over her husband. If only the two weren't so utterly incompatible.

One side of his mouth curved upwards. 'You can tell him what a hard-hearted, mercenary bastard I am.'

'No!' She spoke more vehemently than she intended.

'No?' He looked amused. 'It might be safer for you to renounce me.'

'I would never! Who calls you that?'

'Half the Empress's army for a start. It won't be anything Stephen hasn't heard before. My reputation precedes me.'

'But you're none of those things. If you were, you wouldn't have come back and honoured your promise to my father.' She tossed her head defiantly. 'I won't condemn you to Stephen, not for any reason.'

He regarded her intently for a few moments before he smiled. 'He'd have to defeat me first.'

She picked up another chunk of bread, chewing on it thoughtfully as the implications of his words sank in. It seemed that their marriage protected her even more effectively than her father had realised, providing her with a buffer against Matilda, as well as a defence for her behaviour to Stephen if she ever needed one. Lothar seemed to have thought of everything, as if he were truly determined to protect her. Though it also left her without a side, as if she were stuck in the middle again.

She peered up at him from under her lashes. Strange how, sitting in bed beside him like this, the idea of marriage didn't bother her so much any more, but how did *he* feel about it? She'd been so wrapped up in her own thoughts she'd never even considered his. For all she knew, he'd felt as trapped by the whole arrangement as she had. He'd said something about not wanting a wife...

'I'm sorry if this isn't what you wanted.' She broached the subject nervously. 'My father should never have forced you to marry me.'

'He didn't. He asked.'

'It's still hard to refuse the wishes of a dying man. I wouldn't blame you for resenting it.'

'I was surprised more than anything else. For

your father to ask a man like me… I know I'm
not the kind of husband you would have wanted.'

'I've never wanted any kind.'

'But if you had…' He looked her square in the
eye. 'I would understand if you felt insulted. Or
humiliated.'

'No.' She shook her head quickly. 'I shouldn't
have said those things. I've had time to think this
past week and I know you were only doing what
my father asked. I'm not happy about it, but he
trusted you. I ought to as well. I should never have
accused you of trying to steal my inheritance.'

'It was a reasonable assumption. I'm a blacksmith's son and you're a lady.'

'You're also a better man than a baron like Sir
Guian could ever be. I wasn't insulted.'

Not by that anyway, she added silently. She
was far more insulted by the idea of her husband
being in love with another woman, though saying it aloud would only make her sound jealous…

'I was just angry at the situation. It was a
shock.'

'For both of us, but I want to make the best of
it, Juliana. I hope our truce can still hold.'

He held a hand out and she took it, feeling the
quivering sensation in her stomach flare up again
as he twined his fingers around hers.

'Truce?'

'Truce.' She tried to keep her expression under
control. 'But what will you do if I'm running the
castle?'

He hesitated briefly. 'I'll carry on serving the Empress as before.'

'You mean you'll be leaving again?' The quivering sensation dissipated. *Of course* he'd want to return to Matilda.

'At some point, yes.'

'So we'll live apart, like the Empress and her husband?'

'Not quite like that, but perhaps…in the future…' His expression looked torn. 'In any case, I promise to come back if you ever need me. I'll do everything in my power to protect you.'

She pulled her hand away with a sinking feeling. Considering everything she'd said to him before, it was a reasonable proposal. A kind of part-time marriage. That *ought* to please her. He was offering to let her go on as before, to return to her old role without any interference, only adding his name and reputation, thereby keeping his promise to her father as well as his oath to the Empress. There were so many promises and oaths between them she could barely keep track. Hers to Stephen. His to the Empress. Theirs to each other. How could they possibly *keep* all of them? Which ones came first?

'Juliana…' He seemed on the verge of saying something else, before he stood up abruptly. 'I have to go.'

'Where to?' She felt strangely crestfallen. 'It's still dark.'

'It's almost dawn. I have things to arrange.'

'What things?'

'You'll see.' He pulled his gambeson back over his head. 'You're not in control yet, my lady.'

'But you just said…'

'Not until the morning. First you need to get some more rest. Until then, I'm in charge.' He gave her a conflicted look as he made for the doorway. 'Wife.'

Chapter Twenty-Three

'Lothar?'

Juliana propped herself up on one elbow, staring at the bed with bleary-eyed confusion until she remembered that her husband had gone.

Husband. She said the word aloud, testing its strangeness on her tongue. It wasn't a word she'd ever been fond of, though now it seemed to have lost some of its sting. She looked around the chamber, but all trace of him seemed to be gone. All of his clothing, all the remains of their midnight meal. The only new object was a cup by the bed filled to the brim with something steaming hot and delicious-smelling, like honey mixed with ale and spices.

Eagerly, she picked it up and took a sip, smiling as the warmth reached her stomach. Whoever had brought it must have woken her as they left, though she was glad of the disruption. Whatever her new husband wanted, she had no intention of staying in bed all day. Her mind felt clearer than it had in a long time, as if all the things Lothar had told her the previous night had laid her worries, if not to rest, then to bed anyway. She had a feeling it would take a lot longer to come to terms with everything that had happened, but because of him, she'd made a start. Despite everything—*his* attachment to Matilda and *her* reluctance to be married—he'd been thoughtful and caring and had seemed to know exactly what to say. Maybe being married to him wasn't going to be so bad after all. Maybe they could be friends. She actually felt *eager* to see him again.

She gulped down the rest of the ale and climbed out of bed, splashing her face with water before opening her coffer and exchanging her old tunic for a forest-green surcote trimmed with brown fur. If the cold draught blowing in through the window shutters was anything to go by, she was going to need it. Then she picked up a comb and dragged the prongs through the tangled bird's nest of her hair, wincing at every knot. It took ten long, painful minutes, but finally it was done. She left it loose, tucking the long waves neatly away beneath her headdress, feeling strangely pleased with herself. There. She was ready. Now she just had to find her husband.

She made her way impatiently down the stairs and into the hall, but there was no sign of him, only a couple of maids chattering and laughing together as they stoked up the hearth.

Maids? She stopped dead in surprise. She'd sent all the maids away months ago. What were they doing there now?

'Alys? Maud?' She recognised both of the women at once.

They turned and smiled in unison, dropping into formal curtsies as she hastened forward.

'It's so good to see you again.' She hugged both of them in turn.

'You, too, my lady. We've been so worried about you.' Alys, the older and taller of the two, spoke first. 'Are you all right?'

'Yes.' She burst into a smile, vaguely surprised by her own answer. It was true. She *was* all right. Despite everything that had happened, she really was. It was almost unbelievable when she thought about it. 'But what are you doing here?'

'Ulf came to fetch us this morning. He said he was acting on your husband's orders.' The two maids exchanged glances. 'We wish you all happiness, my lady.'

'Thank you.' She felt her cheeks turn ruddy. Doubtless they'd been as shocked by the news of her marriage as she'd been herself. 'Where is Loth—my husband?'

'Outside, my lady.'

'I see.' She tried to adopt a sober expression. 'In that case, excuse me, but I need to speak with him.'

She fled for the door, her blush deepening as

she heard the maids start to chatter behind her. She'd have to get used to that, she supposed, at least until Lothar left again and things could get back to normal.

She scooped up a cloak from the guardroom and wrapped it tightly around her shoulders before stepping outside. The air was cold, but the sky was a bright, forget-me-not-blue dotted with fluffy white clouds. She felt strangely invigorated, as if she were looking at the world in a whole different light. From her vantage point at the top of the keep steps, she could see that the sky wasn't the only thing to have changed either. All the old inhabitants of the castle seemed to have returned. Farriers, blacksmiths, fletchers, even their children scampering amidst the buildings. It didn't feel like a fortress any more. It felt like a bustling home again.

'Good morning, Juliana.'

She looked down towards the sound of Lothar's voice. She'd been so busy looking around that she hadn't noticed him approach, but now she found him standing directly below the keep steps, freshly bathed and shaved, and yet somehow even more ruggedly handsome than she remembered.

'Good morning.' She gestured around the bailey with a swell of happiness. 'So *this* is what you had to arrange?'

'I thought it was time things got back to normal.' His expression was guarded, as if he wasn't sure what her reaction would be. 'I would have waited to discuss it with you, but I didn't know how long you'd need to sleep.'

'It's a lovely surprise.' She gave him a heartfelt smile. 'I feel much better this morning, thank you.'

'I'm pleased to hear it. Though it might still be best if—'

'No!' She threw her hands up in protest. 'If you tell me to go to bed one more time, I'll throw the mattress out of the window!'

'*That* window?'

He jerked his head up at the small opening and she folded her arms defiantly.

'I'll find a way.'

'I believe you.' There was a glint of amusement in his eye. 'As you wish then, my lady. In that case, what would you like to do today?'

'Today...' she looked up at the sky and sighed wistfully '... I'd like to get out.'

'Out?'

'Yes. Apart from that day we met on the drawbridge, I haven't been outside these walls in five months.'

'Five months?' He gave a low whistle. 'I didn't think of that. I would have run mad.'

'Perhaps I almost did.' She started down the steps. 'But today I'd like to get out, maybe go for a ride...if that's allowed?'

'Why wouldn't it be? You're in charge, remember?'

She stopped on the second step up so that her face was level to his. 'Just checking.'

'Still don't trust me?'

'I'm starting to.'

'Good. Because, with your permission, I'd like to come with you.'

'To *protect* me?' She smiled knowingly, but he didn't respond.

'Partly, though you can take some of your own men if you prefer.'

'Because you on your own is the same as a *few* of my men.' She let out a gurgle of laughter. Apparently she couldn't *stop* smiling today. 'You think very highly of yourself.'

'The Empress once said I was like one of her deerhounds. A good attack dog.'

'That doesn't sound like much of a compliment.'

He grimaced. 'You might be right, though I chose to believe it meant I was good at my job.'

'Maybe she meant you were loyal. To *her* anyway.'

'Maybe.' He arched an eyebrow, as if the comment surprised him. 'In any case, I'd like to get a closer look at the land.'

'All right. You can come.' She jumped down the last two steps enthusiastically. *'Husband.'*

She walked off briskly towards the stables, throwing a quick glance over her shoulder as she did so. Why had she said that? Partly because he'd called her *wife* earlier, partly because she'd wanted to see how he would react—though, judging by the expression of surprise on his face, he didn't know how to. But he'd been right when he'd said they were stuck in this situation together. They ought to try to make the best of it. And he *was* her husband, after all—she was only stating a fact. It was just a word. It didn't *mean* anything else. Even if she was starting to like it.

An hour later she reined in her palfrey, stopping on a ridge that overlooked a deep valley to the east. Together, they'd galloped all along the backbone of the hills, the wind rushing past her ears so fast that her headdress now lay flat on her shoulders, surrounded by a mane of hair as wild and tangled as it had ever been. This was one of her favourite views. As she looked out at the horizon, it was hard to imagine they were part of a country at war with itself. It looked peaceful, the way it once had been—the way it hopefully would be again.

'You're a good rider.' Lothar cantered up beside her.

'I'm out of practice.' She reached forward to pat her palfrey's neck. 'It's one of the few things women are allowed to do that I'm actually good at.' She narrowed her eyes suspiciously. 'Or do you object?'

He grinned. 'I'm not so easily offended. I've seen a woman's legs before.'

'What?'

She looked down, mortified to find that the lower part of her skirt had hitched on to the back of her saddle, exposing her legs all the way from her knees downwards. It must have happened when they were galloping. If it weren't for her woollen stockings he'd be able to see more than just the outline.

'You could have told me!' She wrenched the material down indignantly.

'I just did. And it wasn't easy to catch up. Out of practice or not, you're faster than I am.'

She tossed her head, embarrassment vying with elation. When he smiled like that, she didn't care how much he saw of her.

'When are you leaving?' She dragged her thoughts back on to safer territory.

'What do you mean?' His voice sounded edgier suddenly.

'You said you were going back to the Empress.'

'Oh…that.' A muscle twitched in his jaw, small but unmistakable. 'Not for a while. She doesn't need me until the spring. You're stuck with me until then, I'm afraid.'

'As long as *you* don't mind.'

'Why would I?'

'No particular reason.'

She tried to keep her expression calm as her heart gave a small leap. He sounded tense, but he didn't seem particularly upset about being separated from the Empress.

'Will you tell me what's happening out there?'

She gestured into the distance. 'In the rest of England, I mean.'

'Not much. Not yet anyway.'

'Was the Empress very upset about the Earl of Gloucester?'

'Extremely.'

'It must have helped to see you.'

'Must it? She wanted to discuss her plans.'

'For ending the war?' She couldn't keep the sarcasm out of her voice.

'Yes. In a manner of speaking.'

'What?' She twisted around in her saddle, seized with a rush of hope.

'Her son Henry's coming from Normandy.'

'Oh.' Her spirits sank again. 'I thought you meant it was over.'

'It might be. Most of the Barons have had enough of fighting. More and more are making pacts to stay neutral.'

'So you mean we're just going to stay like this? With battle lines drawn, but no fighting either? It's not war or peace.'

'No, but Stephen's getting older and Henry's a young man. He's a charismatic leader with all the makings of a great king. Given a choice, I believe most of the Barons could be persuaded to side with him.'

'Because he's a man?'

'Not just because of it, but it might tip the scales in his favour. Enough for Stephen to come to a compromise anyway.' He paused, as if uncertain about whether or not to tell her something and then going ahead anyway. 'Matilda wants him to sign a treaty, ceding the throne to Henry on his death.'

'A treaty?' She repeated the word thoughtfully. 'A piece of paper to end a war.'

'Better than a battle.'

'True, but then who wins? If Stephen keeps the crown, but agrees to let Matilda's son succeed him, then both of them win and both of them lose. It makes everything that's happened seem such a waste.'

'War's always a waste.'

'I thought soldiers liked war?'

'Did your father?'

'No,' she conceded the point readily. 'He said that soldiers were a necessary evil, to protect the innocent as much as for fighting battles.'

'He was right.'

She looked at him askance. He'd always seemed like such a born warrior that she'd never considered that he might not want to fight.

'Don't *you* like fighting?'

'There was a time when I did, when it made me feel as if I were moving on from the past. Now...' He gave her an appraising look. 'You seem to have a calming effect on me.'

'Me?' She bit her lip and his eyes followed the movement, flickering with something that made her stomach tighten convulsively.

'Most of the time.' He looked away again quickly.

She swallowed. 'You know, when I first saw you, I thought you were the most terrifying-looking man I'd ever seen.'

To her surprise, he laughed. 'And you said that being compared to a dog wasn't a compliment?'

'I wasn't trying to compliment you. I just wanted to say that I was wrong. You're not so terrifying after all.'

'Not at *all*?' He sounded disappointed.

'Occasionally. When you threatened Sir Guian, for example.' She gave him a pointed look. 'I never thanked you for protecting me from him. I should have.'

'You never told me what he did to you either.'

'No.' She held his gaze evenly. 'I didn't.'

'Will you tell me now?'

She sucked in a breath. Would she? *Could* she?

'It wasn't what he did. It was what he tried to do. I was foolish enough to agree to a private meeting.'

'You said he didn't hurt you.' His voice deepened menacingly.

'He didn't, not as much as I hurt him anyway. He didn't count on my being able to defend myself.'

'When I see him again...'

'You can leave him alone, just like I asked you to.' She reached out impulsively, placing a hand on his jaw to ease the tension there. She didn't want to see the look of fury on his face again. 'Besides, I think you did a good enough job of scaring him last time. Once he finds out that we're married, he'll be quaking in his boots.'

His jaw unclenched finally beneath her fingertips, though his gaze never left hers. 'You're right. I saw him in Devizes and he ran away like a startled hare. The next day I heard he'd ridden back to his estates.'

'Then that's all the revenge I need. I only want peace from now on.'

He took a few deep breaths before agreeing. 'Very well.'

'Thank you.' She pulled her hand away, hardly able to believe her own daring in touching him. What must he think of her? Another part of her didn't care. The sun was past its zenith and the raw winter air stung her throat, but it felt good to be outside and free. She felt almost *alive* again. She was even enjoying her husband's company. He wasn't so terrifying after all, and he was staying, until the spring anyway. No matter how he felt about Matilda, he was her husband and he'd come back to protect her. That was all that mattered for now—and suddenly she knew just how to thank him.

'Come on.' She twitched on her reins. 'I need to show you something.'

'Now? We ought to be getting back.'

'It won't take long.' She was already galloping away. 'You'll be glad of it, I promise!'

Chapter Twenty-Four

❧

'There's a ford?' Lothar stared at the river in disbelief. 'A *ford*?'

'Yes.' Juliana's face was a picture of innocence.

'It's been here the whole time?'

'For as long as I can remember. Only local people know about it.'

He jumped down from his stallion and made his way along the riverbank for a closer inspection. The ford was almost three cart-widths across and in better condition than most of the bridges he'd crossed on his journey through Herefordshire. A troop of soldiers could easily make it across.

'Why didn't you tell Sir Guian?' He looked back at her in amazement. 'You could have ended the siege and sent his army away.'

She gave a small shrug. 'I thought about it, but it would have been the same as giving him the bridge. He was never going to attack us anyway.'

'And when I arrived? I told you we were going to attack! You could have said something then.'

'What was the point? You said that Sir Guian's soldiers would attack us for plunder anyway.'

'I was bluffing!'

'How was I supposed to know that? You looked terrifying, remember? I *might* have said something if I'd thought it would stop you finding my father, but by then you were already inside the castle.'

'So all this time there's been another way over the river...'

She slid down from her palfrey and wandered slowly towards him, eyes gleaming with a look of triumph. 'Why do you think the bridge at Haword is so small? We've never needed a bigger one. Didn't you ever wonder about that?'

He rubbed a hand around the back of his neck, inwardly berating himself for his own lack of attention. He *had* thought about it, briefly when he'd arrived, but then he'd met *her*. Apparently he'd been more distracted than he'd realised. He still was. His jaw was still tingling from where she'd cradled it with her fingers, even if it had seemed more a gesture of comfort than anything else, just like when she'd touched his scar that morning. That was the real measure of his distraction—he'd never let *anyone* touch him there before.

'I should have thought of it. This is better than the bridge.'

'I know.'

He lifted an eyebrow. 'There's no need to rub salt in the wound. Why are you showing it to me now?'

'Because you kept your word and came back, and because you made me feel better last night. I wanted to give you something in return.'

'Doesn't it break your promise to Stephen?'

Her lips curved in a smile that looked both guilty and gleeful at the same time. 'I promised him I'd hold the bridge. I never mentioned anything about a ford.'

'So you didn't tell him about it either?'

'No. I gave him my oath of allegiance, not all my secrets as well. You never know when those might come in handy.'

He gave a shout of laughter. 'You know, if this gets out, it renders Haword's position a lot less important.'

'I know. That's why it's a secret.' She swished a hand over some rushes at the water's edge. 'Though now I suppose you'll have to tell Matilda.'

'Not necessarily. What kind of a lord would I be if I gave all our secrets away? I'll tell the Empress if I ever need to, but since Stephen's not coming now...' he shrugged '...there doesn't seem much point at the moment.'

She smiled and he felt his loins tighten in response. It was the same breathtaking smile she'd worn when she'd come out of the keep that morning. It had caught him unawares at the time, as if she were actually pleased to see him, and the effect seemed to have become more and more arresting with each passing hour. He'd wanted to make her smile again, but he'd never imagined anything quite so powerful—or so potent either. His hands were itching with the desire to reach out and touch her. Just as they'd been that morning, when he'd had to flee her bedchamber to stop himself from gathering her into his arms and showing her just how glad he was to see her again. They were married, but she was grieving and vulnerable. Besides which, their truce was still fragile—and temporary. In the spring he was leaving, not just for Devizes, but for Normandy, possibly for good. Touching her would only complicate matters. He had to remember that—no matter how much he might want to.

'Come on.' He cleared his throat gruffly. 'It's getting late.'

He led the way reluctantly back to the horses. In a couple more hours it would be dark and there was something important they needed to do before then, though he still had to ask her permission. He had no idea what her answer would be. The last thing he wanted was to rush or to force her into anything, but it was too important to delay for long…

'What did you think of *me* when you first saw me?'

'Mmm?' He was so busy thinking about his own question that hers took him by surprise.

'What did you think when you first saw me?' She repeated the words, though her casual tone sounded forced somehow. 'I told you what I thought about you.'

'I thought you were a woman standing on some battlements.'

'Is that all?'

He grasped hold of her palfrey's bridle, holding the animal steady for her to mount. 'I thought that I didn't want to shoot you.'

She froze halfway into the saddle. 'You thought about shooting me?'

'No. I was just being told to.'

'Oh.' She dropped into the saddle with a thud. 'By Sir Guian?'

He nodded and swung up on to his stallion, vaguely discomfited by the exchange. He had the feeling that he'd disappointed her somehow, though he'd only been telling her the truth. He *had* thought she was a woman standing on some battlements. What else did she want from him?

'I thought you looked like a queen.' He wasn't sure where the words came from. 'A Celtic one.'

She looked even more startled than when he'd mentioned shooting her. 'Because I have red hair?'

'It's not red. Not blood-red anyway. It's darker than that, like leaves in the autumn.'

'I like that.' Her head tipped to one side. 'Dark red on a crest stands for victory.'

'There you are then.' He nodded. 'You might beat me yet.'

'Why would I want to do that?'

'To get your castle back?'

'I thought it was *our* castle now.'

'It is.'

'Then I don't need to beat you, do I? Not any more. Especially since you chose *not* to shoot me.'

'I'm glad to hear it.'

'Besides, I quite like the idea of being a queen.' She dug her heels into her horse's flanks, spurring ahead so that he only just caught her next words. 'More than being a stablehand anyway.'

Lothar looked around with satisfaction as they rode back into the bailey at last. All the preparations he'd ordered seemed to be going according to plan, which meant there was only one thing left to do, not that he was any closer to working out *how* to do it. He'd been searching for the right words the whole journey back, but his mind was still a blank. It wasn't a question he'd ever considered, let alone thought about asking before—though if he didn't ask it soon, she'd find out what he was planning by accident.

'Black stands for grief.'

'What?' He twisted towards her in surprise, wondering if he'd missed the start of some conversation, but she seemed deep in thought, apparently oblivious to all the activity going on in the bailey. He was glad about that, but what on earth was she talking about?

'We were talking about crests before.' She gave him a look that suggested her meaning ought to be obvious. 'Black on a crest stands for grief. You always wear black.'

'I've noticed.'

She made a face. 'I *was* about to say something nice.'

'In that case, I take it back. I've never noticed what I wear.'

'I don't want to say it now.'

His lips twitched at her aggrieved tone. 'But I want to hear it. It's not every day someone says something nice about me.'

'I can't imagine why not.'

'Do I have to beg?'

She made a harrumphing sound. 'I'd like to see that.'

'All right.'

He dismounted at once, dropping to one knee in the dirt beside her.

'What are you doing?' She looked around quickly. 'People will see!'

'You told me to beg so I'm begging. Do I have to beseech you as well?'

'No!' She slid down and grabbed his hands, trying to hoist him back to his feet. 'No beseeching!'

'So tell me then. What nice thing were you going to say about me?'

She rolled her eyes when he still didn't budge.
'I was just going to say that black stands for constancy, too.'

'Ah.'

'Because you're loyal.' She sounded faintly embarrassed. 'To the Empress, I mean.'

He frowned at the implication. She'd said something similar earlier.

'To you as well. You're my wife, Juliana, I pledged my loyalty to you, too.'

He glanced down at the light smattering of snow on the ground beneath him, as if the words he wanted to say might be written there somewhere. He felt faintly ridiculous, but now that he'd started, he had to finish.

'Will you marry me?'

Her mouth dropped open. 'I don't understand. We *are* married, aren't we?'

'Yes, but I didn't ask you the first time. Your father did. So I'm asking you now. When I sent Ulf to the village this morning, I made other arrangements as well.'

'What kind of arrangements?'

'For a proper wedding with a feast.' He cleared his throat self-consciously. 'I want to do it properly. There were no witnesses before.'

'Are you afraid that I'll try to deny it?'

'No, but for the avoidance of doubt it would be better if we made the vows formally, in case it's ever called into question in the future.'

He wondered briefly if he ought to tell her

about the Empress's plans for him in that future, before deciding against it. He had a suspicion that mentioning Matilda's name wouldn't persuade her of anything.

'Trust me, Juliana, it's for your own safety. I want everyone to know that we're married. There are plenty of men like Sir Guian in the world, but this way, if any of them dare to touch you again, I can maim them with a clear conscience.'

'Well, when you put it like that...' Her lips curved in that breathtaking smile again. 'When have you made the arrangements for?'

'Right now, if you're amenable.'

Her eyes widened and he felt the band around his chest tighten again. Damn it all, how did she do that to him? He seemed to have no control over his own body any more.

'If you don't want to—'

'No,' she interrupted him, 'it's not that. It's just... I want to do it properly, too. Give me one hour.'

Chapter Twenty-Five

'What do you think?' Juliana ran her hands over the front of her best gown, smoothing out the wrinkles as Alys and Maud exchanged dubious glances. 'What's the matter?'

'It's just…' Alys sounded as if she were trying her hardest to be tactful. 'It's not very pretty.'

'It's my best dress!'

'That doesn't necessarily make it the best choice.'

'Doesn't it?'

She dropped down on to her bed with a dispirited sigh. Her coffer was stacked high with practical tunics in sensible shades of brown and green, none of which seemed remotely suitable as a wedding dress. Hard-wearing and functional, yes. Pretty, no, and she wanted to look pretty for her wedding. She wanted her husband to think she looked pretty, too, though as to why it should mean so much to her...

'It doesn't matter anyway.' She kicked the side of her coffer resentfully. 'He already knows what I look like.'

'Perhaps if we decorated it with some flowers?' Maud came and perched beside her.

'It's winter.'

'A brooch, then?'

She folded her arms with a sigh. She knew her maids were only trying to help, but she was starting to regret the whole idea of dressing up. It was easy for them. Alys's corn-gold hair hung down to her waist like a tumbling waterfall, whilst Maud's wide, hazel-brown eyes seemed to entrance every man who looked into them. They were both naturally pretty, whereas she... She sighed again. She'd been scrubbed, rinsed and brushed within an inch of her life, yet apparently she looked no different to the way she had before. Doubtless Lothar would think the same thing when he saw her. He'd probably just wonder what had taken her so long.

'Are you worried about tonight?' Alys came and sat on her other side.

'Tonight?' She looked up in consternation. Why would she be worried about tonight?

'Has anyone told you what to expect?'

'Alys!' Maud hissed across the bed.

'Well, someone ought to tell her,' Alys argued back. 'Who else is going to?'

Juliana cleared her throat in embarrassment. They were talking about her wedding night, the first official one she'd spend with her husband, as if it were something she ought to be nervous about, and she could hardly correct them without admitting the demeaning truth—that her husband not only thought she looked like a stablehand, but was in love with another woman as well. He wouldn't want to bed her. He'd proven that in the way he'd raced out of her chamber that morning. Whereas she…shamefully, she hadn't wanted him to go. Her body seemed to react in all kinds of surprising ways whenever he was close by, though surely that was just due to the shock of being married—even if she *had* touched him twice in one day, once when she'd stroked his scar in bed, the other when she'd calmed him down that afternoon. Not that he'd seemed to object on either occasion. And sometimes, when he looked at her, it seemed as if he were holding himself back…

'I'm sure there's nothing to worry about.' She tried to sound dismissive.

'You know there'll be a bedding ceremony.'

'A *what*?' She gaped in astonishment. No, she hadn't known that. She'd never even been to a wedding, let alone heard of a bedding ceremony.

'That's when he takes you to bed. Everyone follows to make sure you're really married.'

'But we're already married! We were married two weeks ago.'

'Yes, but not properly. You know...' Alys gave her a nudge '...in bed.'

'You mean we're not properly married until we get into bed together?'

'And the rest.'

'What *rest*?'

'Juliana.' Maud took her hand as Alys rolled her eyes with exasperation. 'Do you know what the marriage debt is?'

She shook her head, torn between wanting to put an end to the conversation and wanting to understand what on earth they were talking about.

'Well, when you're married, your husband has the right to demand certain...*things* of you. To have children, for example.'

'How can he demand that I have children?'

'Well, not children themselves...' even Maud looked embarrassed now '...but the means of making them. If he wants to lie with you.'

'Oh!'

She gulped, appalled by the idea. She'd never imagined that a husband could simply make such a demand. As if having control over every other aspect of a wife's existence wasn't bad enough, now it seemed they could demand that, too! It was wrong, unjust and yet, in her case, not very likely either. Considering that Lothar had only married her as a favour to her father, she thought it highly doubtful that he'd ever demand such a thing from *her*.

'It might hurt the first time,' Alys interjected, 'but only at first.'

'In any case, there won't be a wedding unless we hurry.' Maud jumped back to her feet. 'He'll be wondering where you are. And there's nothing wrong with your gown really. It's perfectly respectable.'

Respectable. She forced her mind back to the matter in hand. 'I just wish I had something in blue. Brides are supposed to wear blue for purity.'

'But that's perfect!' Maud clapped her hands impetuously. 'I can't believe I didn't think of it sooner. Blue!'

'Think of what?' Juliana exchanged confused glances with Alys as Maud charged out of the room suddenly, returning a few minutes later half-hidden behind a vast pile of silk.

'You see!' Maud shook out the material triumphantly, revealing a gorgeous, midnight-blue gown embroidered around the neck and hems with silver thread. 'You *do* have something blue. Your father kept all your mother's old gowns for you to have some day. I air them out every few months.'

'It's beautiful,' Juliana gasped in amazement, 'but I can't wear that.'

'Why not?' Alys stroked the fabric admiringly. 'Somebody should. The colour's perfect for you.'

'I'm sure your mother would have wanted you to have it,' Maud smiled encouragingly, 'especially on your wedding day.'

Juliana reached for the gown slowly, half-afraid to touch something so beautiful. Maud was right. Surely her mother would have wanted her to wear it, though she'd never worn anything of hers before. She'd spent her life hearing about how elegant and ladylike her mother had been. How could *she* possibly hope to live up to such an ideal? Still, it was worth a try...

'You don't think I'll look ridiculous?'

'Trust us.' Maud's smile spread from ear to ear. 'You're going to look stunning.'

Where was she? Lothar marched up and down the hall impatiently, stopping every few minutes to glare in the direction of the stairwell. She'd said she needed an hour, but surely it must have been twice as long already. He'd had time to bathe and shave, for the second time in one day, get dressed *and* make a tour of the bailey in the time it had taken her to...do what exactly? It wasn't as if she ever paid any attention to her appearance! She probably wouldn't even bother to change her gown. In which case, what *was* she doing? If she'd changed her mind, she could at least send somebody to tell him, not leave him waiting like a fool at his own wedding.

'Sergeant?' Ulf waylaid him as he began another lap of the room.

'Yes, Constable?' He tried not to snap.

'There's no need to worry, sir. She never goes back on her word.'

He gave a grunt of acknowledgement. Reassuring as the words were, they also meant he wasn't imagining things. She really was taking a long time. Fuming, he looked down at the plain gold band he'd found in a stall in Devizes, a replacement for Matilda's ring, though why he'd needed to find a replacement was still beyond him. He'd intended to give it to Juliana during the ceremony, though now he was starting to wonder if that was ever going to happen.

Not that it mattered whether she made an appearance, he reminded himself. They were already legally married. Whether she agreed to another ceremony or not really meant nothing at all. He was doing it simply as a further means of protecting her, in case anyone challenged her right to hold the castle in the future. It didn't mean anything to him personally and it wouldn't change anything between them privately either. Even if he felt more nervous than he ever had in his life.

He was scowling in the direction of the stairwell when she finally appeared, clenching his jaw so fiercely that for a moment he found it difficult to breathe. The woman in front of him had the same face and build as Juliana, the same vivid shade of burgundy-coloured hair coiled in a long plait over one shoulder, but everything else about her seemed completely different. She was dressed in a trailing blue gown with a low, square neckline that emphasised the mounds of her breasts to tantalising perfection, not to mention every other curve where the silken fabric clung to her body. Was it really her? He felt as if his senses were reeling, as if he'd drunk some of her poppy-milk medicine again. Surely only that could explain this astounded sensation, as if he were looking at a familiar and yet completely different woman.

'Lothar?' She approached with a nervous expression, peering up through her eyelashes as if she were afraid of what he might be thinking. The gesture reminded him of the first time they'd met, when she'd been trying to lure him inside the castle. She'd looked at him in the same way then, but the difference had been that he'd known it was a pretence. Now he didn't know anything except that this time, if she were trying to seduce him, then she was very definitely succeeding.

Not that he could let himself be tempted. She looked even more like a queen—one who deserved better than him. Never mind the fact that he was leaving. In a couple of months at the most, he'd be crossing the Channel for Normandy, possibly never to return. Even if he cared for her, which he wasn't capable of, even if he was worthy, which he wasn't, even if he wanted to, which he definitely did, he couldn't lie with her and then simply leave. It had been hard enough leaving Haword the first time.

'Are you ready?'

His voice sounded harsh even to him and her expression wavered slightly.

'Yes, but I have something for you first.' She held out a blue ribbon. 'It's for luck. May I?'

He nodded silently and she reached up, wrapping the ribbon around his bicep so gently that he found himself wanting to bend down and kiss her right there and then. He turned his face away instead, stamping down a fierce rush of desire as her fingers skimmed over his forearm. For luck, she'd said. Considering every other obstacle between them, he had a feeling they might need as much of that as they could get. He might need it to help keep his hands off her, for a start. He'd definitely need it to keep his body under control for the next few months. If this was what being married to her was going to feel like, then the sooner he left, the better.

'Let's hope it works.' He offered an arm gruffly and steeled himself for her touch. 'Shall we?'

Juliana looked down at the gold band on her finger, then back at the hall, dazzled by the sight and scale of the decorations. Yule was almost upon them and the room had been decked out early with garlands of holly and ivy, laurel, mistletoe, rosemary and bay, as if everything green outside had been transplanted indoors. There were even evergreen boughs, decorated with brightly coloured ribbons and beads, so that it looked less like a hall than a forest lit up with a hundred glittering candles. The bailey had been decorated, too, filled with row upon row of make-shift tables, all illuminated by torches, so that everyone in the area could be accommodated for the wedding feast. Everyone seemed to have come, too, filling the castle with noise and excitement, colour and laughter, all the things that had been absent for so long. Even in her father's day, she'd never seen the place look quite so magnificent. The whole effect was breathtaking.

The feast itself had come as an even bigger surprise. She'd expected chicken stew at the most, but instead she'd been presented with a trencher of goose and partridge. To top *that* off, she'd discovered a bowl of candied fruits set on the table in front of her, delicacies which must *surely* have come from Devizes, though her new husband hadn't touched any of them, as if he'd bought them especially for her.

She sipped nervously at the cup of wine that he'd poured her. He was drinking ale, as usual, but tonight she'd wanted something stronger. The ceremony had gone well, the feast even better, and if she drank, she could almost believe it was all real and not just a marriage forced on them by circumstance. Besides, she needed courage for the bedding ceremony ahead. It was getting late and surely they'd be retiring soon…

The knot of anxiety in her stomach twisted at the thought, accompanied by the first stirrings of a headache. The gentle harp and flute music that had started the evening had been replaced first by fiddles and then increasingly raucous singing. Now their soldiers seemed to be comparing English and Angevin drinking songs, competing as to who could sing the loudest. Her ears were ringing, but at least *they* were in a celebratory mood, which was more than she could say for her husband. He'd looked at her so strangely when she'd first come down to the hall that she'd felt all her newfound confidence evaporate. Then he'd seemed almost determined *not* to look at her since. He'd been severe and stern and as much like a statue as she'd ever seen him, as if the ceremony were just a chore he wanted to get over with. When he'd asked her to marry him in the bailey, he'd seemed to genuinely care about her answer, but now he seemed to have no feelings at all. They appeared to be right back where they'd started.

Well, she hadn't tolerated it then and she wasn't going to tolerate it now.

'You haven't mentioned my gown.' She rounded on him accusingly.

'Haven't I?' His tone was impassive.

'No.'

'It looks good.'

'Good.' She repeated the word flatly.

'*Very* good. It's just not what I'm used to.'

Her temper flared. 'No, I'm sure the Empress has much finer gowns.'

'What does the Empress have to do with it? I meant that I'm not used to seeing you in something so…' he seemed momentarily lost for words '…colourful.'

She pursed her lips. If colourful was the best thing he could think of to say about it, then she might as well not have bothered.

'It's time we went upstairs.'

'For the bedding ceremony?' Her voice seemed to have turned into a squeak.

'Yes.' His gaze swept over her face and then away past her shoulder. 'It's expected.'

She swallowed apprehensively as she stood up, trying to suppress a rising sense of panic as she walked towards the stairwell. She could hear Lothar's footsteps behind her, then others, a whole cacophony of footsteps as the revellers followed them up to her chamber. What were they going to do—watch? This was the worst, most humiliating thing she could ever have imagined! Surely her father had never intended for her to go through anything like *this*!

'My lady?' Alys was already waiting in her chamber. 'Shall I help you with your gown?'

'Please.' Her hands were shaking so much she doubted she'd be able to undo any of the ties herself.

Out of the corner of her eye, she saw Lothar enter the room behind her and start to disrobe, tossing his boots casually into one corner as if he weren't remotely concerned about what was happening. She felt sick. This wasn't the way marriage was supposed to be, was it? With a cluster of people standing outside their door waiting for them to do…what? She tensed as Alys drew the gown over her head, leaving her naked except for a knee-length shift. Surely Lothar wouldn't take her to bed just to provide witnesses to their marriage? It was so cold, so emotionless. Why were witnesses important anyway? She looked over her shoulder to see a crowd gathered outside, though mercifully no one was making any attempt to come in. Quickly, she fled to the bed, jumping in and wriggling under the covers.

'There you are.' Lothar followed Alys across the room as she made to depart, giving an exaggerated bow to their audience before slamming the door in their faces. 'They've seen us together.'

'You mean that's it?' She sat up in surprise. 'I thought they had to see us in bed?'

'They've seen us half-dressed in a bedchamber. That's enough.'

She lay down again, her whole body sagging with relief. 'So what now?'

'Now I suggest we get some sleep.'

He pulled his tunic over his head and she squeezed her eyes shut, shocked by the sight of his naked chest. She'd thought of him as a statue often enough, but now the comparison seemed even more apt. His torso was so well defined he might as well have been carved from marble, the muscles of his stomach like waves that had been petrified, as solid and unyielding as rock. As if she hadn't felt inadequate enough before!

'I could sleep in the chair if you prefer?' He sounded hesitant.

'No.' She opened one eye cautiously. 'As long as we're just sleeping.'

His expression clouded for a moment and then cleared. 'So you thought the bedding ceremony meant…'

She pulled the covers up over her face, trying to hide her embarrassment. 'I wasn't sure.'

'No wonder you looked so scared.'

'I did not!' She hauled the blanket down again, stung by the accusation.

'You were shaking.'

She opened her mouth to argue and then closed it again. 'Well, maybe I was, but you can't blame me. I didn't know what to expect. We've never discussed…*that.*'

'You're right, I should have thought of it.' He sat down on the edge of the mattress, almost as far away from her as it was possible to get. 'You've no need to fear me, Juliana. I won't touch you. This marriage is only for your protection, remember?'

'So you don't want me to pay the marriage debt?'

The words were out before she could think better of them and his shoulders stiffened visibly.

'I wouldn't expect it of you, no.'

'Oh.' She felt an unexpected sense of disappointment.

There was a brief silence before he spoke

again, his voice sounding calm and measured, as if he were choosing his words with care. 'Though you could still demand it yourself.'

'What do you mean?'

'Just that the debt works both ways. You could ask me to pay it, too. I can't refuse if that's what you want.'

She bit her lip, not knowing how to answer. Never in a thousand years would she ever do anything so brazen, but the images it brought to mind were…intriguing.

'*Do* you want me to?'

She gasped, suddenly realising how incriminating her silence must sound. 'No!'

'Ah.' His tone was expressionless. 'Then we ought to get some sleep.'

He blew out the candle and she rolled away, determined to put all thoughts of marriage and debts and beds out of her mind, though she had a feeling that any such attempt was already doomed to failure. How could she *not* think about them lying beside him? Surely it wasn't possible to feel any more mortified.

'Juliana?' His voice sounded softer.

'Yes?'

'You looked beautiful tonight. I should have told you before.'

'Oh.' She felt her heartbeat accelerate. No one apart from her father had ever called her beautiful before, but he sounded like he meant it.

'Nothing at all like a stablehand.'

She gave a tremulous laugh. 'Thank you.'

'The next time I say anything like that you have my permission to hit me again.'

'You think I need your permission?'

This time it was his turn to laugh. 'No, I suppose not. Goodnight, Juliana.'

'Goodnight.'

She closed her eyes, struck with the feeling that it was going to be harder to sleep now than ever.

Chapter Twenty-Six

'What are you doing?'

Juliana lifted her head to find Lothar staring at her with a bewildered expression from the doorway.

'A tapestry.' She didn't know whether to feel amused or offended by his reaction. 'I've never made one before. What do you think?'

He took a cautious step into her chamber, as if afraid that her behaviour was some kind of trick. 'What is it?'

'Just a border so far. You can say it's a pretty pattern, if you like.'

'It's a pretty pattern.' He looked relieved. 'Wouldn't you rather be outside with a sword?'

'It's actually not as dull as I expected. Maud's helping me.' She arched her eyebrows. 'I thought you didn't like me fighting anyway?'

'As long as it's not with me.' He stretched out

in the chair opposite. 'Your father was right, a woman ought to be able to defend herself.'

'I have you for that now, don't I?' She gave him a teasing look.

'You do. For now.'

She turned her gaze quickly back to the tapestry. Until the spring, he meant, when he had to go back to the Empress. Which also meant soon. The thought caused a pang in her chest, but at least he wouldn't be gone for ever. A lot of men spent their springs and summers away from their wives and families at court or on campaign, only returning home in the winter. Their marriage wouldn't be so unusual in that regard.

'I'm sure the Empress will be able to spare you from time to time.'

She peered sideways at him, though the mention of Matilda seemed to make his expression cloud even further. Was he pining for her? she wondered. He didn't seem to be. As far as she knew, he hadn't sent or received any messages since his return from Devizes. He'd actually been in a surprisingly good mood for the past two months. During the days he'd ridden, trained his men and helped out with any tasks that needed doing around the castle. She'd found him carrying barrels to the taproom, grooming horses in the stables, even shaping horseshoes in the smithy. As promised, he'd left the day-to-day running of the castle to her, only offering help or advice when she asked for it—something she found herself doing more and more. It was surprisingly pleasant to have someone to share her ideas with, so much so that the evenings had become her favourite part of the day. They spent that time together, playing chess or backgammon, or just talking, always together, though also always amidst other people in the hall. They were rarely alone together. He'd slept in her father's old chamber ever since their wedding night and she was always the first to retire to bed. As much as he seemed to enjoy her company, he seemed equally determined never to escort her upstairs or share a room with her. On one occasion, she'd tried staying up late to see if she could make him go to bed first, but he'd stayed in his chair until she'd been unable to stifle her yawns any longer. Then she'd listened at her door when she'd finally gone back to her room, hearing his footsteps go past just a few minutes later.

That was the one awkward part of their truce. Obviously the marriage debt scared him even more than it had her, though in that case she wondered why he'd told her about *her* rights in the first place. She'd absolutely no intention of throwing herself at any man who didn't want her, but his avoidance only added insult to injury, as if he found her so unattractive that he preferred to stay in a crowded hall rather than run any risk of it. Of course, he was sitting in her chamber now, she thought bitterly, though that was probably only because it was the middle of the afternoon. He probably thought he was safe.

'There's something I need to tell you.' His voice sounded alarmingly serious all of a sudden. 'About Matilda.'

She stabbed her needle into her finger with a jolt. She'd dreaded the thought of this conversation, had been afraid it was coming, though she'd hoped to avoid it. He was about to tell her that he was in love with Matilda. She stifled an exclamation. Wasn't it bad enough that she knew it already? She didn't want to suffer the indignity of hearing her husband say it out loud.

'Can't it wait?' She sucked her finger to staunch the flow of blood. 'Maud's gone for some more thread, but she'll be back any moment.'

'No.' He reached behind him, pushing the door shut with an ominous thud. 'It's important. I should have told you before, but… I thought perhaps the circumstances might change.'

Circumstances? Her stomach contracted. What did he mean by *circumstances*? If he'd thought their marriage might affect his feelings for Matilda, then clearly he was about to tell her otherwise…

'What I'm about to tell you goes no further than this chamber.'

She held back a snort. Of course it wouldn't go any further! Did he really think she'd want to trumpet the fact of her husband being in love with another woman?

'Very well.' She lifted her chin up stiffly. If she really couldn't stop him, then she could at least listen with dignity.

'Matilda's going back to Normandy.'

'*What?*'

'You remember I told you about her hopes for a treaty?' He leaned forward in his chair. 'Well, she's handing the fight over to her son. Henry FitzEmpress will take her place when she leaves.'

'But… She's leaving?' She felt utterly astounded. That Matilda, the woman who'd dubbed herself *Lady of the English*, might abandon the country she'd fought over for so long was well-nigh unthinkable…

'It won't be easy for her.' He seemed to be watching her intently.

'No, I suppose not.'

'For me either, but she needs me now more than ever. I don't have a choice, Juliana.'

She frowned, trying to comprehend what he was telling her. She'd been too shocked by his first statement to pay much attention to the rest, but now he seemed to be trying to defend himself, to forestall some kind of argument.

'What don't you have a choice about?'

'About going back to Normandy with her.'

'*Normandy?*' She was on her feet, her needle clattering to the floor, before she even knew she intended to stand up.

'Yes.' He stood up, too. 'She wants me to go with her.'

'Since when?'

A guilty expression crossed his face. 'Since she told me in Devizes.'

'That was two months ago!'

'As I said, I thought the circumstances might change. I didn't know if she'd go through with it.'

'And now you are?'

'If she'd changed her mind, I would have received word by now.'

She gripped the back of her chair, feeling as if the room were spinning suddenly. 'So when are you leaving?'

'She told me to return to Devizes when the weather started to clear. It's clearing now. I ought to leave in the morning.'

'*Tomorrow* morning? And you're only telling me now?' She gave a bitter laugh. 'Of course! I don't know why I expected any different. *She's* your Empress, I'm just your wife. I hope the two of you will be very happy together!'

'What's that supposed to mean?' He looked shocked.

'What do *you* think it means?'

'Juliana, I'm only following orders.'

'Then who am I to stand in the way?' She started forward angrily, suddenly desperate to get away from him. 'Now if you'll excuse me, I have better things to do than talk about *your* Empress.'

'Wait.' He took a step to one side, blocking the

way so that she almost walked into him. 'There's something else.'

She stopped a hair's breadth from his chest. She wanted to pound on it with her fists. What else could there be? She felt enough of a fool already. If she didn't get out of there soon then she'd either throw something at him or start crying and she wasn't sure which was worse. How could he do this—abandon her just when she was starting to get used to him? She hadn't wanted a husband, but he'd *made* her get used to him! More than that, she'd enjoyed spending time with him. Their evenings together had meant something to *her*. Hadn't they meant anything to him?

'What?' She met his gaze furiously, determined not to show any of the pain she was feeling.

'The Empress wants to see you, too, before she leaves.'

'Why?'

He paused briefly. 'She wants to know if you can be trusted after what happened with your father.'

'I thought you said she understood about that?'

'She did, but she still wants to know she's leaving Haword in the hands of someone she can trust.'

'She isn't!' Anger flared again. How dare he! Now of all times, how dare he demand her allegiance to the woman he was running away with? 'I told you I gave Stephen my oath.'

'That was before we were married.'

'So naturally you expect me to abandon my loyalties for yours? Why *should* I be loyal to her?'

'Because I vouched for you!'

She stiffened in shock. 'Why?'

'Because I know how much Haword means to you. I didn't, *don't*, want you to lose your home.'

She swallowed, trying to make sense of a confusing tumult of emotions. Gratitude, resentment, jealousy... She didn't understand any of it. *Why* had he taken such a risk? If he'd vouched for her, then he was responsible for her actions, even in Normandy. It bound them even closer together—just when he leaving!

'Why did you do that? You knew I gave my oath to Stephen.'

A shadow fell over his face. 'Would you really surrender Haword to him if he came back?'

'Yes, if you're not here.'

'Even after I vouched for you?'

'You shouldn't have! You had no right to say anything on my behalf.'

'I'm your husband.'

'My husband who's leaving!'

He ran a hand over his face. 'You know it doesn't work that way, Juliana. You can use my name to hold the castle. You don't have to break your oath.'

'Then you're just like every other man, after all! You think I should just hide behind you as if I don't have a mind of my own.' She shoved both of her hands hard against his chest. 'Well, maybe I *want* to support Stephen. Maybe I *like* Stephen!'

He caught her wrists as she raised them again. 'Meaning what?'

'He was very courteous to me. More than *some* people I could mention.'

'He's a traitor who stole the crown! Or do you value courtesy more than loyalty?'

'Hypocrite!' She wrenched her wrists away. 'How can you talk about loyalty? You've been in love with another woman since we met!'

'What?'

'With Matilda.' She jutted her chin out, not caring how jealous she sounded now. Since they were being honest with each other, she might as well be completely honest. 'Or are you going to deny that you're in love with her?'

'Yes!' He staggered backwards, looking thunderstruck. 'Of course I'm not in love with her. What on earth made you think such a thing?'

'Because you said she was beautiful and that she saved you, and that you'd give your life to save her if necessary. Why else would you say all those things?'

'Because she's my Empress! Not because I love her.'

'But…' The look of genuine bewilderment on his face made her conviction waver, replaced by a flicker of hope. 'You mean you're *not* in love with her?'

'I don't love!'

They stared at each other in silence for a long moment before he swore softly. 'Hell's teeth. I don't love anyone, Juliana. I don't love, I don't care and I don't *feel*. I can't. It's not who I am.'

She sucked in a breath. 'Not at all?'

'No.' His voice sounded convincing enough. 'I told you, I protect people. That's what I do.'

She felt her brief sense of elation drain away. So he wasn't in love with Matilda. That fact should have made her happy, but his explanation only made her feel worse. She still came second, even to a woman he wasn't in love with, and now it seemed that there was no hope of him ever caring for *her* either—just when she'd realised with terrible, acute certainty that she wanted him to. Because she cared for him.

'You promised my father you'd protect me.' She tried to keep her expression calm. 'Or don't I matter next to Matilda?'

'Of course you do. I'll always come if you summon me.'

'From Normandy?'

'Yes. I'm leaving my men here to protect you, too.'

'So you're abandoning all of us?'

His expression looked pained. 'I'm leaving you in command of Haword. Isn't that what you always wanted, *your* command, *your* castle, without a husband to interfere?'

She whirled away from him at the words, storming towards the far corner of the room. If she couldn't get to the door, then she could at least put as much distance between them as possible!

That *was* what she'd always wanted, but he'd no right to use her own words against her.

'Isn't that what you always wanted, Juliana?' His footsteps pursued her.

'Yes!' She spun round as he grabbed her arm. 'But that doesn't mean I still do!'

His jaw tightened. 'Juliana, you've been trying to get rid of me ever since I arrived.'

'That's not true!' She tried to pull her arm away, but he held tight this time. 'I only wanted to get rid of you at first. These past few weeks…' She bit her lip.

'What?' He tugged her against him when she didn't answer. 'These past few weeks what?'

'I don't know! They've just been different!'

His chest heaved as if he were trying to control some emotion. 'I know, but I have to do my duty. I have to go with the Empress. She needs me.'

She inhaled sharply, his close proximity making her breath come in short bursts. 'What about your duty to me? What about the marriage debt? How do you intend to fulfil *that* part of your promise from Normandy?'

'You said you didn't want me to.'

'It's not about what I want!' She tossed her head, feeling as if she'd just argued herself into a corner. *Was* that what she wanted? Even if it was, she didn't want *him* to think that she did. 'It's the principle. How am I supposed to have an heir?

How do I have a child with a man in a different country? Who will inherit Haword?'

'You want me to get you with child?' The pupils of his eyes widened suddenly.

'I…' That wasn't what she'd meant, not exactly, but the deep rumble of his voice was sending a potent thrill racing all through her body from the top of her head down to the tips of her toes and she didn't know what to say. What she'd meant was that she wanted him to kiss her once more before he left, to hold her, to remind her of how it felt to be touched, the way he'd touched her the first day they'd met. What she'd meant was that it wasn't fair, that nothing, in the whole tangled mess of their separate allegiances, was fair. Their marriage might have been an arrangement to protect her, something they'd both agreed to for the sake of her father, but she didn't want it to be just that any more. She wanted something else, something more…something that he'd said was impossible.

'Juliana.' He let go of her arm, trailing his fingers up her back and around her shoulder-blades. 'Is that what you want?'

Instinctively, she tipped her head back, letting his lips find her throat whilst her hands drifted up to his chest. She felt a soft tug, followed by a slackening sensation, as if he were pulling on something, though it took her a moment to realise it was the laces of her gown.

'Juliana?' He repeated her name in a hoarse

whisper, his lips skimming the hollow space above her collarbone. 'Is it? You need to tell me.'

'Yes.' She breathed the word, answering a different question to the one that he'd asked her. The last thing she wanted was to be left carrying the child of a man who was about to leave her, but she could let *him* believe that, couldn't she? Better for him to think it was all she wanted. It wasn't as if the reason really mattered. He was her husband and he wasn't in love with another woman. No one else would get hurt and if he wasn't capable of feeling then he wouldn't care either way. She was *allowed* to ask him to pay the marriage debt. There was nothing wrong in it…even if, somehow, it didn't feel quite right either.

'No.' She pushed her hands against his chest abruptly.

'What is it?' He lifted his head at once.

'Not like this, it's wrong.'

'Does it feel wrong?' His eyes were smoky with what looked like, what surely had to be, desire.

She shook her head. 'We still can't. Not because of a debt.'

'Forget the debt, Juliana.'

He growled the words as his lips found hers again, his tongue plundering her mouth with a hunger that made her feel dizzy. This kiss was different to the others, fierce and demanding, as if he were trying to stifle any protest. She felt a giddy rush of elation, though whether from the feeling of his lips or the sensation of breathlessness she hardly knew. This definitely didn't feel like the calling in of a debt. It felt like something far more powerful, as if he wanted her as much as she wanted him. *More* even, judging by the way he was scarcely letting her up for air.

She gasped as the fabric of her gown fell over her shoulders and pooled loosely around her waist. His hands pushed it down and she found herself wriggling to help him, writhing her hips until it slid the rest of the way to the floor. Then he reached down, so swiftly that she barely had time to wonder what he was doing, tearing her stockings away before seizing the hem of her under-shift and pulling it over her head.

She held her breath as cold air met her skin. She was standing completely naked in front of a man who was looking at her in a way she'd never imagined possible, one that made her feel exposed and strangely powerful at the same time. There was no condemnation or criticism in his eyes, only desire. For her. All her embarrassment evaporated under the heat of his gaze, replaced by her own sense of need. Tentatively, she reached out and unbuckled his belt, letting it fall to the floor before grasping the ends of his tunic, mimicking his earlier actions as she tugged the fabric over his head. Then they both moved together at the same time, hands meeting skin as he dipped down and lifted her up into his arms.

'Wrap your legs around me.'

She did as he said, twining her legs around his waist as he pulled his head back to look at her.

'Are you certain about this?'

She nodded, meeting his gaze with a look of utter certainty. His eyes were smouldering more fiercely than she'd ever seen them, yet there was tenderness there, too. If she wanted, she could still put a stop to this, but she didn't want to. She knew that with every part of her being. Even if it were just going to be this once, she wanted this, whatever this was, to happen.

He carried her across the room, lips seeking hers again as he lowered her gently down on to the bed, then pulled back as if he intended to move to one side. She didn't let him, tightening her legs around his waist to draw him down on top of her instead. He resisted for a moment, before his eyes seemed to spark suddenly, and then she lost all power of description. She was only aware of the weight of his body on hers and the intoxicating feel of his mouth on her skin, trailing a pattern over her throat and breasts, causing a hunger that seemed to eclipse every other thought or sensation.

'You're beautiful, Juliana.'

She heard the words through a haze, intent upon running her hands over the strong muscles of his back. His hands were busy exploring her, too, tracing the curve of her waist and hips as if he were trying to memorise every inch of her

body. Was he? The thought made her go cold for
a moment, reminding her that he was leaving.

'Juliana?' He lifted his head, as if sensing the
change, and she forced a smile.

'Show me what to do,' she stretched up to
whisper in his ear and felt a shudder run through
his body.

'It might hurt at first.' He grasped one of her
hands and pressed his lips against her fingertips.

'I know. Alys and Maud told me.'

He shifted backwards and she sat up, thinking
she must have said the wrong thing.

'Where are you going?'

'To remove my hose.' He looked faintly
amused. 'Didn't they tell you I needed to remove
them?'

'Oh… Yes.'

She lay down again and rolled on to her side,
trying to hide her confusion. Alys and Maud's description hadn't exactly made matters clear, but
she didn't want him to guess just how little she
knew. Then the bed dipped again and she felt a
warm hand on her ankle, trailing its way slowly
up her leg, past her knee, over her hip and the
curve of her bottom, and she felt her fears start
to dissipate.

'Tell me if I hurt you.' His voice sounded
strained. 'I'll stop.'

She nodded and then his hands were back
around her waist, rolling her over as he stretched
his body on top of hers. She twisted her arms

around his neck, pulling his face downwards, kissing him with all the hunger she knew she had only one day to satiate as he nudged her legs gently apart. This was it, the thing that Alys and Maud had told her about, and yet it didn't feel painful. It felt…

She cried out as he pushed deep inside her, every muscle in her body clenching at once. A mistake. This had definitely been a mistake! She wanted to tell him so, but his lips were still moving gently, his body hovering motionless above hers in a way that was less painful already. She let out a breath of relief. Perhaps it wasn't so bad after all. The tightness actually seemed to be easing, so much that she even wanted to move herself. She tried it and felt a rush of pleasure spread out from between her legs to her stomach, like the tremulous, fluttering sensation she'd felt before, only stronger. Curious, she tested it again and the feeling intensified.

'Juliana.' Lothar's voice sounded hoarse.

'Am I doing it wrong?' She froze instantly.

'No. Just tell me when.'

'When what?'

'When I can move.'

She hesitated. Would that hurt? She tried moving her own body again, rolling her hips in a slow circling motion, and this time he groaned aloud.

'You can move.'

She said the words tentatively—was utterly unprepared for his reaction. He pushed so deeply into her that she cried out again, though this time the feeling was less pain than pleasure. When he moved back and pushed again, she felt as though she were in the grip of some fever, as if all the blood in her body had rushed to her stomach in a searing hot torrent. It was like nothing she'd ever felt before. New, surprising and so unimaginably intense that she didn't want any of it to stop. Instinctively, she followed his rhythm, advancing and retreating beneath him until he gripped her arms suddenly, pushing them both down into the mattress.

'Wait.'

His voice was a growl, but she didn't heed him. The feeling in her stomach was building to something, she could sense it. If she stopped now, then it would go away and she didn't want it to. She wanted to feel *it*, whatever *it* was, right now. If he were leaving, then this might be the only chance she ever had to find out.

'Juliana!'

The way he cried her name pushed her over the brink. She heard herself cry out, too, feeling as though she'd left the bed somehow, as if she were being tossed and turned in the river beneath her window. Her whole body was trembling, convulsing with some primal reaction that made her mind feel numb. She was vaguely aware of his body shaking, too, though he pulled away from her first, leaving her with a strangely empty feeling as he rolled on to his back. She hadn't wanted him to go, but perhaps that was how it worked.

Then she forgot everything else, surrendering herself to the vibrating sensations still rippling through her body. Perhaps she'd ask him about that later, about why he'd moved away… It was the last thing she thought before she fell asleep.

Lothar stared at the wooden rafters above his head. The sky outside the window was darkening fast and the candle beside the bed was burning so low that if he didn't get up and replace it soon, it would go out. He still didn't move. He couldn't. His wife was sleeping peacefully against his shoulder and he didn't want to disturb her— wanted to savour the feeling of her in his arms for a while longer.

He shouldn't have slept with her. No matter how much he'd wanted to, he should never have given in to the temptation. He was leaving. He'd spent the last two months reminding himself of that fact over and over again, warning himself to keep away from her, not that he'd been able to. Instead, he'd convinced himself that he was strong enough to resist, even though every evening they'd spent together had felt like a slow torture, as if he were taunting himself with what he could never have. It hadn't helped that she'd seemed to grow more and more desirable each day, her skin taking on a healthy glow as her eyes gradually lost their dark shadows. Even the curves of her body had started to fill out again— he'd spent enough time looking to notice—so that he'd had to use all the self-control he possessed to stay in his chair in the hall every night, allowing her enough time to reach her chamber before going to his own room upstairs. If he could he would have slept in the hall, but he hadn't wanted to start any rumours.

Now it seemed he'd succeeded in restoring her health, but failed in his other, more important resolve. On the very last day, he'd failed, unable to resist when she'd mentioned the marriage debt. Then he'd been unable to fight his desire any longer, telling himself it was something he had no choice over, though deep down he knew he'd taken her because he'd wanted to, because he wanted her more than any woman he'd ever met. She'd said she wanted a child, but he'd failed her even in that, pulling away at the last moment. The thought of leaving her had been bad enough, but the idea of leaving her with a child while he left for another country had been more than he could bear.

He tightened his arm around her instinctively, burying his face in the deep red mass of her hair. It still smelt of honeysuckle. There was a thin sheen of sweat on her skin and he had to wrestle the urge to stroke it away. If only... He tensed, gripped with an emotion he hadn't felt for as long as he could remember, so powerful and all-engulfing that he felt as if his chest were being squeezed in a vice.

No!

He leapt out of the bed, flinging her away so forcefully that she woke up at once. It couldn't be *that*. He wasn't capable of *that*. He had to get out of there.

'Lothar?' She sounded alarmed. 'What's the matter?'

'Nothing,' he answered gruffly, pulling his clothes on without turning around. 'I have things to prepare. So do you.' He risked a quick look over his shoulder and then wished he hadn't. Confusion and hurt were writ plain on her face. 'We'll be leaving early.'

She didn't say anything, but he could feel her eyes on his back, watching as he raced for the door. He had to get out. The room seemed to be closing in around him and he needed some air—air and space to clear his head and breathe, to let his heartbeat return to something resembling a normal pace.

If only…

He flung the door shut behind him and rested his head against the wood. There was no if only… He wasn't capable of *if only*. For a terrifying moment, it had felt as though he might be, as if what he'd thought was a stone in his chest was actually just a hard shell cracking open, splintering apart to reveal a real beating heart underneath. But that couldn't be true. It wasn't possible—and if it was then he didn't want to know what was inside.

Chapter Twenty-Seven

⁓⁓⁓⁓⁓

They left Haword at dawn, riding the interminable, two-day journey to Devizes in near-silence, the few words they spoke sounding unnaturally loud, as if every background noise were being absorbed by the cold. Lothar had chosen half a dozen soldiers as an escort, but even they stayed mute, seemingly afraid to disturb the close atmosphere that hung so heavily in the air around them, as if the world itself were holding its breath.

He couldn't remember ever feeling uncomfortable with silence before. For most of his life he'd actually favoured it, but now it felt oppressive, reproaching him for what he'd done. He'd managed to pull himself back together, but he had the unnerving suspicion that whatever balance he'd found was fragile, liable to shatter at any moment. All he knew was that his wife deserved better. She deserved someone capable of loving her, not an empty vessel like him. She'd given herself to him and he'd taken advantage of the situation, taking her innocence and offering nothing back in return. The stricken look on her face when he'd left her chamber afterwards had haunted him almost every moment since.

'There's Devizes, sir,' one of the guards called out.

He drew rein, reluctant to go any further as he spied the great tower of the castle in the distance. Another hour and the brief interlude of their married life would be over. As much as he'd told himself it was for the best, that Juliana would be better off without him, actually confronting that fact was another matter. But he had no choice. He couldn't disobey the Empress's orders any more than he could change who he was—and who he was wasn't anywhere near good enough.

They rode on towards the city gates and he led them through a throng of people towards the keep.

'Find some quarters for the night.' He dismounted and handed his reins to one of his soldiers.

'Just for tonight, sir?'

'Yes,' he answered tersely, wishing he knew the real answer to that. 'Hopefully you'll be able to go back to Haword in the morning.'

He turned away to avoid further questions. He didn't believe Juliana was in any real danger from the Empress, just as long as she didn't say anything foolish about her allegiance to Stephen. He trusted that he'd made her see sense about that, though he also knew that pushing her on the subject would avail nothing. Hopefully she'd be pragmatic enough not to say anything too incriminating. Then, with any luck, she'd be able to leave with his men again tomorrow.

'It's huge!'

The sound of her voice behind him made his chest constrict almost painfully. He'd missed her voice, he realised, even if it had only been absent for two days. How much more would he miss it after a week, a month…a year? He turned to find her staring up at the keep with a dumbfounded expression, as if she'd never seen anything like it. Probably she hadn't. It *was* immense, built entirely of stone and not yet thirty years old. He ought to have considered how intimidating it might appear to someone who'd spent most of her life in the country, but he hadn't dared look ahead to this moment. Now she seemed so overwhelmed that he wanted to lift her down from the horse and wrap her up in his arms, but he daren't do that either. For the sake of his sanity, if nothing else, he had to get her to the Empress as quickly as possible.

'It's just stone. Come.'

She gave a visible gulp as she slid out of her saddle, landing with such an ungainly stagger that he leapt forward instinctively, grasping hold of her waist to steady her.

Their eyes met and for a moment he thought he'd been attacked. Surely only that could explain the visceral jolt that tore through his body as if someone had just shoved him hard in the chest. It took a few moments to realise that the sensation had actually originated in his hands, as if the very touch of her were enough to send all of his senses reeling. He tried to loosen his fingers and found himself gripping tighter instead, his muscles refusing to obey his commands. At that moment, he didn't know which of them was steadying the other. He had the startling impression he might fall if he let her go.

'We should go in.'

Her voice had a pleading note he'd never heard before, breaking the spell somehow, and he tore his hands away with an effort, keeping only a light hold on her elbow as he steered her past the castle guards and towards the great hall. At the last moment he slowed down, trying to think of something to say, some words of comfort or reassurance, but as usual there was nothing. Nothing he could think of to make either one of them feel better. Then it was too late and they were in the hall itself, the ambience of the room shifting subtly as they entered, as if everyone inside had been waiting for them.

'Lothar!' Matilda's voice rang out from where she stood in the centre, surrounded by her usual cohort of soldiers and courtiers. 'You've come back at last.'

'As promised.' He dropped down on to one knee, looking out of the corner of his eye to make sure Juliana did the same. 'It's good to see you again, Empress.'

'Is it?' Matilda made her way regally towards them. 'Yet the roads have been passable for a week.' A murmur of amusement rippled around the hall, though there was nothing amused in the look she gave him. 'I was almost ready to ride into Herefordshire and fetch you myself.'

'Apologies, Empress, but there were matters that required my attention.'

'I'm sure.' Matilda's blue gaze fixed on Juliana with a predatory gleam. 'And here she is. Welcome to Devizes, my dear. You must favour your mother in appearance.'

There was a momentary pause before his wife answered. 'They tell me so, Empress.'

'Though you have your father's eyes…' Matilda's voice softened as she placed one finger under Juliana's chin and tilted it upwards. 'He's dead, then?'

'Yes, Empress.'

'I'm sorry. I wonder what he would have thought about our meeting like this.'

'I don't know, Empress.'

'No, I suppose not. But perhaps we ought to discuss it in private, so we can get to know each other properly.' She waved a hand in the air imperiously. 'The rest of you may leave us. That includes you, Lothar.'

'Empress?' He felt a shiver of unease. The look in Matilda's eyes was like that of a falcon that had just spotted a smaller bird—easy prey. Not that Juliana was easy prey. Far from it. She had her own talons, but the last thing he wanted was to leave her either to fight or to fend for herself.

'Wait outside the door if you wish, Lothar.' The order was unmistakable. 'In the meantime, your wife and I have a lot to talk about. You may *go*.'

Juliana closed her eyes, torn between regret and relief as the great oak door closed with a reverberating thud. The journey to Devizes had been almost unbearable, every moment in her husband's company a humiliating reminder of what had happened between them. In the bright light of day her behaviour had seemed even more shameless than it had felt at the time. She couldn't defend herself *or* what she'd done. She'd practically asked Lothar to take her to bed, deluding herself into thinking he might want *her*, too. As if realising how much she cared for him wasn't bad enough! She didn't *want* to care for him, but she did, and now she'd gone to bed with him, the feeling was even more heart-wrenchingly painful. Even the memory of their lovemaking was tarnished by the way he'd behaved afterwards. He'd barely even looked at her, as if all he wanted was to go back to Matilda and forget.

'Come, my dear.' Matilda hooked an arm through hers, pulling her towards a low couch by the fireplace. 'I've heard so much about you, I feel like I know you already.'

'Thank you, Empress.' She perched on the edge of the couch with a growing sense of trepidation. If anyone else had been fooled by the other woman's show of friendship, she certainly hadn't. No matter what Lothar claimed, she had the feeling that she wasn't going to be forgiven for surrendering to Stephen quite so easily. She felt like a condemned woman, waiting for the axe to fall.

'Your father was a good man.' Matilda sat down opposite. 'I valued him a great deal.'

'He would have been pleased to know that, Empress.'

'I valued his advice, too. Even if he *did* think I was fighting a losing battle.' The blue gaze narrowed in on hers suddenly. 'He was clever enough to recognise the truth when he saw it.'

Juliana caught her breath, knowing she ought to deny it, but unable to lie quite so blatantly. 'He died loyal to you, Empress.'

'I know. *Unlike* his daughter.'

She felt a prickle of goosebumps, as if she'd just walked into a trap. She couldn't deny that fact either. She couldn't even regret her disloyalty. If she had to, she knew she'd make the same choices all over again. The only question now was what Matilda would do to her, not that she particularly cared. After what had happened with Lothar, she could hardly feel any worse. But Matilda seemed to have moved on already, lost in her own train of thought.

'You know when Robert, the Earl of Gloucester, was captured, I had to exchange Stephen for his release. Some people said it was sentimental and womanly of me, that I should have left him to rot where he was, but he was my half-brother. I cared too much to abandon him, even though it meant starting the war all over again. Sometimes we don't have any good choices. I think your bargain with Stephen was one of those.'

'You do?' Juliana couldn't keep the surprise out of her voice, scarcely able to believe she was going to be let off the hook so easily. 'I know I've no right to your forgiveness, Empress.'

'I give it anyway. In all honesty, I wish your father had been a little *less* loyal. If he'd surrendered to Stephen when he'd had the chance, he could have come here and been properly cared for.'

Juliana bristled at the insinuation. 'I did my best.'

'I'm sure you did. That wasn't what I meant. And at least you were with him, taking care of him. When my own father died I was miles away in Anjou. We were arguing at the time over the rights to my dower castles. I know what it is to be estranged from a parent.'

'We weren't arguing, my lady. He never knew about my agreement with Stephen, but...' She drew her brows together, struggling to put all the tangled emotions of the past few months into words. 'I still felt it there, somehow, like a barrier between us. When he told me to marry Lothar, I thought that maybe he suspected something, that he was punishing me.'

'I won't deny that I was surprised by your marriage, but is that how it feels, like a punishment?'

'No.' She dropped her eyes under the intensity of the other woman's scrutiny. 'But I never wanted to be married. I always thought I could manage on my own, like a man.'

'Even men are forced to marry sometimes, but you're right, it's different for us. If a woman is unmarried, she isn't taken seriously, and if she is married, she cedes her authority to her husband. But there *are* exceptions, with the right kind of man, of course. Take my first husband, Heinrich. He was loving, considerate, and he treated me with respect, as an equal. I miss him dearly. A marriage like that is the goal, don't you think?'

'What about your second husband?'

The blue gaze flashed. 'You're a brave woman to ask me about Geoffrey. Our marriage isn't *quite* so harmonious, as no doubt you've heard. Being in different countries might be the only thing that stops us from fighting each other, but our marriage was necessary from a political perspective. My father thought in those terms, you see, and in those terms, he was right. Geoffrey *was* the best choice politically. But I don't think your father would have chosen a husband for you in quite the same way. I don't think he would have bound you to any man he thought wasn't good enough.'

'He wanted someone who could protect me.'

'Then he chose well, but I doubt that was *all* he wanted. He would have wanted you to be happy, too. Don't forget, he knew Lothar, knew what kind of a man he is. Isn't it possible he thought the two of you well suited?'

Juliana took a deep breath, stalling for time before she answered. *Was* it possible? In truth, they were surprisingly well matched. The two months they'd spent together over the winter had proven that. Up until two days ago, the time she'd spent in his company had been almost perfect. What had happened in her bedchamber had shown they were compatible in other ways, too, or so she'd thought... Not that it made any difference. He was still leaving her and going back to Normandy with Matilda, the woman who would always come first, the same woman who was talking to her now as if *she* had any kind of choice in the matter.

'It doesn't matter.' She shook her head resentfully. 'If I *have* to be married, then I want a husband who can love me back.'

Matilda swept to her feet suddenly, moving towards a small table and pouring out two cups of wine.

'You know, when I found him in Bamburg, he was just a boy, but he seemed older. He was too stern for a child, too hard, as if a part of him had turned to stone. It was a full year before he smiled again.' She handed her one of the cups. 'Not that he makes a habit of it now.'

'He says you saved him.'

'His life perhaps, though as for the rest...' Matilda sat down next to her this time. 'Did he ever tell you about his mother?'

'He said his father killed her.'

'What about his scar?'

'That his father did it, too.'

'Did he tell you they happened at the same time?'

'No.' She shook her head, aghast.

'We only spoke about it once, on the night I found him. I asked him why he'd run away from home and he told me that his father had been hurting his mother, that he'd tried to stop him, and she'd come between them.'

'You mean she was killed trying to protect him?' She gasped at the horror of it.

'That was the one and only time he ever mentioned her to me, though I think perhaps he told your father, too. Afterwards, he became like my shadow. At first I thought he was clinging to me for comfort, as some kind of replacement mother. I didn't have the heart to send him away, but after a while, I realised it wasn't comfort he was looking for. He was just looking, watching and waiting, as if he were bracing himself for another fight.'

'I thought that, too!' Juliana sat up excitedly, almost spilling her wine. 'The first time I saw him, I had the feeling that he was waiting for something to happen. He looked dangerous.'

'And now?'

'Now?' She blinked. Now she thought of it, he hadn't looked that way for a while, not for a month at least. In their evenings together he'd seemed almost relaxed. 'No, not any more.'

'Then you've achieved more in a few weeks than I have in twenty years. I put him into guard training as a boy because I thought it might help him. Now I think it might have made things worse.'

'I don't understand.'

Matilda sighed. 'I only gave him a way to use his grief, not to get past it. I don't believe he's ever been able to get past that day when his mother died. He's spent his whole life blaming himself for her death, protecting *me* because he wasn't able to protect *her*. Every battle he's fought on my behalf has been an attempt to put that right.'

'But he'll never be able to...' Juliana pressed her lips together, heart aching at the thought of a small boy blaming himself for his mother's death, trying to put right whatever mistake he thought that he'd made. 'That's why he's so protective. I thought he was in love with you.'

Matilda let out a particularly un-regal-sounding laugh. 'He cares for me as much as he's able. He has a strong sense of duty, I know that, but I

don't think he's let himself *feel* anything since the
day she died. Until he met you, that is.'

'No.' Juliana resisted the temptation to believe
the words. 'He doesn't care for me. He says he's
incapable.'

'He wants to be. There's a difference. He's kept
his feelings buried away for so long he thinks he
doesn't have them any more, but if anything, he's
capable of feeling too much. I've taken him for
granted, too. I thought he couldn't change, that
he'd never want to leave me, but two months ago
he did something I never expected. He lied to me.'

'Empress?'

'He told me that you'd hold Haword for me if
Stephen returned. If you're William's daughter,
then I know better.'

She swallowed nervously. 'I swore an oath,
my lady.'

'I know.' Matilda patted her arm, the atmosphere of menace evaporating. 'When I told Lothar to bring you here, I thought it was because I
wanted to punish you. Now I know I just wanted
to look at the woman he cared about enough to
lie to me. I wanted to see the two of you together.
And when he walked out of that door just now he
looked at you in a way I've never seen him look
at anyone before, as if he truly loves you.'

'He doesn't. He said—'

'I doubt he knows it himself, of course,'
Matilda continued. 'But he does. And if he's finally found someone to care about, then perhaps I

can let him go after all. Just as long as he doesn't get hurt.'

'I'd never hurt him!'

'Not deliberately, perhaps, but you could and badly. If you've managed to open his heart again, then I'm glad of it, but underneath that hard exterior, he's vulnerable. I can forgive you for everything else, but if you hurt Lothar then I'll lead an army into Herefordshire myself. I don't ask you to renounce your oath to Stephen, but I do expect you to put your marriage vows ahead of it. If you have to choose, then I expect you to choose Lothar. Not me, not Stephen, but him. Can you promise me that?'

'Yes, Empress.' She found herself nodding even before Matilda had finished speaking. 'But what about Normandy? He says you need him.'

'Typical man.' Matilda rolled her eyes. 'I'll miss him, but I'll manage. I want him to have a chance at happiness, too. Besides, he's a stern enough companion at the best of times. I don't need him acting the lovesick swain as well. Better that he stays here.'

'But…' Juliana lifted her shoulders and then let them fall again helplessly. 'What if you're wrong? What if he really *can't* love? What if he doesn't want to stay with me?'

'Those are risks, but ones worth taking, don't you think?' Matilda gave her a pointed look. 'Come now, I didn't expect William's daughter to give up quite so easily. Do you love him or not?'

'It's not that simple.'

'Well, decide and be certain. If you love Lothar, then take him, but I won't part with him for less.'

'What do I say to him?'

Matilda's gaze softened. 'If you love him, then you need to be the strong one and tell him. He won't do it first. Tell him he loves you, too, for pity's sake. Force some sense into that stubborn head of his.'

'I can't just…'

'You can.' Matilda raised her cup as if she were making a toast, sapphire eyes glinting over the rim. 'He's just a man, Juliana. Tell him you love him. It might be the only thing that can save him.'

Chapter Twenty-Eight

‘Lothar!’

He swung round at the sound of Matilda's summons, charging towards the door so fast that if a guard hadn't opened it, he might simply have barged through.

‘Empress?’ He came to a halt a few paces away from where the two women sat side by side, one regarding him with a look of hauteur, the other staring at the floor as if she wanted to sink through it. His hopes plummeted.

‘I've reached a decision.’ Matilda stood up languidly. ‘Your wife has pulled the wool over your eyes, Lothar. I can't trust her not to side with Stephen once I'm gone. She cannot remain as chatelaine at Haword.’

‘But, Empress…’

‘It seems to me there are only two choices,’ Matilda spoke over him. ‘Either we send her

packing off to Stephen, or somebody has to stay
and keep an eye on her. Under the circumstances,
I believe you're the only fit man for the job.'

'Me?'

'Would you prefer me to send another man?'

'No!'

'I thought not.' Matilda's lips twitched as she
picked up an ermine cloak and swung it loosely
around her shoulders. 'After all, she's *your* wife,
Lothar, and you know how difficult those can be.
Just ask my husband.'

'I thought you wanted me to accompany you
to Normandy, Empress?'

She placed a hand on his arm almost tenderly.
'Of course I want you to come with me, but you're
still a young man. I was wrong to abuse your loyalty. You ought to lead a life of your own, not just
follow mine. I'll miss you, Lothar, but now your
wife has something important to tell you.' She
squeezed his arm before sweeping on to the door.
'I suggest you listen to her. In the meantime, I'll
make sure you're not disturbed.'

'I don't understand.' The floor seemed to tilt
slightly as the door closed again, leaving him
alone with his wife. The possibility of Matilda
offering to leave him behind had never even occurred to him. Now he didn't know how to react.
'What happened?'

Juliana looked up finally, meeting his gaze
with a look of chagrin. 'I told her the truth.'

'You *told* her you'd give Haword back to Stephen?'

'Not exactly.' Her cheeks flushed. 'But I told her I couldn't break my oath if he came back. You knew that was the best I could do.'

'Yes.' He rubbed a hand over his eyes. 'I suppose I did.'

'I'm sorry. I couldn't lie.'

'I know.'

'I'm sorry I've put you in this position, too. I know you wanted to go with the Empress.'

He pulled his hand away from his face with a dull sense of surprise. 'It's not a question of what I *want*. It's a question of duty. Who will protect her now?'

'She has other guards.'

'It's not that simple. It's my job.'

'Why?'

He moved across to the fireplace, leaning one arm against the mantel. 'It's just what I do, who I am.'

'Because of your mother?'

He froze. Standing next to the roaring fire, he felt his whole body go frigid. 'What do you mean?'

'The Empress said that she died trying to defend you.' Her footsteps moved towards him. 'Will you tell me what happened?'

He swayed slightly as the room seemed to tilt again. *Could* he tell her? He didn't want to talk about it, yet somehow the words seemed to be coming out anyway.

'It was all my fault. My mother was good at evading my father's blows. She knew how to protect both of us, but one day when he hit her, I decided I was a man so I picked up a poker and charged at him with it. He put out a foot and kicked me backwards. My head hit a table on the way down.' He gestured towards his scar. 'I remember lying on the floor. There was so much blood I could hardly see, but then I felt his hand on my shoulder, heaving me back to my feet. I knew he was going to punish me, badly this time, but then my mother stepped between us. She said something, I don't know what because my ears were still ringing from the fall, but he let me go and then...'

'Then?' Her voice prodded him gently.

'Then she fell. Right next to me. Her arm landed on my stomach, as if she were wrapping it around me, but her eyes were open and I knew...' The pressure in his chest was building again, stretching almost to breaking point, though he seemed to be powerless to do anything to stop it. 'She just lay there staring, but I knew she couldn't see me.'

'I'm so sorry.' She rested a hand on his shoulder. 'But it wasn't your fault.'

He shook his head. 'If it hadn't been for me, he wouldn't have been so angry. He might have left us alone. I thought I could protect her, but I couldn't.'

'You still weren't the one who killed her. You can't blame yourself.'

'I failed her. I wasn't strong enough.'

'You were just a boy.'

'I should have got up.'

There was a short silence as if she were considering.

'Didn't you tell me that I shouldn't blame myself for betraying my father?'

He frowned. 'Yes.'

'Didn't you say he would have forgiven me anything?'

'Yes.'

'If your mother was prepared to get between you and your father, then she loved you. She wouldn't have blamed you and she wouldn't have wanted you to spend the rest of your life blaming yourself either. She would have wanted you to be free. Just like Matilda wants you to be free now.'

He half-turned around. 'You don't understand. When she found me, I felt as though my mother had sent her somehow, as if she were giving me a second chance. That's why I have to protect Matilda.'

'So you love Matilda like a mother?'

'*No!*' He pulled away, resisting the idea. 'Juliana, we've been over this. I told you, I don't love. I protect people, that's all.'

'And you'd rather protect her than me?'

'No, it's just…easier.'

'Why?'

'Because it is.'

There was another long pause before she spoke again, her voice sounding strained suddenly. 'If it's about the other day then I'm sorry. I should never have mentioned the marriage debt.'

'What?'

'I'm sorry if I made you feel indebted.'

'Indebted?' He swung around this time, staring at her incredulously. 'Is that what you think, that I took you to bed because of a debt?'

'I thought you couldn't refuse.'

'I can refuse whatever the hell I want!'

'So you didn't feel indebted?'

'No! I wanted…' He raked a hand through his hair. 'I wanted you, Juliana. I've wanted you since the first moment I saw you. Couldn't you tell?'

'I thought so, but I wasn't sure. And then, you still wanted to leave…'

'Not because of that.'

'Was it…bad?'

'Bad?' He spluttered in shock. 'No, it was…' He sought for a way to describe it and came up with nothing. As usual, words were beyond him. In which case, there was only one way to show her how much he wanted her. He wrenched her into his arms, grinding his lips against hers with a fervour that seemed to envelop the whole of his being. His senses were reeling with the force of his need. He wanted to tear her gown away and bury himself in her. He wanted to take her right now and every day afterwards. He wanted her more than he'd wanted any woman in his life. But he *couldn't* love her…

'I want you, Juliana.' He pulled away again, breathing heavily. 'But it's impossible.'

She staggered slightly, raising a hand to her swollen lips. 'You mean you want me *and* you want to leave me?'

'Yes.' He sank down on to the couch and put his head in his hands. 'I don't know to explain it, but when I lost my mother, it was the worst pain I ever felt. I never want to feel that way again. I *won't* feel that way again.'

She hesitated for a moment and then sat down beside him. 'Caring for someone doesn't just involve pain.'

'No? Look at you and your father.' He regretted the words instantly. 'I'm sorry.'

'It's all right. My father suffered at the end, but for most of my life he made me feel happy and loved. He raised me in a way he thought would make me happy, too. He let me be myself. And he'll always be here.' She pressed a hand to her heart. 'Just like your mother is still there in yours.'

He dragged in a breath as the constricting sensation in his chest seemed to burst suddenly. He'd heard troubadours sing about broken hearts, but this was different, as if it weren't so much his heart, but the stone around it that was crumbling, not just into pieces, but into dust that could never be put back together again, unleashing all the pent-up emotions he'd kept hidden away for twenty years. She was right. His mother *was* still there. Along with all the pain and the loss and the suffering, there was love, too. He clamped a hand to his chest, overwhelmed by the onslaught of feeling.

'You don't have to be afraid.' She wrapped an arm around his shoulders.

'What if I can't protect you?' He didn't recognise his own voice. It sounded guttural, like an animal in pain. 'If I failed the Empress it would be bad enough, but if I failed you... If I lost you... I couldn't bear it, not again.'

'You won't fail me.'

'Juliana...'

'No. Listen to me, I never wanted your protection. I've been telling you that from the start. I can take care of myself.'

'It's what I do.'

'But it's not what I *want*. If that's all you can offer, then you *should* leave with Matilda.'

'I don't want to.' His shoulders heaved at the admission.

'Then stay.'

'I don't know if I can change, Juliana. I don't know if I can love.'

'Then we'll find out together.'

He turned towards her, resting his forehead against hers. 'You deserve better.'

'I know.' She smiled softly. 'You're just a man.

But you're my husband, too, and I won't give up on you.'

He closed his eyes briefly. 'I'll do my best.'

'Good, because if you don't come with me, then I'd rather go straight to Stephen.'

'What about Haword?'

'I don't want it without you, not any more.' She reached up and pressed her hand gently against his scar. 'I want you, no matter how damaged you are. You don't have to say it, but I will. I love you, Lothar. Whatever happens in the future, I love you and you love me, somewhere deep down inside. And I'm not going back home without you.'

Chapter Twenty-Nine

Haword Castle—1153, five years later

'He's here! Lower the bridge!'

Juliana shouted out to the warden, pressing a hand to her stomach as she felt a sudden, violent kicking, as if the baby inside shared her excitement, too.

'There now.' She smiled tenderly. 'Your father's home.'

She made her way down the steps, compelled to move slowly for once, so that by the time she reached the bottom, Lothar was already waiting, his stern features breaking into a wide smile when he saw her. She felt the breath stall in her throat. After five years of marriage, her feelings for him were even stronger than they'd been on the day when she'd first told him she loved him—the day when she'd told him he loved her, too, and he…well, he'd neither confirmed nor denied it. He'd never been able to say the words back, but she'd come to realise it didn't matter. He proved how he felt about her every moment they were together. He made her feel beautiful and desirable and happy. His smile wasn't something she could have ever imagined when they'd first met. That was enough.

'Wife.' He pretended to reach for her hand and then hauled her into his arms. 'I suppose it won't make any difference if I say you ought to be resting, not climbing the battlements?'

'Not a whit. It's your fault for staying away so long.'

'Were you up there pining for me?'

'Maybe a little.' She laughed and nestled against him, burrowing her face into his gambeson and breathing in the familiar, reassuring scent of him. 'I'm just glad you're home.'

'So am I.' He pressed a kiss into her hair. 'I'm getting too old to be riding all over the country on Henry's business.'

'Not too old, I hope.' She tipped her head back and smiled seductively at him. 'I still have some uses for you.'

'Then I'll do my best to oblige.' His eyes darkened in response. 'But first I have some good news for once.'

'You don't mean…'

'Yes.' His lips curved in a smile. 'Stephen's

agreed to a treaty. When he dies, Henry will be King.'

'So the war's over?'

'As good as.'

She let out a sob and squeezed her arms even tighter around him, tears flowing down her cheeks.

'Why are you crying?' He looked confused.

'Because I'm so happy!' She laughed. 'I can't believe it's finally over. It's been so long.'

'Too long. This should have been over years ago, but it means that England's a safer place for our children.' He raised his hands to her cheeks and rubbed the tears away with his thumbs. 'Speaking of which, where is he?'

She sniffed, bringing her emotions back under control. 'Ulf's giving him archery lessons. They've become inseparable recently. How do you think I was able to climb up on the battlements without being chided? Come on.'

They walked arm in arm to the far side of the bailey, where a small boy was aiming an arrow at a round target.

'Lift your shoulder!' Lothar bellowed and the boy spun around, dropping the weapon with a yelp of glee as he came hurtling towards them. Juliana took a step to one side quickly, making room as he leapt headlong into his father's arms.

'Careful!' Lothar tossed him up into the air and then caught him again, ruffling his dark hair affectionately. 'That's your little brother your mother's carrying.'

'Sorry, Papa.'

'Sister,' she corrected him. 'This one's a girl.'

'How can you tell?'

'Because William here hardly moved at all. Whereas this one…' She laid a hand on her stomach knowingly. 'She never stops kicking. Definitely a girl.'

'With red hair.' He smiled. 'I hope so, too.'

'But I want a brother!' William looked indignant. 'Someone to do archery with.'

'If she takes after her mother then she will.'

'But it *might* be a brother?' The little boy still sounded hopeful.

'We'll see, but I've learned to listen to your mother. She's the Empress around here.'

'Empress?' She lifted an eyebrow and he grinned.

'Would you prefer Queen?'

'No, just chatelaine. That's all I ever wanted.' She reached up and planted a kiss on his cheek. 'Until a great woman told me I could have something better.'

'Will you come and do archery with me now, Papa?'

'Soon.' Lothar put the boy down, looking serious again as he nudged him back towards Ulf. 'I just need to tell your mother something first.'

'What is it?' She felt a flutter of panic. 'What's wrong?'

'I've been thinking about names for the baby.'

'Oh.' She exhaled with relief. 'Is that all? Don't tell me—Matilda for a girl?'

'Gisela. My mother's name.'

'Oh.' She was speechless for a few moments. It had been five years since they'd last spoken about his mother and she'd been starting to think that the subject was closed for ever. 'Gisela. I like that, but are you sure?'

'Yes. I think she would have liked a grand-daughter named after her.'

'I think so, too.' She clasped one of his hands, twining their fingers together. 'Is it getting any easier to think of her?'

'A little. I try to remember the good times now. We had some of those, too.'

'I'm glad.'

He squeezed her hand. 'So am I.'

'You know, there was something I always wanted to ask you…' She paused. There had never seemed a good time for the question, but she was afraid that if she didn't ask it now then she wouldn't have the courage again.

'Yes?'

'About your father…' She hesitated again before ploughing on. 'I wondered if you ever saw him again after you ran away?'

'Did he ever come looking for me, you mean? No.' His mouth twisted bitterly. 'But I found him. I went back to Bamburg a few years after Matilda took me in.'

'Oh.' She tensed. 'What happened?'

'He was drunk in a tavern. He didn't even recognise me.'

'Did you…?'

He shook his head. 'No. I thought I wanted to avenge my mother, but he was no danger to anyone any more. It wouldn't have been a fair fight. That was what I wanted, to fight him on equal terms, but there was no chance. So I walked out and left.' He sighed heavily. 'For as long as I can remember people have looked at me as if I were some heartless monster. I don't blame them. I wanted to seem that way. I just never realised it made me look exactly like him.'

'You're not heartless. I knew that from the second day I knew you.'

'As soon as that?' He gave a low chuckle and then sobered again. 'When I found him in that tavern, I told myself I didn't feel anything, but I did. I think it was pity. Despite everything, I pitied him, for all the waste that he'd caused. It took me a long time to understand that I was wasting my own life, too, though I think your father realised it. Part of me could even suspect that he planned all this from the start.'

'What do you mean?'

'I think somehow he knew that you were the only possible woman for me. I told you, he was a clever man.'

She smiled. 'Perhaps he knew you'd be good for me, too.'

'We're good for each other.' He wrapped his arms around her and gazed down tenderly into her face. 'It's taken me a long time to come to my senses, to realise something I should have said a long time ago.'

'Yes?' She held her breath, hardly dared to hope…

'I love you, Juliana. I'm still not good enough for you, but I love you. I always have and I always will. And this time I'm back for good. I've asked Henry FitzEmpress to release me from his service.'

'You have?' She felt as though all her dreams were coming true at once. 'What did he say?'

'He said yes. He knew I'd send word to his mother if he didn't.'

She flung her arms around his neck, holding him as tightly as she was able. 'In that case, how about Gisela Matilda for the baby? I think we owe the Empress that much.'

'Perhaps we do.' He leaned down, his lips hovering over hers. 'I'm done with fighting, Juliana. Are you ready for a quiet life with me?'

She nodded eagerly, stretching up on her toes for his kiss. 'I'm ready.'

* * * * *

*If you enjoyed this story,
you won't want to miss these other great reads
by Jenni Fletcher:*

*THE CONVENIENT FELSTONE MARRIAGE
MARRIED TO HER ENEMY*

MILLS & BOON®

& HISTORICAL

AWAKEN THE ROMANCE OF THE PAST

MILLS & BOON®

EXCLUSIVE EXTRACT

Read on for a sneak preview of
COMPROMISED BY THE PRINCE'S TOUCH
by Bronwyn Scott
the first book in the daring and seductive series
RUSSIAN ROYALS OF KUBAN

'I am a prince who cannot return to his kingdom. I, too, must be careful with whom I associate.' Nikolay's voice was a caress, low and husky with caution. It was not caution for himself, but for her; a warning Klara realised too late.

His mouth was on hers, sealing the distance between them. He kissed like a warrior; possessive and proving, a man who would not be challenged without choosing to respond in kind.

Her mouth answered that challenge, her body thrilled to it. This was what it meant to be kissed, not like the few hasty kisses she'd experienced during her first Season out before it was clear she'd been set aside for the Duke. That should have told her something. Well-meaning gentlemen held their baser instincts in reserve, they didn't kiss as if the world was on fire. There was nothing altruistic about Prince Nikolay Baklanov when it came to seduction and he wanted her to know. As a warrior, as a lover, he took no prisoners.

Two could play that game. Her arms went about his neck, keeping him close, letting her body press against and softness of her. She let her tongue explore his mouth, her teeth nipped at his lip as she tasted him. There were things she wanted him to know as well. She was not one of his spoiled students. She would not be cowed by a stern look and a raised voice. She was not afraid of passion. Nor was she afraid to take what she wanted, even from him. She was good at showing people what she was not. It was easier than showing people what she was: a girl forced to marry, a girl who knew nothing about where she came from, a girl caught between worlds. Her hands were in his hair, dragging it free of its leather tie. She gave a little moan of satisfaction as his teeth nipped at her ear lobe.

At the sound, he swore—something in Russian she didn't need to understand to know what it meant: that their kiss had tempted him beyond comfortable boundaries. He drew back, his dark eyes obsidian-black, his voice ragged at its edges as if he'd found a certain amount of satisfaction and been reluctant to let it go. But there was only that glimpse before the words that indicated this might have only been a game played for her benefit, to show her what it meant to poke this particular dragon. 'Forgive me,' he began, 'I did not intend…'

Cold fury doused the newly stoked heat of her body. 'Yes, you did. You've had every intention of kissing me since we met.'

'Touché.'

DON'T MISS
COMPROMISED BY THE PRINCE'S TOUCH
BY BRONWYN SCOTT

Available January 2018
www.millsandboon.co.uk